MOONSTALKER

A KNIGHT IN BUFFALO

Christofer Nigro

I0620597

Cover Art: rizkynugraha

https://www.fiverr.com/rizkynugraha

Special thanks to Gordon Long and Matt Hickman for their adept editing chores and advice; and to David MacDowell Blue and Lungga Creatives (https://ldnrdnt.com/) and (rdnt.arts@yahoo.com.au) for helping me put the finishing touches to the cover.

Christofer Nigro

Dedications

This novel is dedicated to my grandmother, Gertrude "Trudie" Nigro, for loving me as much as anyone possibly could despite our various disagreements over the years; to the memory of my grandfather, Thomas J. Nigro, for being a father figure throughout my life and the remainder of his after I came into this world despite all of our differences; and mother Patricia Nigro and my uncle, Thomas F. Nigro, for putting up with me my entire life and helping me whenever they could; and to the memory of my aunt, Concetta "Connie" Denisco, for always supporting me and believing in me; and to the memory of my Uncle Pete and Aunt Marie for likewise always supporting me and seeing the good in me.

... To the memory of my friend Dennis MacMillan Jr., for teaching me what it's like to be courageous in the face of the greatest adversity of them all; to my many other friends who honored me by seeing positive qualities in me; and my many colleagues in the creative arts for helping me fulfill my lifelong dream of putting my ideas to paper (particularly Jean-Marc Lofficier for giving me my first big break).

... And to the many creative minds, past and present, who helped forge the super-hero genre from its dramatic beginnings to its gradual ascension from the fringe of cultural acceptability to the mainstream over the past 80 years... with special thanks to Jerry Siegal, Joe Schuster, Bill Finger, Bob Kane, William Moulton Marston, Otto Binder, Gardner Fox, Jack Kirby, Joe Simon, Stan Lee, Steve Ditko, Alan Moore, Mark Gruenwald, Frank Miller, Mark Millar, Paul Levitz, John Ostrander, Geoff Johns, and many others too numerous to mention for their bold vision and the lifelong inspiration they provided to me and so many others for several generations.

Table of Contents

Part 1: The Law is Blue; Justice is Gray

Chapter 1: Blackboard Jungle

Alan Perez casually loitered about the decrepit outer building of Riverfield High where he was supposed to be attending classes. Two of his compatriots in voluntary absenteeism -- that would be Teddy and Alfredo -- stood beside him. As usual, Alan found skulking around the exterior of the building preferable to attending classes which he felt taught him nothing he actually needed to know for surviving on the mean streets of Buffalo, New York.

Specifically, these were the streets centered on the Queen City's infamous East Side, near the notorious collective of boulevards that bore the seemingly innocuous moniker of the Fruit Belt. No exotic fruits of any sort grew in this cold region of the northeastern United States; the streets in this section of the Empire State's second largest city were named after a variety of produce for no reason that Alan ever knew.

Of course, no farmers were present to till these contemporary urban neighborhoods. In the place of such hard-working people of the earth, various street gangs appeared over the past few years to claim their share of the city's ample available "turf." There were times when Alan savored the thought of leading a powerful and prosperous street gang himself. The idea of the prestige and quick wealth that could come his way through such an enterprise was highly tempting. However, a large percentage of his fifteen and a half years on this planet were instead taken up with intense martial arts training and related mental disciplines.

He was lucky enough to have been chosen by one of the world's greatest instructors, Master Kai, who claimed to have traveled to Buffalo from his native Japan to escape "bad debts" and build a new life. The formidable old man never elaborated on what these "debts" consisted of, though; and Alan -- along with the rest of his instructor's small chosen circle of students -- never dared considered asking at any rate. You spoke to Master Kai only if he spoke to you first, and you followed all his rules to the letter.

Alan was highly elated to be chosen to train in such a heavily esoteric merging of several formidable martial disciplines from throughout the breadth of Asia. This included an eclectic and smooth blending of koga-ryu ninjitsu, isshin-ryu karate, judo, and the Chinese techniques of tiger and dragon-style kung fu, with a good helping of the Korean art of hapkido thrown into the mix. Alan also received a large degree of training from Kondra, a young female expert gymnast and acrobat who worked with Master Kai as an adjunct instructor. Alan never forgot the many things he learned from Kondra in addition to -- and often alongside -- acrobatics.

All of these disciplines were combined in a unique form of combat training Master Kai had christened Teng-ryu. Alan was never charged a single cent for any of these years of intensive studies, and that was quite fortuitous considering the challenged financial situation of his household.

When Alan thanked his enigmatic sensei for the free training, the young boy remembered the diminutive but mighty Oriental instructor, who was half Chinese and half Japanese with an inkling of Korean blood, look at him with his steely gray eyes and saying the following: "Nothing in this world is for free. Payment and debt do not come only in the form of currency or material compensation. This training will come at a cost to you that will include, among other things, carrying on the disciplines I am teaching you to a new generation. The Teng-ryu training must be preserved, for the purpose it serves in this world will one day become clearly evident."

As it turned out, Alan became one of Master Kai's two prize students. A few he had chosen had unfortunately "washed out," as the instructor expected; whereas others became quite daunting in their own right. However, none of the other successes achieved the level of skill acquired by Alan and his fellow stand-out, Kenny Chapman.

The modern generation of Master Kai's Teng-ryu legacy was quickly growing, and by age fifteen, Alan had mastered most of the disciplines required of him. He felt all the hard work and training demanded by Master Kai constituted one of the three best uses of his time. Hence, he devoted many hours per week to these studies over the past several years. When not training in armed and unarmed combat or meditation techniques by Master Kai, he was doing acrobatic training with Konda; or learning all about pharmacology and incendiaries by his instructor's disciple Matoi, an expert chemist and herbalist who is alleged to have served for years as a member of some shadowy black ops government agency.

Alan considered the second best use of his time to be mastering the musical arts, as he practiced diligently as a disc jockey (i.e., *DJ*), learning to use a drum machine with great alacrity. It was his goal to successfully break into the hip hop scene by forming his own "crew" and earning a fortune in that vocation. He believed his technical skills for using technology to synthetically produce music, along with his general streetwise manner and cunning, would one day serve him well in achieving this goal.

The attractive young man considered the third best use of his time wooing the opposite sex, something in which he proved equal to all of his above described talents. Having recently been divested of his virginity, along with the huge pride that comes with that for an adolescent male, Alan was now ready to take on the world of amour in addition to that of musical creativity. He actually saw the two pastimes as being complimentary to each other, with one allowing him greater ease into the other.

Yes, Alan Perez had many plans and goals for the future. But at this point, he could hardly conceive what destiny would have in store for him.

***

Alfredo took a puff of a joint and offered it to Alan, who swatted his friend's hand away. "Man, didn't I tell you that I don't do recreational pharmaceuticals?"

"Geez, dude, you don't gotta lay on the hurt," Alfredo replied distressingly. "All I did was offer. And it's not like you don't sometimes take that herbal shit…"

"That's for meditative purposes, not recreation," Alan abruptly corrected Alfredo. "If I want my body to function properly, I can't pollute it."

"Man, you pollute your body every time you scarf down those fries at McBurger's," Teddy noted aloud. "I heard that shit clogs your arteries with cholesterol that slowly builds up 'til it causes a heart attack."

"I *have* to eat food," Alan retorted. "Sometimes, I *need* to use an herbal aid, like peyote, to open my mind for access to… other levels of thought. But I don't ever need to smoke that junk just to feel 'good.'"

"You really gotta lighten your ass up," Teddy lectured to Alan, thinking he could get away with it since he was his oldest friend.

"My ass is already light enough," Alan replied with obvious sarcasm, the comment being an allusion to the light skin tone he had due to his parents being an interracial couple.

"Ya'll know what I mean," Teddy responded with some irritation. "I swear, you been acting even more spaced since we both saw the weird blue flash that lit up the night sky. I think the bloggers are callin' it the *Warp Event*, or some shit like that, right? Anyways, it's almost like since that weird ass light show, you're more driven than ever before, if that's even possible."

"That flash made me feel… weird," Alan noted. "It gave me visions. Made me realize that life is short, and I need to have a purpose. A certain teacher of mine gave me a purpose long before that, and now I know that I need to see it fulfilled."

"Whatever ya say, man," Teddy responded and motioned to Alfredo to hand him the blunt.

Alan, however, kept scanning the poverty-stricken neighborhood surrounding the school with his small, darkish eyes, thinking of all the ways he could improve this city if only it was under his benevolent protection. Or *control*.

Chapter 2: Ghetto Plights

Alan calmly walked the several blocks from the bus stop to his home on Buffalo's Upper East Side after leaving school. The squalor surrounding him was depressing to many, not to mention a public relations nightmare for the mayor, but to him it was simply what he had always known. He viewed it as *home*, plain and simple. Alan knew it could use some improvement, but he never considered such an upgrade to constitute a major transition to a new way of life.

If the ghetto was really so bad, he often mused to himself, then why did some of the best aspects of black culture like the blues, rap, hip hop, and related genres that added so much to American culture emerge from earlier versions of it?

Alan believed that someone would always have control over these impoverished streets, but it would be most fortuitous if the person controlling it had the best interests of the inhabitants at heart. If such a leader were to emerge, he contended, the ghetto could come to be duly recognized as a culturally respectable locale one could be proud to be identified with. That leadership situation would be a highly beneficial alternative to the gangs and drug pushers who currently sought to achieve a parasitic type of relationship with the common residents, preying upon them and sucking them dry of what little they had. This was something he needed to do something about.

The young ghetto dweller's silent musings were interrupted when his attention was attracted by a ruckus ensuing directly across the street. He turned to see four young men whom he clearly identified as members of the much-feared street gang known as the New York Boys holding an older man up against the wall of a local deli.

Scanning the situation more closely, Alan could see that the older man was Mr. Gifford, a sometimes curmudgeonly but well-respected hard worker who ran the store for many years. Three of the gang members held him while the fourth, lead gangbanger had his left hand firmly grasped around Gifford's neck.

Alan's first instinct was to mind his own business, but then he remembered one of the main tenets Master Kai had always taught him: Those who have the ability to help unfortunates in a precarious situation have an obligation to do so; otherwise, the darker elements of the world will ultimately prevail. It then occurred to Alan that the skills he spent the past several years mastering made him one of those individuals who carried this obligation.

He thus concluded that his own well-being had to take a back seat to these principles. If he valued personal consequences too much, then he wasn't truly worthy of being one of the chosen few to carry on the tenets of the Teng-ryu system.

With that decided, Alan strode quietly but rapidly across the street to offer Mr. Gifford what help he could -- which he knew to be a lot. The young man also realized this would be a good opportunity to test his hard-earned skills in an uncontrolled street setting. Despite his appreciation of the glamorous notoriety which rap artists sometimes referred to as the "thug life," he always kept the code of honor he was taught in Master Kai's dojo as the foremost influence guiding his personal conduct.

As Alan reached the other side of the street, he could hear precisely what this quartet of New York Boys were hassling the grumpy store manager over.

"Didn't we tell your old ass the consequences of holding out on us?" the leader of the group asked.

This leader was known by the street name Shank, and he was an up and coming street soldier for the New York Boys. The brutal, muscular hellion continued to grip Gifford's throat tightly, leaving dark bruises on the man's light brown skin.

"I give you people more than enough as it is every month!" Gifford protested through the pressure constraining his larynx. "I ain't holding out nothin' on you! You demanded a certain percentage, and that's what you got!"

"Funny how our cut seems to get lower every month," Shank retorted.

"Well, business has been getting lot's worse lately," Gifford alleged, "which shouldn't be surprising considering how your gang scares everyone away from here!"

Shank pointed his right index finger a mere inch from Gifford's left eye. "Don't fuck with me, *tarado*," the young street soldier firmly stated. "We know your store isn't hurting like you say. You give us the rest of the percentage you owe us, and maybe I won't hurt you *too much* for holding out."

"That's enough." All four gangbangers turned their heads to see Alan, the author of that bold verbal command, standing a few feet behind them.

"And who the hell are you supposed to be?" Shank asked with a combination of annoyance and amusement. "Are you this old dude's nephew? Or maybe his rent boy?"

His three compatriots laughed.

"Get the hell outta here while you still can, you stupid kid!" Gifford hollered at the young Samaritan.

"Your homophobic remark just pissed me off all the more," Alan quietly replied, with just a tinge of rage discernible in his tone. "Now let him go."

"Don't interfere with our business operations, man," Shank spat. "If you want to live on these streets, you follow our rules."

"Rules that hurt rather than help the people who live under them are made to be broken," Alan replied with firm resolution.

"I don't have time for this shit," Shank decreed. "Leopard, go ice that *pendajo* while I get back to business here."

"Word," Leopard said quietly as he rushed towards their challenger.

Standing in a calm "at ease" stance until the last possible moment, Alan delivered a brutal front kick to Leopard's diaphragm that immediately stopped the heavily-built gangbanger's charge. Gasping in agony from the air abruptly forced from his lungs, Leopard never saw Alan's follow-up kick to the bridge of his nose coming. The burly man's cartilage was crushed with a spray of blood as the 250-pound thug was knocked flat on his back.

"Son of a bitch," one of the other three gangbangers said to himself in surprise. "Did ya see what he just did to Leopard? *Leopard*, man!"

"Tear that dickhead a *new* asshole!" Shank commanded to Malcolm and Cam, the other two gangbangers comprising his crew, who quickly complied by rushing at Alan in unison.

Taking advantage of the leader's distraction, Gifford struck the strongly built young man in the side of the face, stunning him. The angry deli owner then leapt upon the off-kilter street soldier and the two went sprawling on the ground.

In the meantime, as Malcolm and Cam both rushed to simultaneously tackle Alan, their target suddenly semi-somersaulted to the left of them while simultaneously delivering a brutal spinning kick directly to Cam's jaw. The area where the bone connected to the facial muscles cracked audibly, and Cam sunk to the ground. He spit two of his teeth detached by the kick onto the sidewalk before grasping his dislocated jaw.

Without wasting so much as a second, Alan focused the energetic adrenal "high" now coursing through his lithe form like water through a high-pressure hose into an attack upon the second of his assailants. Before Malcolm could even attempt to take a swing, Alan delivered a vicious spear hand thrust to the young thug's trachea. This caused his opponent to fall to the ground while grasping his swollen throat and uttering a series of loud gagging sounds.

With that brutal task accomplished, Alan turned to notice both Shank and Gifford back on their feet trading blows, with the older man determined to pummel his younger foe into submission and holding his own to an impressive degree in the process.

Forced to accede to the best course of action, Shank turned and fled while shouting, "Both of you are dead, man! I'll be back, and I won't be comin' alone!"

Gifford ran up to the young man who had assisted him and gave him an angry shove.

"Stupid punk kid!" the older man shouted. "You're damn lucky I was here, or those bastards would have killed you!"

Alan snickered and said, "If you say so, Mr. Gifford. Are you okay?"

"Yeah, I think so. My throat just hurts a bit. But I need to close up shop and get out of here before they come back. It's just not worth runnin' a business in this part of the city anymore. Nothing but trash around here."

"Are you seriously going to let those thugs run you out of the 'hood? You've had that store ever since I was a kid."

"You still *are* a kid! That shows exactly how much you know about reality. If your parents are smart, they'll get the hell out of this place too."

"We own a house here. This is where our lives are established."

"Really, kid? Let's see how all that goes now that you went and pissed those bastards off. That means you're officially on their radar, now."

Alan's small, dark eyes flickered as he realized the man had a point that needed to be considered. And strongly.

Chapter 3: A Knight is Born

As the chill of evening fell over Buffalo's East Side, Alan Perez took a meditative sitting position in his bedroom. This was one of the disciplines he most valued having learned from Master Kai, for it provided him with a sense of peace and mental clarity he rarely experienced in his everyday waking state. He always looked forward to these nightly contemplations which enabled him to access a higher state of consciousness. This particular evening, however, was to begin a major turning point in his life. And it was something his meditative state could scarcely have prepared him for.

Despite his deep trance, the young martial artist's hearing remained acutely alert. Master Kai always made it clear that one must always maintain a constant status of preparedness while in a meditative trance. That was why Alan still heard the familiar sound of his front door opening, and his father, Bradford, entering the house following work.

This time, however, the sound of his father's entrance wasn't as familiar as it usually was: Alan clearly heard Bradford *stumble*, rather than walk, in the door. He then heard his mother, Lenore, run into the front room in an alarmed manner, shouting his father's name. Within a split second, the young man was out of trance state and at his parents' side.

Upon rushing into the front room, which was directly outside his bedroom, Alan saw his mother helping his father to remain on his feet. The older man had clearly been worked over severely, as he had a swollen left eye and a stream of blood seeped out of his left nostril.

"Bradford, what the hell happened?" Lenore demanded to know.

"Those son of a bitchin' gang members," Bradford stammered out painfully as he was helped into a comfortable chair. "They did this to me as I stepped out of the car. They said to consider this a 'message' for our son to stay out of their business."

Alan's heart suddenly felt as if it had skipped several beats.

Lenore turned towards her son with a livid expression. "Alan, what did those punks mean by that? Are you getting involved with those animals? Answer me!"

Alan gritted his teeth. "I'm not involved in the sense of joining up with them, if that's what you mean. I just had an… altercation of sorts with them the other day."

"Jesus Christ!" Bradford shouted. "What type of altercation are you talking about?"

"They were beating on old Mr. Gifford outside of his store, because he refused to pay them a 'fee' for operating in their 'territory.' So, I intervened and… helped him fight them off."

"My god!" Lenore exclaimed. "Alan Theodore Perez! You could have gotten yourself killed or seriously hurt! Because of that, your father *was* hurt! And he could have been hurt much worse, or even killed! What the hell were you thinking?"

"Was I supposed to just stand there and let them hurt Mr. Gifford?" Alan replied while sternly standing his ground. "I'm sick of those scum doing whatever they please because nobody ever does anything about it. The police sure as hell don't give a damn. Mr. Gifford stood up to them, so helping him by doing the same was the least I could do."

"I think he did the right thing, Lenore," said Bradford, while rubbing his sore eye and applying a handkerchief to his bleeding septum.

"That's a load of bull, Bradford!" his wife insisted. "You two are practically all I have! I don't want to lose either of you because your son is so pig-headed!"

"Mom, it's because almost everyone thinks like you do that these punks have the power to do things like this in the first place," Alan rejoined. "We have the advantage in numbers, but most people prefer to cower at their boots. That spineless attitude is what did this to Dad and Mr. Gifford, not me for doing something about it!"

"Alan, the majority of us are not violent animals like those gang members are!" Lenore decreed. "That's why we don't just pick up knives and clubs and go beat them down! Yet you want to be just like them! Well, look what happened to your father because of that."

"No, it happened to Dad because most people think we should just sit back and take it!" Alan lamented. "Otherwise, those punks would be afraid of us, instead of the other way around! Is it any wonder they feel free to do whatever the hell they want to us? To take whatever they want from us?"

"Imagine how bad this city would be if everyone acted like them!" Lenore bewailed. "This is what you get for thinking like they do, Alan! More violence! Remember what I always told you? Violence just begets more violence, not solutions. But you never wanted to listen!"

17

"Acting in self-defense, or in defense of others, is not being like them, Mom!" Alan responded. "Do you see me beating up on people for money or turf?"

"I knew it was a mistake to let you take those martial arts classes," Lenore stated glumly. "They teach you to try solving everything with violence."

"That's a total load of bull, Mom!" Alan shouted. "I'm really good at it, and it's not only kept me out of trouble, but it taught me a lot of things, so I don't have to be a coward every time someone with a knife demands a 'fee' from me for living in 'their' territory!"

"Who do you think you're talking to, young man?" Lenore queried rhetorically.

"No one I should respect, that's for sure!" he replied curtly. "Not if you want your son to be a coward!"

"Listen, enough of this, both of you," Bradford interjected. "They didn't hurt me too bad, and I don't want this family torn apart because of those bastards."

"It's being torn apart because your son acted just like them!" was Lenore's loud retort just before storming out of the room.

Alan strolled over to his father and carefully checked his injuries. "Dad, I'm sorry. I should have foreseen this. I'm sorry I talked to Mom that way too, but it really pisses me off when she…"

"Alan, both you and your mother mean well, I know that," Bradford calmly interrupted. "Helping others and standing up to thugs like that is what we should all do. But your mother is right in the sense that very few people are willing to do that, and because of this, the few who do stand up to them are taking a huge risk, both for themselves and for their families. So please think about both points before you go jumping into something like that again."

Bradford then stood up, gave his son a reassuring pat on the shoulder, and headed for the bathroom to clean himself up. Alan remained standing in the front room seething with rage. His great determination to stand up to the gangs taking control of the ghetto areas of Buffalo was now tempered by his concern over making his family a target again.

***

Though Alan's first instinct was to go after the New York Boys and begin dealing with them in piecemeal fashion immediately, he realized that he would need to plan first. Master Kai always taught him never to rush into a situation without thinking through all the available options and likely consequences first. So, he would carefully conceive a plan, just as he had been trained to think.

As a child of the streets, Alan didn't agree with his mother that violence was always a bad thing. He further believed that this was the only language the gang mentality understood, and the only thing they respected and potentially feared.

He would need to put the fear into them and smash their operations to pieces, but he also knew that most of his neighbors were too "civilized" to do anything about it, other than make reports to the police and hope they acted on them.

After spending several hours in tranquil meditation in a lotus position, Alan came upon what might have been the ideal solution to this problem. It was one that would enable him to vent all his built-up anger against a deserving target. More importantly, it would simultaneously give him a useful outlet for the multitude of skills he mastered via the extensive teachings of Master Kai and his staff.

He thought back to Master Kai's summer training camps in the wilderness of the Southern Tier which he attended for years in addition to the regular classes in the city dojo. While his parents believed he was attending run of the mill martial arts camps for exercise and recreation more than anything else, in reality Master Kai and his team put his finest students through a grueling set of training that would make a Marine Corps boot camp seem easy by comparison.

Among many other things, the sensei showed his students how to design and construct full-body synthetic chain mail outfits that enabled them to fight full contact, both with and without weapons, as well as how to make them very cheaply. The students learned sufficient stealth techniques to sneak up on a deer and kill them with a shuriken through the eye from several yards away. Evading the forest rangers while doing this was another part of that training, something Master Kai never hesitated to put them through despite its illegality.

The students would further practice their stealth techniques by sneaking into conventional summer camps unseen and return with non-valuable items they pilfered from there, such as the counselor's notepads and shoe horns. They each ran challenging obstacle courses until every single student navigated them in a time frame that would rival any Olympic athlete. Further, they learned to expertly track both human and animal quarry though just about any type of environment.

One of the most useful and unique skills Alan learned was to perceive solid objects in the dark by a form of training that strengthened his retinas and optical muscles beyond that of normal human level. It was an exceedingly difficult attribute to develop and master; in fact, Alan became the only one of Master Kai's students to learn this ability. It was a form of reverse-nyctalopea that he referred to simply as "night vision."

Working feverishly over the next month, Alan constructed a charcoal gray chain mail body suit that resembled the popular late 20th century conception of a ninja outfit. The cowl covered his eyes as well as the rest of his head, however. It was porous enough for him to breathe properly, it muffled the sound of his voice, and he covered its eye holes with grayish plastic lenses that were opaque on the outside.

The modified tabi boots he wore had thick rubber soles that aided him in moving silently and made him appear slightly taller than his natural height of five feet ten inches. He was well-disguised, with an outfit that could blend into shadow and offer some resistance to blades, small caliber arms fire, bludgeoning, and the natural elements.

The outfit was also filled with an array of hidden pockets and a tight-fitting gray utility belt that held his arsenal of sickle-shaped shurikens, which he learned to make on his own from ceramic that he easily procured from his wood shop class and nearby garbage dumps. The sharpened edges of this hard ceramic had the same penetration power as those made of metallic alloys but were obviously no problem getting through metal-detectors.

Alan also constructed a solid plastic bo staff that he could pull apart to form two sickle-bladed kamas, with each section hidden in a holster on the opposite side of his belt. He could retract the blades – which were made of hardened, razor-sharp nylon -- and use them as hardwood batons. This he also learned to make from materials that he could readily obtain from Mr. Izo's Pottery shop located right next to Master Kai's Dojo, which was a business that was secretly owned and run by the martial arts master and his staff respectively.

The fairly popular pottery shop -- located on Carlton Street, just a few blocks away from Alan's home on Jefferson Avenue, and just outside the current limits of the New York Boys' turf -- helped to finance the school along with training fees from the regular students who attended ordinary Tai Chi classes, and supplements from certain investments back in Asia which the Master rarely even alluded to (but possibly has something to do with tea and jewelry).

His gray costume was punctuated with a crimson half-moon symbol on the chest area. This insignia was light enough to be seen in the open for providing symbolic value, but not enough to give him away when concealed in shadows.

Through Alan's training with Master Kai's associate instructor Matoi he learned the art of constructing small, easily concealable incendiary containers out of nitrogen he acquired from common fertilizer. By mixing them with several other cheaply obtained chemicals they would cause a powerful detonation upon strong impact with a hard surface.

He also designed small palm-sized plastic containers that, instead of detonating upon impact, would crack open to release a rapidly spreading smoke-like mist that he could use to confuse his opponents or cover an escape. He referred to these as his "darkout bombs"; his night vision would enable him to see rough shapes in the dark gray clouds, whereas his opponents could see nothing.

As Alan sat in his room putting the finishing touches on this mesh outfit, he noted two other major inspirations that convinced him to go the "lone masked avenger" route.

One of them was his collection of reprint pulp magazines featuring characters like The Black Centipede, The Masked Avenger, and The Black Shadow, along with comic books starring Raptor. The youthful martial arts master always received untold thrills by reading about darkly-clad vigilantes who operated outside the law, and who observed no rules other than their own when it came to halting the activities of those who preyed on the innocent. Some would kill without hesitation, whereas others had a code against killing under any circumstances despite the hurt they delivered to their foes. Alan still had to ponder which methodological and ideological route he would follow.

The second inspiration were the real costumed metahumans who began appearing on the scene over the past few years. Their appearances followed a series of mysterious celestial manifestations that occurred over various locales which the press and scientific community referred to as the Warp Events. Alan had personally witnessed the major Warp Event that recently manifested over Western New York. He saw it as a cosmic portent of things to come.

After learning about the debut of the metahuman vigilante called Centurion on Buffalo's West Side two months previous, he viewed that as the portent reaching fruition. It served to bolster his inspiration to take what he read about in fiction into the realm he experienced as reality. He believed that he finally realized what Master Kai meant when he told his students how the barriers between imagination and reality were often quite fragile, needing just the right type of catalyst to breach these boundaries.

Alan knew that he lacked impressive superhuman powers like those possessed by Centurion, let alone truly heavy-hitters like Ultimus, but he didn't consider this a major impediment. The martial arts master was confident that his great set of acquired skills, both in unarmed combat and with the use of simple but effective weapons, would more than make up for his lack of superhuman abilities. He would put Centurion and even Ultimus to shame by showing them how to clean up a city. He knew he wouldn't be able to wipe out the gang all in one fell swoop, but he had no problem with using a combination of physical and psychological warfare to whittle down their numbers over a period of time.

He looked at the completed gray uniform spread out on his bed and began musing to himself.

By using this uniform and a code name, the gang and other criminals won't know who I really am. I'll stay out of the public radar, and become something like a living symbol, an urban legend that will terrify the gangs. I once read that criminals are, at heart, a superstitious and cowardly lot. I don't believe that, of course. But they are human, and because of that, they can experience terror and confusion if faced with a threat they cannot identify or easily stop.

I don't have money at my disposal like the alter-egos of those pulp and comic book heroes, but I'll prove I can make do without it. I'll prove you need not be a billionaire to effectively confront crime and evil on the streets. You don't need elaborate gadgets or super-scientific weapons, either. You just have to be very good at certain skills and know the mindset of the individuals you oppose. I think Sun Tzu said that somewhere in The Art of War.

Of course, I'll need a code name. I'm going with Moonstalker, because… well, why not? It just sounds cool. And since I'll be operating mostly at night, I can't think of a better symbol of light within the darkness than the Moon. Not to mention how the half-moon resembles some of the sickle-shaped blades I'll be using. Quite apropos, if I do say so myself.

Chapter 4: Baptism of Fire at St. Luke's

St. Luke's Church is a venerable structure of Catholic worship that has stood proudly for nearly a century in the infamous Fruit Belt section of Buffalo's East Side. It's served the spiritual needs of its congregants for well over 100 years, and the Romanesque aesthetic of its architecture has long been an imposingly familiar sight to generations who lived here.

For the past four years the church has been under the stewardship of Father Merle Harris, a worldly and stern but good-hearted priest in late middle age. Since Father Harris's order had assigned him to this church, he has become well known and respected amongst the local community for his attempts to improve living conditions for the hard-working people of this largely impoverished area.

To the new type of alpha predator emerging in this section of the city, however, the apostolic edifice and what assets it had was simply another target and potential source of tribute to those who would be the streets' equivalent of feudal lords.

It was a frigid Friday evening in early March as Harris stood alone in the spacious rectory of the church filling up the wine chalices in preparation for the weekend masses. Since he became pastor he had insisted that several masses be conducted on Saturday as well as Sunday to accommodate various groups of parishioners with differing schedules and language preferences. He strongly believed that such open-ended accommodation would keep the waning number of congregants from diminishing any further and could actually serve to bolster the number in attendance. This extended mass schedule had gradually shown promising results since the church had fallen under Harris's watch.

The tall and lean priest had since grown accustomed to every single shadow and sound that was typical in the rectory at this time of the evening, when illumination was provided by nothing more than a long row of lit candles. Though it seemed as silent as ever, Harris could not get over the feeling that something was amiss that night, as if he wasn't alone. With a slight bit of nervousness, he glanced at the large oaken doors located several meters down the pathway leading through the pews. Even in the low luminescence of the candlelight, Harris's 20/20 vision could clearly discern the locked deadbolt chains around the handles of the door. This provided him slight reassurance, but he still couldn't get over that pervading sense of unease.

Worrying that perhaps he had seen films like *The Omen* once too often, Father Harris silently admonished himself to continue his preparations for the weekend activities and stop being afraid of the dark. Nevertheless, he felt it justified to walk to the tables containing the multiple rows of candles and light another several wicks if the extra illumination would provide him a more relaxed state of mind.

So, the nervy clergyman walked the several feet over to the table area, looking to make sure that every shadow he laid eyes upon was familiar to him. Considering that he saw no movement outside of the flickering dance produced by the small plumes of flame that slowly consumed each candle wick, he once again reminded himself to stop being so foolish. *Just light the extra candles and get back to the job, you silly old fool,* he silently critiqued himself.

As Harris stepped up to the first wick of the unlit candles, he pulled the lighter from the pocket of his robe, clicked the lever with his thumb, and heard the slight "vwoosh" of the flame bursting from the tip. The illumination immediately surrounding him increased as the flame appeared, and he moved it towards the waiting wick of the first unlit candle from this row. It was then that something made him casually glance to his side, where he caught sight of the pock-marked, beaming visage of a young man with three gold teeth that gleamed in the oxidation-produced light.

Shouting in surprise, Harris dropped the lighter, whose flame died as it clattered to the floor. His instinctive move to back away from the tables was halted when he bumped into another, quite solid human body standing behind him. This other young man's strong hands clasped over the priest's arms, holding him firmly in place. The first intruder with the grinning countenance moved closer to Harris, and within a moment a shiny steel stiletto blade was pointing but an inch from his face.

"Don't make another sound like that, priest," his young accoster said in a cold raspy voice. "You may consider yourself a man of God, but to us you're just another sheep in the 'hood, and I'll cut you all the same."

Harris looked around as four other young men, all well-built and clad in similar attire, stepped from the shadows of the pews and surrounded him. They were multi-racial in composition, but all had skin punctuated with lines of scar tissue obviously incurred in combat, along with tattoos on their arms in the image of a serpent coiling around a modern-looking building.

Forcing himself to gather nerve, Harris spoke with a tone of authority that he was determined to maintain in this church despite what he stood up against. He took his spiritual duties seriously, and he was confident that God would provide him the aid he now desperately needed, even though he could not guess what form it might take.

"What is the meaning of this?" Harris demanded. "How dare you sneak into this holy sanctuary and desecrate it."

The thug standing in front of him moved the blade a third of an inch into the priest's right nostril. "Watch it, Father," the young man said in a more menacing tone. "See, we're the New York Boys, and we dare anything. God doesn't run these streets, *we* do. And we expect the people running His house to pay the same fee for operating here as any other business."

"What are you talking about?" Harris replied with a high degree of incredulity. "This isn't a place of business, and you know that. The church is entirely non-profit…"

The young man swiped the blade to the left and inflicted a small but deep cut on the lower part of the priest's nose that interrupted the holy man's spiel. "Don't get technical with me, priest! We know this place gets lots of donations, and your operating fee is gonna come out of that. And word has it those chalices of yours are made of real silver. I'm sure one of ordinary glass would work well enough for wine sipping, so consider the silver ones as part of the fee. What else do you got in here that we should know about?"

Harris gritted his teeth, realizing from the wound just wreaked on him that these young men meant business, and would give no special deference to a man of the cloth. They were clearly the Devil's brood, and he found himself silently praying for an agent of the angels to come forth and drive them from the sacred grounds they were now violating with their evil. The clergyman briefly glanced at a nearby statue of the archangel Michael, armed with his sword, and quickly found himself appreciating the warrior aspect of the Heavenly forces.

"Don't make me ask you again!" the gang lieutenant yelled.

The heavily-built leader of this collection crew followed his words with a hard punch to the priest's stomach. Harris gasped in agony, his hands moving to his lower abdomen as the breath was forced out of his lungs. He couldn't help falling to his knees, but he quickly forced himself to stand and face these intruders once more. Maybe he wasn't a warrior, but he was a man of God and the pastor of this church, and he wouldn't fail to stand and face the forces of evil directly. Harris saw this as a very strong test on his spiritual resolve, and though he wouldn't provoke these men unnecessarily, he wouldn't falter before what they represented either.

"How… how did you boys get in here?" he asked as he recovered his breath.

The gangbanger leading the glorified home invasion grabbed the lapel of Harris's robe, pulled him closer, and put the blade up to his throat, its razor-sharp tip slightly piercing his skin. "I ask the questions here, not you! Now, I'm gonna ask you once more, and this time you better give me an answer. Where do you keep the donations and chalices, and what else do you got in here that we'd be interested in besides those silver drinking cups?"

Before any type of response could be so much as contemplated, a distinctly audible but low whooshing sound briefly entered their airspace. Its source was a ceramic sickle-shaped blade hurled from the far side of the pews which sunk deep into the flesh of the gang member's wrist. He shouted in both surprise and pain while dropping the stiletto to the floor with a loud clanking sound.

"What the hell!" one of the other gangbangers in the invasion crew hollered as he pulled a .45 from his belt.

However, the gun-wielding thug found his movement interrupted as another sickle-shaped shuriken flew out of the shadows and pierced his shoulder. He exclaimed a series of expletives as he discharged the gun, but the injury ruined his aim. As a result, the shot was inadvertently directed downwards, with the bullet ricocheting off the hard marble floor and ripping into his calf. He shouted in agony again, only this time he fell to the ground, the muscles of that leg ripped apart by the invasive lead projectile.

Harris slipped forward as the crew leader that was holding his person released his steely grip. The young criminal then drew his own blade in preparation for facing this other uninvited antagonist. In contrast, the priest didn't consider this newcomer, whoever he was, to be the least bit unwelcome. The man of the cloth looked deep into the darkened area between the pews and saw a mysterious gray-garbed figure emerge from the shadows, almost resembling a living silhouette of fury.

"Back off from that priest," a fearsome but muffled voice emanated from the figure. "Do it now, or I'll hurt the rest of you a lot worse than the first two."

"Shit, that's the guy who did this!" the pock-faced leader bellowed as he attempted to pull the shuriken from his bleeding wrist without severing a major artery. "Ice him! Now!"

The figure stood in an "at ease" stance, readying himself for the coming attack. This was the martial arts master's baptism of fire in a place known for a much different sort of baptism, and he was determined to not only succeed, but to do so in a manner that left a very strong impression. He recalled all his years of training, and he cleared his mind entirely of thought, entering a state where he "expected nothing, but was ready for anything" as Master Kai called it.

One of the gangbangers screamed like a rage-maddened animal and rushed towards the offending figure. The gray-attired vigilante easily caught the felon's intended haymaker in an arm lock and slammed his palm down on the elbow. The bone was pushed clear through the flesh on the opposite side. The warrior scream previously emitted by the young man now mutated to one of unbridled agony at the cruel and grotesque compound fracture visited upon his limb.

The figure then slammed his elbow into the center of the gang member's nose, crushing its cartilage into a mass of crumpled tissue. The brutally injured young malcontent fell to the ground in horrific agony as blood spurted from his now deformed nasal passages like miniature geysers of crimson ink.

"Jesus!" one of the other gangbangers shouted as he extended his own blade and prepared to enter the melee.

"How ironic that now, when you're the prey instead of the predator, you cry out for Jesus in this church," was the icy response from the charcoal-attired invader.

I could not have said it better, Father Harris couldn't help musing to himself.

Unable to see as clearly in the dark as the figure standing in opposition to him, the gangbanger nevertheless lunged at the dim shadow of his enemy. As he swung his blade towards the throat area of the figure, he found his arm intercepted by a hard stick-like implement. The impact with the small hardwood staff immediately fractured the bone in the center of the arm, causing him to drop the blade. Within a split second this move was followed up by the steel-hard bludgeon smashing him on the skull, which ripped a small chunk of flesh out of the cranial region just above his temple.

Yet another member of the crew was now lying unconscious on the floor as blood seeped from the gaping wound and congealed into a thick puddle resembling a huge Rorschach blot.

Moonstalker then separated the staff into two batons and holstered them in sheathes built into each pant leg. He was determined to finish off the last two hand-to-hand, as he felt the practice would be useful.

Not being foolish, and having overcome their initial surprise, the last two gangbangers attacked in unison. Placing one of his hands on a large wooden pew for support, the ninja-like warrior executed a high side kick that struck the front attacker in the throat. The man's larynx felt like it had been punctured with a two-by-four as the amazing force of the kick sent him careening into his fellow gang member who stood directly behind him.

The second attacker wasted no time in pushing the fallen form of his compatriot off him and jumping to his feet. But as impressive as his speed was, it paled before that of his opponent. No sooner had the young ruffian returned to a standing position than his nose was shattered with a brutal palm heel strike. He instinctively covered his face as blood flowed through the cracks of his fingers like water through a strainer. Moonstalker followed this with a kick to the diaphragm that knocked the gang member several feet backwards, where his spine smashed into the first marble step leading up to the rectory's temple.

Father Harris watched in astonishment as the figure then trod entirely from the shadows, revealing his charcoal gray outfit in all its frightening glory. Now only the leader of the invasion soiree remained, and he was still trying to remove the shuriken embedded in his wrist.

"Having some trouble?" the figure queried in an iron tone. "Here, let me help you with that."

The vigilante tore the sickle-shaped shuriken from the gang leader's wrist, obviously ripping open at least one vein in the process. This caused blood to spurt from the flesh as if heated by a pressure cooker. The young gangbanger with the pock-marked face and gold teeth screamed in terror and agony just before he squeezed his wrist with his other hand in a desperate attempt to staunch the blood loss.

Harris cautiously but reverently approached the gray-clad figure before him. "Thanks be to God that you arrived," he said. "Who are you, son?"

"You can call me Moonstalker," the young vigilante told him. "That's what you can call me too, scum!" he said in the direction of the terribly bleeding gang leader.

"Awww man, I'm gonna bleed out, help me," the emaciated criminal said in a whimpering plea.

"You'll only bleed out if the pastor here doesn't care to call you an ambulance," Moonstalker replied with sardonic glee. "Something tells me he will, though. It would serve you right if I made you come back here and mop up your blood from the floor. And the blood from your fallen comrades, too, since they'll be in no condition to so much as wipe their own asses over the next several days. I'm going to leave you relatively intact, so you can deliver a message to the rest of your gang:

"These streets do not belong to you. They belong to *me*. These are my people. You don't prey on my people anymore. If anyone does, I will prey on *them*. Do you understand?"

"Awwww, man, this hurts..."

Moonstalker kicked the gang lieutenant in the side of his face, picking a spot below his temple that would cause maximum pain without knocking him out. "I asked you a question. *Do you understand?*"

"Yes! Shit, man! Just get me a goddamn ambulance!"

Moonstalker kicked the gang leader once more, this time in the right leg, which caused him to howl in pain anew.

"Don't take the Lord's name in vain here again! You've violated this sacred place enough already for one night, don't you think?"

"Sorry, man… shit…"

Moonstalker turned to Harris and handed him a key. "This is how they got in. It seems one of your parishioners who has access to the rectory made them a copy of the key you provided for them. I'm not yet sure if that person did this after being shaken down by the gang, or if one of the more trusted members of your congregation is in the gang's pocket. I advise you to watch your flock a bit closer in the future, Father.

"In the meantime, call the police to haul out this human detritus. And call an ambulance for them if you feel like it. I don't think you'll be needing me anymore tonight. Just a janitor. But if you ever do in the future, I'll be here again."

With that made clear, the vigilante sped off into the darkness of the pews and promptly vanished from sight, before Harris could say anything to him. The priest had no idea how Moonstalker had managed to either enter or exit the church. But he actually felt safer that this strange warrior had the means of doing so, especially now that he knew the gang had their own means of ingress.

As a man of God, Harris was well aware that he was supposed to be against violence as a resolution to any problem. But he also considered himself a student of history as well as a realist, and consequently he knew that sometimes force had to be matched with a strong counter-force. He readily understood that not everyone could be expected to take up the warrior mantle, but he earnestly believed that those who had such a talent should put it to use in defense of the common people, rather than using it against them. As far as Father Harris was concerned, people who excelled in the way of the fist had as much a place in the world as those whose specialty was the way of the heart.

Sometimes necessary evils need to be tolerated to face down greater evils, the pastor quietly convinced himself. *No doubt that warriors on the side of the angels have their use in the world. After all, Michael himself carries a sword.*

The pastor of St. Luke's figured this Moonstalker may have been the answer to some of his most fervent prayers to help clean up these surrounding neighborhoods. Perhaps he was intended to be a living component of Michael's sword right here on Earth.

***

Medino, the pock-faced lieutenant who led the failed church invasion crew two evenings previous, was released from the hospital. He now had to face the true leader of the New York Boys, the self-declared master of Buffalo's East Side, to explain his failure, along with the exact cause of it. Having just left a church, he found himself actually praying that the much-feared young man who was known only as Assailant would show him the same degree of mercy that Moonstalker had the previous night.

The street lieutenant stood in a large room which was part of a Harrisstone building located in the heart of the East Side. It was decorated with a fancy assemblage of furniture and technological amenities purchased with illicitly acquired funds. He was on his knees on the woolen rug covering the floor in front of the large leather chair that intentionally reminded all who beheld it of a throne. On it sat a young man of prodigious build.

The fearsome personage who was seated on the makeshift throne stood to reveal his daunting height of well over six feet. He wore a sleeveless leather jacket that exposed the impressive musculature rippling beneath the skin which covered his massive arms. The upper half of his face was concealed by a thin leather mask with eyeholes that exposed his impassive hazel eyes. His skin was mocha-toned, and that along with a slightly noticeable Spanish accent marked him as being of Hispanic heritage. The front of the jacket was unbuttoned to show off a dark shirt emblazoned with the neon-colored symbol of the New York Boys.

His intimidating attire was completed by a pair of black khaki pants that allowed his huge frame full freedom of movement. Additionally, leather gloves with exposed fingers fit snugly over his hands.

"Did you seriously let one man do all this to you, *padre?*" Assailant asked in an icy deep voice.

Medino was unable to force himself not to quiver as if he were sitting atop a shifting tectonic plate. "It-it wasn't my fault, boss. Seriously, he came outta nowhere, and he wasn't like a normal man. He was dressed something like a ninja, and he had these sharp things that he threw like…"

"*One man!* You let *one man* do this to you?"

"Oh, c'mon, please, boss, I told you what happened. He wasn't like no other man! He said these streets were his now, and he did this to us, and…"

Before Medino could utter another word, each side of his face was seized by Assailant's powerful hands. The hapless man's whole body was then lifted into the air as if he weighed less than a sack of sugar. The pressure brought to bear on his cheekbones by that grip was so tremendous that he clearly felt both retinas detach in his eyes.

"Boss, I'm sorry… please don't…" were the last words he managed to choke out before the brutal leader of the New York Boys sunk his thumbs into the front of his throat and pushed until the man's trachea was crushed inwards. The whole deed took but a few seconds.

The pock-faced field leader vomited a quick torrent of blood, while his eyes turned a pinkish-red as numerous vessels burst behind the lenses. A feeling of intense disappointment pervaded Assailant's bellicose mind as he let the human carcass in his hands fall to the floor, an act which stained his expensive woolen rug with splotches of crimson. He didn't mind, though; he knew the sight of the dried blood would provide an important reminder to the rest of his crew, particularly whomever would replace Medino as his one of his main street lieutenants.

"One man," he said to the corpse before him, as if it could still hear his gripes. "*Estúpido idiota.*"

The business at hand completed, Assailant turned to the three members of his crew in attendance. All of them were struggling hard not to show any emotion over what they had just witnessed, including fear. They all managed to remain stoic in appearance, but their colossal leader could still feel the terror emanating from them like a breeze of air. He noted to himself that their fear tasted sweeter than kiwi.

"Come over here and drag this *pendejo* out of my sight and throw him in the incinerator," the bulky gang leader firmly ordered. "Make sure his bones burn along with his flesh, but you can keep one of his fibula for my dog. Also, save his jacket for me; I always liked it. And on your way back, one of you grab me a tuna sub from the deli. I just worked up a bit of an appetite."

Chapter 5: Serpent in the School

Riverfield High School was a building that looked to be about 100 years old. Its intercom system barely worked, and virtually everything else about that institution of secondary education was sub-standard. This paucity of resources extended to the quality of equipment for the sports teams, the text books, the computers in the social media lab, and the attention paid to the attendance list in the office by the underpaid truant officers. It was, along with North Park, one of the two Buffalo secondary schools which were hit particularly hard by the mayor's recent cuts to the city's education budget. Especially considering these two schools didn't have much before that either.

Alan was thankful that the science chemistry lab was kept mostly up to date, however. This was not because he enjoyed science classes, but because various substances were kept there that he had use of in making his various chemically-based paraphernalia. This particular set of skills, courtesy of Master Kai's adjunct instructor Matoi, would serve his new career as a costumed vigilante quite well.

Like most people on Buffalo's East Side, his finances were tight; hence, his access to the chemistry lab was a godsend to a non-millionaire crime fighter who had to place the utmost importance on mastering the art of frugality. Moonstalker couldn't be a comic book hero like Raptor, but he was determined to become the type of vigilante who was more than formidable enough without bottomless pockets.

Despite being early in May, the Buffalo air had a typical chill to it as Alan approached Riverfield High shortly after eight in the morning. As was often the case, many girls looked at him yearningly as he walked past, with several of them making a point to offer him verbal greetings and a hug. He was quite proud of the popularity his attractiveness to the opposite sex afforded him.

Of course, Alan placed equal value on his reputation as a physically tough customer, having always realized the respect granted to males in his crowd who displayed impressive physical prowess. He had proved himself in several fights over the years, all the while being careful to use but a minimum of his incredible martial arts skills. As a result, even those among his peers who hated him tended to keep this fact to themselves.

The school looked quite run down on the outside, being about as attractive to the eye as a swollen cold sore on a person's lip. The interior didn't look much better. Despite disliking school, he knew that he had to tolerate this daily ritual to acquire the all-important diploma. His alacrity with computers was almost as impressive as his affinity for the martial disciplines, and his lack of interest in academics belied the strong intellect he possessed in regard to philosophy and psychology. His expertise with using technology to create music was also well known and respected across the East Side.

As Alan confidently strode down the hall towards the corridor where his locker was situated, the young man's eyes focused on a distressing sight. One of the other students, the athletic Tony Kirkland, was very clearly "putting the movies" on the lovely Shanice Morris. She was a freshman whom Alan had eyes for since the beginning of the year, and he knew he was one of the few boys in the school who had a realistic chance of winning a relationship with her. He knew little of Kirkland, save for his similar reputation of being tough and a fine football player.

It didn't much matter to Alan Perez who Kirkland was, however. The secret vigilante feared no one and had healthy respect for few. Moreover, he had spent the past week getting to know Shanice and wasn't about to let another boy steal her interest away.

Alan walked towards the two conversing students, believing this would be a social situation he could handle with the typical degree of ease for any high school student that enjoyed his reputation. Little did he realize how wrong that comforting thought would turn out to be.

Alan confidently approached Shanice while looking askance at Kirkland. "What's up, babe?" he said, making his interest in her quite obvious to his basketball star rival. "I just wanted to make sure I got the correct digits you gave me last week."

He pulled out his cell phone and accessed his address book with a few taps to the device's screen, a gesture designed to emphasize the point he was making.

Kirkland looked Alan up and down, as if sizing him up. "Excuse *you*," he said firmly. "If you don't mind, I'm trying to ask this beautiful lady out."

Shanice giggled in response to his comment before greeting her other suitor. "Hey, Alan. 'Sup?"

"My bad for interrupting, man," he told Kirkland, "but I just wanted to make sure I got Shanice's number correct, since I already asked her out. Maybe you'll get a chance with her if I fail to please. Not likely given my record, but a brother *can* hope, right?"

Shanice giggled again and gave Alan a mock slap on the arm. "You're so bad, you know that?"

"Are you playing with me, man?" Kirkland queried with an expression that suddenly turned darkly malevolent.

Alan met his gaze with an equally acidic, unwavering stare. Shanice could now sense the tension building between the two, and casually stepped between them. The situation she saw developing before her was no longer flattering or amusing in the least.

"Chill, both of you, okay?" she requested nervously. "Alan did ask me out first, but it's not like…"

"… because if you are," Kirkland interrupted her to continue, "then you should know exactly *who* you're crossing first."

The tall, well-built young man unbuttoned his school jacket just enough to let Alan see the green emblem of the New York Boys emblazoned on his tee-shirt. Shanice winced when she laid eyes on that much-dreaded symbol. Alan showed no sign of fear but was forced to acknowledge what he was now getting himself into.

"Word has it that you already got in our business," Kirkland said, poking Alan in the rib cage with his index finger hard enough to elicit a sensation of pain. "Don't you think your dad had enough the first time? Stay out of my way, this girl is part of my turf now. Do you understand me, man?"

Alan was infuriated, and it took every iota of his well-honed mental discipline to avoid inflicting mortal harm upon the revealed gangbanger right then and there. Shanice was no angel, but she did take her future seriously, and didn't see herself as the "prized possession" of a dangerous gang member. She no longer found Kirkland's attentions remotely gratifying, and her fear became palpable.

"Look, Tony, you're cool and all that," she all but stammered, "but Alan did ask me out first. Maybe we can arrange something in the future though, okay?"

Kirkland's malign glare then shifted from Alan to Shanice. "Are you saying you're taking this loser over me?"

The girl was no coward, having grown up in a rough neighborhood, but this was one of the New York Boys standing before her. She needed to handle the situation with much deference to that fact.

"No, no," she said, frantically trying to defuse what was brewing. "It's not that at all. But he asked me first, so it's just polite and ladylike to give him a shot before going out with another boy."

Kirkland then shifted his aspersive glare from Alan back to Shanice. He gritted his teeth as if rapidly becoming overwhelmed by rage. This culminated in his punching one of the locker doors so hard that he actually left a visible dent in it. The strongly built adolescent exhibited no sign of pain after doing this, which caused Shanice to further recoil. Alan remained impassive at the display.

The young gang member then turned and treaded down the hall, stopping briefly to turn around and point a menacing index finger at the two standing before him. He then huffed off down another corridor.

"Jesus," Shanice said while gasping as if trying to stave off a panic attack. She then looked at the attractive face of the young man standing before her. "Alan, I'm sorry, I didn't mean to start anything."

He gently took her hand. "Don't worry, okay? Everything'll be all right."

"But he's one of the New York Boys. Did you see...?"

"I told you, everything will be okay. I promise. Are you up for a bite to eat this afternoon?"

"But what about our classes?"

"Exactly. What about them?"

*****

Five hours later, Alan and Shanice were enjoying an afternoon repast in a local restaurant called the Tasty Spoon. The two admired each other's features from across the table as they munched on a simple but well-prepared meal. This was a popular dining spot due to its reputation for good food at very reasonable prices. Despite being treated to this culinary pleasure by Alan, his date was clearly suffering from anxiety.

"Are you sure we aren't going to get into trouble for ditching school, Alan?" she asked.

"Nah," he replied with all full assurance. "Just so long as we signed in during morning roll call, as far as the office is concerned, we were there the whole day. The staff has too many other things to worry about in that school than making sure every student attends every single class. I have connections with the attendance staff in the office anyway. Same with the security crew."

"How did you get so damn important?"

"Just by being myself, I suppose."

Shanice couldn't help giggling at the response. "But you can't just ditch school like that. Don't you want your education? Don't you want to get out of his hell hole eventually and make something of yourself?"

"I'm guessing I just don't define 'education' in the same way you do. At least in terms of identifying it with schooling. I'll finish high school, because I know how important having that piece of paper we call a diploma is. As for getting out of his 'hell hole,' I'd rather work on changing it into something that isn't so hellish rather than just up and running away."

Shanice looked at her date with a pensive expression as she chewed a few leaves of salad. "You know, Alan, despite having a natural gangtsa-ish swagger, you're really very different than that. You're really smart, but not in a nerdy way. More like in a really educated but street wise way, if you get what I'm saying. Geez, I must be making a fool out of myself right now."

Alan beamed in a reassuring fashion. "Don't worry, you know guys don't get turned off when a girl gets nervous on a date. You're doing fine. I'm glad to find there's more to you than just the face and figure of a model."

"So that's not the only thing you're after then?"

"Babe, if that was all I was after, then I would be pursuing dippy girls who were walking trophies, not one who has your personality qualities, including fully operating gray matter in her skull. And I was quite impressed to see that you aren't turned on by punks like Kirkland."

"Of course not. He scares me. And since I'm really starting to like you, Alan, I'm scared for *you* now too."

"Didn't I make you a promise?"

"Yes, but, well… look, the New York Boys are no joke. And I heard you already crossed them before. You need to be careful. Please."

Alan glowered at his date. "So, you're doubting my ability to keep that promise? How can I consider dating a girl that doesn't trust my word?"

He then quietly reminded himself to keep both his ego and his temper in check. This constituted a negative quality of his persona that had cost him more than one friendship and relationship in the past.

"Chill, Alan. I'm just concerned about you, okay? I won't apologize for that."

"It's appreciated, but I don't need the concern. I'll keep safe."

She forced herself to form a weak smile. "I know."

"Cool. And with that out of the way, I know someplace we can go to be alone. My friend Ty and his mom won't be at home for a few hours, and they've always trusted me with the key to their place. If you're up for it, of course."

"Alan, isn't that moving, well, rather fast?"

"Can you think of a good reason to go slow?"

"Several."

"And how good are those reasons, when you really think about them?"

"Good enough. I'm not going to let you use me, Alan. Don't think you're the only one with a sense of pride."

"Fine. I get that, but it was never my intention to use you." He shrugged past this awkward point in the conversation. "So, back to school then? Or might you be down for a trip to the mall?"

"Ha! You know they won't let us in there without adult supervision. Not in the middle of a school day."

Alan grinned that mischievous smirk of his again, an expression Shanice was already becoming quite familiar with. "I beg to differ, babe. The school isn't the only place where I have friends in high places."

Once again, he heard his date's appealing giggle in response. "You're on, then. I may have pride, but I'm not against breaking the rules to have some fun."

Alan smiled, paid the check, and took Shanice's hand as they left the counter. The two then departed the diner together, preparing to grace the mall with their presence.

It would turn out to be a most unwise decision.

Chapter 6: Melee at the Mall

Alan entered the Main Street Mall hand-in-hand with Shanice while displaying a demeanor of complete nonchalance. He secretly felt quite privileged to be accompanied by a girl as attractive as the one now holding his hand. She was African-American with a bright caramel skin tone, long braided ebony hair, and a body weight perfectly complimentary for her five foot, four inches of height. She felt equally ecstatic to be in his company, considering how attractive she knew he was amongst the female population in their school.

Nevertheless, Shanice couldn't help feeling a bit of reticence at breaking the rules of the mall. She couldn't help wondering whether Alan was serious about his "friends in high places" status being applicable outside the school.

"Are you sure about this, Alan?" she queried. "That security guard over there is looking at us funny."

"Are you doubting my word again?" he asked with a noticeable hint of exasperation.

"Alan, I just don't want to get into trouble, or my 'rents won't let me go out with you…"

They were cut off when a large security guard approached them.

"Alan," he said in a deeply intimidating voice, clearly recognizing the young man. "You know that you and that young lady are not supposed to be here now."

"Hey, you know I always have a school pass, right, Jerry?" Alan responded with that smirk again.

"Can I see it?"

"Certainly," Alan assured him as he produced a folded piece of paper from his pocket.

Jerry perused the notice and smiled in a reassuring manner. "I figured you had this. You know I have to check anyway, right? It's part of the job description."

"And I'm mighty glad you do your job so well, Jerry," Alan said with a convincing smile of his own. "The mall is all the better for it."

"And the young lady?" Jerry asked, causing Shanice to tense up.

"That pass was for both of us," Alan said calmly.

"Oh, okay, no problem then," Jerry replied.

As the guard walked off, Alan glared at Shanice with an expression that could only be described as a combination of satisfaction and annoyance.

"Now do you see that I'm not one to tell any stories?" he said.

"Yes, I can," Shanice responded in a mollifying manner.

***

The couple spent the next forty minutes visiting various shops in the mall, as well as talking and joking around as young people often do. Shanice was unusually easy to get along with, and she couldn't help noticing that Alan's sometimes prominent ego was balanced by his charm, confidence, wit, and intelligent way of looking at the world. She had some reservations about him but couldn't help her feelings from growing increasingly deeper as she spent more minutes with the young man.

The East Side girl felt safe with Alan Perez in a way she didn't with any other boy she had gone out with before. It was something the striking girl could judge quite well despite her young age, as her attractiveness had always assured that boys often displayed an open interest in her for a few years now.

Yet Shanice was still determined not to be used, and not to just let Alan have his way regarding all things. She had a healthy sense of self-worth, and she would make this clear to him. Still, the girl wanted to do this in a way that wouldn't invoke the incendiary temper she could tell that he had underneath his affability.

Even though Shanice well knew that she had her pick of any number of other boys, the young lady was mindful that the same held true for Alan when it came to his own choices among the girl populace. She didn't want it to come to this if it was possible to establish a mutual understanding between them that effectively tamed his ego.

Towards the end of those forty minutes, Alan was in the Sound Factory store showing off his knowledge of musical equipment. He was discussing the intricacies of one particular drum machine that he was most impressed with.

"See this here?" he said. "The TR-8 combines the best rhythm-making technology of the two highest-performing drum machines of the '80s. You know, back in the Stone Age when DJ's were still scratching vinyl records on a turntable to make the music skip to a certain beat?"

"I wouldn't know," she replied with a sardonic grin. "I wasn't there to see what the Neanderthals of that decade did."

Alan met her grin with his own. "Ha! Yup. You can easily duplicate all of that with this machine, and a lot more besides. It's really pricey though, going for over $500.00. But I'm determined to save up for it. The gigs I get in the clubs now should let me save up enough within a few months. Then I'll get even better gigs and be able to produce fully professional material that I can sell under my own label through my web site."

"Cool. Doesn't your 'rents mind that you play some of these clubs at all hours on the weekend? I mean, just to be honest, some of those places can be, well, you know... sort of seedy."

"I'm not sure how they feel about it, since it never occurred to me to ask them."

"You mean, they don't know about this career of yours?"

"Not entirely. No need to get into it with them. I can't rely on them to pay my bills forever, and they have enough on their plate even now. I need to do my own thing, and I'm not going to wait until I turn eighteen to start doing that. And I'm not going to do it working for McDonnie's or King of Burgers."

"I hear you, but..."

Alan cut her statement short by putting his index finger over her lips to signify she needed to be quiet.

"Am I not entitled to my opinion?" she asked at a low decibel.

"It's not that. Look outside the shop, but without making it obvious you're looking. Don't panic, and don't say anything above a whisper."

She did as requested to the best of her ability, and saw something that made her feel the urge to urinate in her pants on the spot.

Five members of the New York Boys, easily recognizable by the brazen display of the gang's logo on their shirts and characteristic green headbands, were standing across the railing just a few yards outside the Sound Factory. Clearly, Alan's buddy Jerry and the rest of the few security guards in the mall did nothing to deter them from congregating there as a group, let alone from entering the mall at this hour in the first place. She also couldn't help wondering why someone didn't simply call the police.

"Oh my God, Alan, what do we do? Are they here for us? Did Tony say something to them already? He had his cell phone with him today, he could have called them or something..."

"Calm down. I know it's not easy to do that right now, but you have to keep calm if you don't want to draw their attention to this shop."

"And to answer your question, I honestly don't know. Gangs don't usually like getting involved in personal skirmishes between their members and civilians. But they do make exceptions at times. And they may simply be doing surveillance as a personal favor for him while checking on their turf.

"This mall is in the downtown area, outside the perimeter of the East Side, and I had no idea they had extended their territory this far. They may be planning on knocking heads with the State Boys, since they're getting quite close to encroaching on their turf."

"Geez, Alan, you sound like you're doing military strategical thinking or something. You may be tough as nails, but like you said, we're just civilians. We're not police officers."

Alan wanted to berate his pretty paramour for what he considered the cowardly and apathetic attitude displayed by so many civilians when confronted with these gang members. He wouldn't need to have taken up the mantle of Moonstalker in the first place if the average person would refuse to cower from bands of human predators and rely entirely on the unpredictable appearances of law enforcement officers to protect them. But he realized this wasn't the time to get on her case about that. His open strategical musings had already sounded odd to her.

"Listen to me carefully," Alan said firmly. "You take my hand, and we're going to walk out of this shop. We will walk fast, but *do not* start running. That draws attention. We're going to walk over to Wentworth's, which will have a lot of customers. Let's do it now, don't question anything."

Since Shanice was determined to get home unscathed and taken by Alan's confidence in the face of possibly extreme danger, she did as he requested. Wanting to look unbothered by the situation, the young woman walked as fast as she could without escalating into running. The gang members initially showed no interest in the couple's departure, but they then suddenly stepped away from the railing and began walking behind them. *Oh geez, are they following us?* Shanice couldn't help asking herself that as terror began to overcome her thought processes.

Though Alan didn't look back, he noticeably picked up his pace when the gang members began walking behind them. He seemed determined to keep at least twenty feet between the gangbangers and the two of them. Though it seemed to take an eternity to the trembling Shanice due to her state of mind, it was mere minutes before they reached the typically crowded clothing store called Wentworth's.

After walking quickly inside, Alan and Shanice navigated several aisles of clothing. The hanging collections of attire provided something of a cover for their movements thanks to the large amount of sartorial product on display and customers looking around. He then made his way to the dressing rooms in the back, specifically the section where the women changed.

"Grab some clothing off the rack, make like you're going in there to change. And stay in there until I tell you it's okay to come out. This won't be the first place they look, since you're with me. They'll figure we're shopping together."

"What are you going to do?"

"I'm going to sneak by them, find Jerry, and let him know there are gang members here possibly looking for trouble. He'll get on the dispatch and mobilize the other guards, maybe call the police."

"You seriously think he doesn't already know they're here, Alan?"

"I don't have time to argue! Just listen to me, okay, goddamn it?"

Shanice was taken aback by Alan's display of anger, but she had to concede that he appeared to know what he was doing thus far. She was also quite street wise, but he seemed more than simply that; he appeared to be a natural tactical thinker, as if he had spent years in the military. So ultimately, she nervously nodded her head and did as he requested.

Alan then used all his stealth training to move about the clothing store virtually unseen. He had no doubt, like Shanice surmised, that Jerry knew the New York Boys were there. Their presence was quite conspicuous, and he realized the security guards of the mall either felt they weren't paid enough to risk dealing with the likes of them, or they had been paid by the gang itself to "look the other way." He expected no help from them; at least, not intentionally.

Alan managed to slip out of the clothing shop without incident, and he noticed that three of the gang members were standing about five feet from the entrance. He pretended not to notice them as he headed towards the rest room area. Alan further noticed that Tony Kirkland was not among them, and that they appeared to recognize him and show interest in his departure. They quietly walked behind their target, trying not to make it known they were scoping him.

Within minutes, Alan dashed into the bathroom. He figured the two who didn't trail him would continue to look for Shanice, so he needed to deal with this quickly. The men's room was empty save for the visible feet of a single man sitting in one of the stalls. Hopefully, if anything went down other than what was in his bowels, he would have the common sense – or healthy fear – to stay seated.

Walking into another stall, Alan reached into his coat pocket and pulled out what resembled nothing more than a square of cloth. But in actuality it was a simple but highly useful invention he was taught to make at the dojo. It was a charcoal outfit designed to be resistant to tearing but thin enough to be easily folded and stored in a pocket. It was a pull over garment that had a barely visible seal in the back which, with practice he already had, could be donned within mere seconds. The garment included a sewed-on mask complete with one-directional view eye lenses that could be pulled over the head. He usually made a point to wear clothing that allowed him full freedom of movement, so it wasn't difficult to fit this uniform over it. It had cloth sandals that slipped over his sneakers to conceal them.

It wasn't nearly the quality of the regular uniform Alan had worn as Moonstalker, but it would do in a pinch. Wearing it lessened the risk of his being identified should he make a mistake while having to go into action unexpectedly. The young warrior was well aware how he needed to find a way to modify his regular, Kevlar-coated outfit so he could carry and get into it as easily as this one (he thought it was silly and impractical to wear a costume under his regular clothing like comic book heroes often did). But for now, this would have to do.

Hidden in a pair of pockets sewn into his regular pants were two small retractable hard plastic batons that served as the only weapons he had on hand right now.

I need to modify my nylon utility belt, so I can wear it in concealed fashion when I go out, he noted to himself.

As the disguised Alan Perez walked out of the stall in makeshift battle garb, he realized that his timing was off in a major way. One of the gang members stepped into the men's room just in time to see the vigilante head for the door. *Damn it!*

"Hey, what the f…" was all the young thug could get out of his mouth before Moonstalker delivered a lightning-fast side kick to his sternum.

Taken by surprise in addition to the force of the expertly placed blow, the gangbanger was sent crashing through the door of the stall that was occupied by the man moving his bowels. *Damn it, I didn't mean to knock him through thru that stall. Now I just endangered a civilian!*

"What the holy hell?" the man on the toilet screamed as shards of the wooden door flew over him and a 210-pound gang member suddenly landed on his lap.

Forcing himself to shrug off the effects of the blow, the gangbanger leapt off the hapless civilian's lower extremities and attempted to rush his opponent. He was stopped dead with a powerful reverse punch to the face by the gray-clad champion, the blow augmented by the hard baton he had gripped in his hand. The cartilage of what was once the ruffian's nose exploded into a spray of blood and mucous as he once again flew back and into the trapped civilian.

The hapless civilian was in the midst of quickly leaping off the toilet and pulling his underwear up, only to be knocked back onto the porcelain seat by the force of the gangbanger smashing into him. This time the thug was no longer conscious, and his blood now covered both the walls of the stall and the shirt and underwear of the man he landed on.

"Oh God Jesus!" the besieged civilian shouted. "Please get him offa' me!"

Moonstalker knew he had to stop this person from screaming, as understandable as it was. Before the terror-stricken civilian could utter another sound, he was silenced when the vigilante's dark-gloved hand suddenly clasped hard over his mouth. Moonstalker's hooded face then moved close to the man's own visage as he put his upward pointed index finger to his lips, indicating that he wanted the man to cease making all sounds.

"Shhhh…" he told the shaking gentleman softly. "I'm sorry, but you need to stay quiet and wait a few minutes before leaving this stall. More of this is about to happen out there. Get out of this mall as quickly as you can. Sorry to interrupt your shit, and sorry that I got this fool's blood all over you and the rolls of toilet paper. But that's okay, you don't have time to wipe your ass now anyway"

The man nervously nodded his head, too terrified to do anything else. Moonstalker then graciously dragged the insensate gang member off the man and departed the rest room with surprisingly little sound. The civilian stayed put as ordered, not the least of which because he now actually needed to be on the porcelain throne another several minutes for reasons other than heeding the vigilante's words.

***

The youthful warrior was thankful to find out that the other two gang members who followed him to the rest room didn't wait directly outside of the door. The plan was clearly for their one member to look in the rest room and verify for them that Alan had entered. He knew any second now they would both find it suspicious that their point man didn't report back to them, so the gray-garbed vigilante hid in the corner of the large encasement that led to the rest rooms.

As the first of the other two gangbangers rounded the entrance of the encasement, he barely saw the sole of Moonstalker's foot slam into his face courtesy of an extremely fast side kick. As the ruffian instinctively put his hands over his smashed septum, the vigilante rushed forward and delivered a roundhouse kick that knocked the pain-debilitated gang member back against the second floor railing with such force that he then toppled directly over it. He fell the 25 feet to the ground below, landing in a large enclosure of plants directly in front of Jerry the security guard.

"Damn!" Jerry yelled. "What the hell kinda shit is this?" He quickly pulled out his mobile radio and called the other guards in the mall over the dispatch. "We got an incident here! As in one of those thugs was thrown right off the goddamn second floor! No, I'm not exaggerating! Get your asses over here and call the goddamn police! Damn those gang members!"

Back up on the second floor, the third gang member had witnessed what Moonstalker did to his blood brother, and quickly figured the one who had entered the rest room was now similarly dispatched. Shouting in fury, he pulled out a pocket knife and lunged at his opponent.

Moonstalker put his years of intense full contact training to use by evading three very quick slashes of the knife. He then caught his opponent's arm and pounded a baton against the joint directly below the elbow, snapping it like a twig. The vigilante made sure to maintain the incredibly painful grip as he slammed the gang member senseless against the metal railing.

"Your gang isn't welcome here in the mall," Moonstalker told his bleeding adversary with icy cold authority. "Or in this area of the city. Don't you ever let me catch any of you following civilians around again. Don't ignore this warning if you want to continue being able to so much as wipe your ass without help."

After making sure his opponent heard him clearly despite the blinding pain being inflicted on his broken arm, Moonstalker slammed the gangbanger's forehead against the railing again. This gave the young thug a concussion that ensured he was out of the fight completely. The charcoal-attired crime fighter then ducked down the corridor leading back to the clothing store, dodging several terrified customers in the process.

"Holy shit!" one of the women he ran past shouted. "Was that the vigilante reported on the news? It kinda looked like him!"

"I dunno," a fellow shopper replied while recovering from being startled. "It didn't look like that Centurion guy, the one who shoots those blue rays out of his hands, so I guess it was. Damn, I wish I had my phone in my hand so I coulda' taken a pic, but he came outta nowhere and moved so damn fast!"

***

Moonstalker ran back into the clothing store, determined to get the drop on the two remaining members of the New York Boys before they discovered Shanice. He also knew what just ensued was too much for Jerry to ignore, and the police were also almost certainly on their way. Hence, he needed to avoid an altercation with both while insuring that his (hopefully) new girlfriend was safely extricated from the mall.

Moonstalker's stealth and speed were sufficient that few of the customers noticed him enter Wentworth's, and he disappeared into the various aisles of clothing before they could say anything, let alone before they could attempt to snap pics or take footage with their phone cams. He made his way to the women's dressing area and noticed the changing room he left Shanice in was still occupied. One older rotund woman just exited the changing partition next to that one and upon seeing the strangely garbed vigilante her mouth gaped open wide with startled awe. She was obviously about to scream, and he had to make sure she didn't.

Before the terror-stricken lady could utter a sound Moonstalker pulled a pair of women's panties off of one of the racks and shoved it into her mouth, which quickly silenced her as he held the back of the woman's neck with his other hand.

"Shhhh…" he said to the lady while motioning his index finger in front of his lips again. "Back out of this area, don't make a sound, and leave the store now. Sorry I had to do this, but the safety of people is at stake right now."

The older woman did as she was instructed and walked out of the changing section in robotic fashion due to being in a state of shock, without even bothering to remove the panties stuffed into her mouth.

No sooner did Moonstalker turn back to the door behind which Shanice was concealed than one of the two remaining gangbangers suddenly emerged from a nearby aisles in front of him. The two quickly locked eyes, both of them taken by surprise. *Damn it, rookie, you need to be more careful,* the vigilante admonished himself.

"What the hell?" the gang member shouted as he drew a firearm.

Moonstalker reacted with impressive speed by hurling one of the mini-batons directly at his opponent's face. They were designed to be thrown if necessary, and he had practiced doing so for long hours. The airborne bludgeon struck the gangbanger over the bridge of his nose, caving in the top of his septum, but not before he got off a shot with his gun. The dark-attired champion dived out of the way, but there was a rack of clothing preventing him from moving more than a foot to the side. As a result, the bullet grazed his left arm.

Moonstalker forced himself to grit his teeth hard so he wouldn't yell out in pain. *Son of a bitch! You stupid rookie!*

Luckily, the injury to his opponent's nasal passage caused him to lose his balance and fall back into another rack of clothing. Ignoring his own pain, Moonstalker rolled on the floor, recovered his thrown mini-baton, and smashed the gang member over the head with it, cracking his skull and knocking him cold.

The vigilante could hear Shanice screaming inside the door since the gun went off. He needed to get her out of there fast, but before he could do that, he had one more opponent to account for. This time, however, he didn't need to go looking. The final member of the New York Boys in the store came running into the changing room area to help his partner once he heard the commotion.

Realizing that he was rapidly losing blood, Moonstalker wasted no time in acting. He pulled a woman's bra off a nearby display, ducked past the thug rushing in his direction, and ensnared his throat in the bra's flexible strap. He then used the woman's undergarment as an improvised garrote, squeezing it with all his might so that it closed his adversary's windpipe.

The young thug's eyes practically popped from their sockets while he gasped in agony as his lifeline to the precious oxygen around him was cut off. Despite the fiery agony in his left arm, Moonstalker pooled his willpower and kept on the pressure, ensuring he did sufficient damage to the gang member's trachea to take him down. In short order, the man fell to the cold hard floor with his swollen tongue protruding from his mouth. He landed with his eyes wide open, and the skin of his throat marred by a dark purple discoloration.

Thankful it was now ended, Moonstalker dropped the stringy garment and checked the wound on his arm while trying to staunch the flow of blood. The problem wasn't over yet, though. Jerry suddenly turned down the aisle, and he caught sight of the strangely garbed figure before him.

"What the hell...?"

"Sorry, man," Moonstalker said casually as he rammed his elbow into Jerry's face, causing him to keel over. He then delivered a close handed chop to the area of his carotid artery, using just enough force to send the security guard into unconsciousness from the sudden shock to his circulatory system.

The gray-attired crime fighter quickly removed the outfit from himself, folded it back into a square, and re-secured his mini-batons into the hidden pockets of his pant legs. The pain this caused his injured left arm was severe, but he forced himself to endure it with every erg of his well-honed will. He then knocked on the locked door to the changing room where Shanice was hiding.

"Babe, it's me," Alan said loud enough for her to hear clearly. "The police are here, and everything is okay"

Relieved beyond measure, Shanice opened the door, only to see the blood rushing from the wound in her boyfriend's left arm.

"Oh my God, Alan, you're hurt!"

"Yeah, the bullet from that punk grazed my arm. But it's okay, we have to get out of here."

"It's not okay! For God's sake, you've been shot!"

Alan grabbed her arm with his right hand. "We'll take care of it when we get out of here, okay? I'll call Ty on my cell to come and pick us up. Now take my hand and follow me."

Shanice then noticed the three bleeding men lying unconscious on the floor.

"Alan, what happened to those gang members? And isn't that your security guard friend on the floor?"

"Yes, they had an altercation with Jerry and they all got knocked out."

"My God, was Jerry shot?"

"He wasn't, he'll be fine. Let's just get out of here, now!"

Confused, rattled, and not knowing how else to react, Shanice did as Alan demanded. Following his instructions, they both managed to sneak out of the store.

The two other guards rushed down one of the adjacent aisles of Wentworth's and failed to see the fast-moving Alan and Shanice slip out the entrance. The young man called for his friend Ty to send them a ride as they hurried down the flight of stairs which led to the exit of the mall.

Chapter 7: The Vigilante Spirit

It was a dark and chilly December evening just past 11:30 PM as a small crowd of people from the surrounding neighborhoods congregated within the heated back room of Fred Gifford's Orange Street deli. Fred himself addressed the people he had known and served as customers for more years than he was comfortable admitting. This time, though, he harbored a noticeably more serious expression on his face than his long-time friends and patrons were used to. Once the respected older gentleman saw that he had his audience's rapt attention, he softly cleared his throat and began his spiel.

"So, the way I see it, people, the question is this. Are we going to continue letting just one man fight all our battles for us? Or are we going to follow his lead and show those punks that these streets belong to *us*, not them?"

These queries were followed by several seconds of uncomfortable silence. Just as Fred was tempted to break the quiet himself, his old friend and steady customer Howie Kendall raised his arm and responded.

"Fred, if you're talkin' about that guy in the gray ninja outfit who's been kicking a lot of gangbanger ass lately, including that ruckus down at St. Luke's, well, um… need I remind you that the law would consider him a vigilante?"

"Yes, Howie, I know what a dang vigilante is," Fred snarked back. "He's also the only one in this damn city who stands up for us. We sure as hell don't stand up for ourselves, 'cause if we did, then Moonstalker wouldn't be around in the first place."

"But, Fred, I think you're missing Howie's point," neighborhood hair dresser Nell Moss said. "I don't like these punks pushing us around anymore than you do, and I hope you realize that. But dealing with the gangs is the police's job. If we all go outside the law, then very soon there won't be any more law, but just a bunch of angry people running around and beating up on anyone who done pisses them off."

"Oh, come on now, Nell," Fred replied with annoyance. "You're saying we don't know where to draw the line? That we can't tell the difference between someone who assaults us and demands we give a share of our hard-earned money to them 'or else,' and someone who just happens to look at us the wrong way or whose dog happens to take a dump on our lawn? We're not stupid and uneducated, ya know."

"I didn't say you or any of us are dullards, Fred," Nell responded in irate fashion, "so please don't be putting words in my mouth. I'm just saying that even smart people start acting really dumb and uncivilized when they let anger and fear get the better of them. I don't want to see us becoming no better than those gang members."

"Oh please, Nell!" Fred snapped. "You've been watching too many of those movies on the Lifetime network."

"C'mon, Fred, she's right," Howie interjected. "We have the police for a reason, and they operate by procedure for a reason. That Moonstalker guy you're so keen on is no better than the gang members, far as I'm concerned. No one in this neighborhood elected or appointed him to go out busting asses like that. This cat has some serious issues, and you're suggesting that we follow in his bootsteps?"

Fred gritted his teeth, raised both his hands, and responded to these criticisms with more heated zeal. "People, let's all keep in mind that we didn't elect or appoint these police officers either. The mayor and that fat ass chief of detectives does all that, and those men live in a safe part of the city with lots of personal guards protecting them, like, 24/7. It's easy for them to call the shots and insist that we don't defend ourselves.

"But since we gotta rely on a bunch of people in blue uniforms who don't answer to us, and mostly don't even live in our neighborhoods, and who only answer our calls when they're good and ready, well… as I see it, the only one we have as a guardian who *really* looks after us is Moonstalker."

"I can see what Fred is saying," opined local grocery store worker Kenny Smith. "I mean, I'm terrified whenever my mom and sister leave the house. Sometimes it's days between the times I see a cop car patrolling our streets. I'm sick of being scared. It's bad enough that Mr. Gurney has to give them money, so they don't thrash both him and his store; but every time I see two of those gang members stroll in there like they own the damn place to collect from him… well, I'm just sick of having to keep my mouth shut and do nothing."

"It's kept you alive, hasn't it?" former schoolteacher Edith Hall countered. "You're not the police, Kenny, and you're a good boy, not some violent vigilante. I've known you since you were a pup, and your mom and sister would be devastated if something happened to you. If you see those punks come into the store, just sneak off somewhere and call the police on your cell phone. Let them do their jobs and don't do anything you're not trained to do!"

"I don't even think he should do that, Edith," opined bus driver Lem Simpson. "If the gang finds out he was the one who called the cops, they could do a retaliation thing on him or his family."

"See, this is exactly the type of bullcocking attitude I'm talking about here!" Fred bemoaned. "We're too afraid to even call the police to do their jobs because of these punks! Fear of retaliation is one of the things they use to control us. If most of us stood up to them like Moonstalker does, they wouldn't have taken control of our neighborhoods like this in the first place!"

"Seriously, Fred, do you remember what happened to the father of the young man who helped you when those bastards were hassling you?" Edith asked. "I'm sure the Perez boy is thinking twice about taking the law into his own hands now."

"What Alan did was brave!" Fred exclaimed in defense of his young patron. "He actually looked out for someone other than himself and his own family. His father was retaliated on because the gang knew that none of us would back him up and would instead be cowering in our houses and pretending we didn't see anything. They knew the police would play dumb and not do anything about it, at least not before they got their day's share of free donuts and coffee. I owe that boy my life, and many of us owe our lives to Moonstalker."

Fred then turned his attention to the opposite end of the room. "Isn't that right, Father Harris?"

Fred was clearly addressing the man of the cloth sitting quietly with a contemplative expression on his face. The pensive clergyman looked up for the first time during this gathering when he heard his name called.

"Yes, that's right," Harris answered Fred in a tone devoid of any emotion. "Either of them are welcome to visit the chapel pantry for free bacon and eggs any time."

"Father Harris, you can't be agreeing with Fred here," Howie said. "You would never condone stepping outside of the law."

"There are laws higher than those written by man," the priest replied sans any change in his stoical expression. "I'm not here to judge, but merely to listen. We should all consider doing the same. Please go on, Mr. Gifford."

***

Darius McCain was a young lawman who differed markedly from the typical law enforcement officer serving the 8th Precinct. This was the division that had the infamous Fruit Belt in their jurisdiction, but unlike the majority of patrol officers in this precinct, Darius wasn't adverse about doing his job to the fullest. Hailing from a family who raised him with a strong sense of ethics despite the urban cesspool in which he spent his formative years, this young man was determined to uphold the principles of law and justice as was expected of one holding his station.

It was now a few months past his second year on the job, and Darius had already seen many things that horrified his fervently brave soul. But that only increased his determination and sense of purpose as a protector of the city. He would do his job even if it killed him; and with the rise of the New York Boys in this area of the city, he knew that his life may very well be the price he must ultimately pay to uphold the principles he swore an oath to.

Nevertheless, Darius McCain always felt the shiny eagle on the police badge symbolized a higher power than the dull green dollar sign. It was a belief had yet to waver despite eighteen months of exposure to the cold, hard reality of the municipal law enforcement vocation.

Due to recent budgetary restraints that all his fellow patrol officers complained about to no avail, Darius was patrolling the evening thoroughfares of Buffalo's Main Street sector sans a partner. He made a point to spend a good portion of his time patrolling the streets where there resided small family businesses which were among the last few to resist paying "protection" money to the gang members.

The young officer spent every waking moment on patrol dreaming of taking down the shadowy and reputedly extremely dangerous leader of the New York Boys, who was known simply but chillingly as "The Assailant." No real name was attached to this sinister figure, and it was said that this reportedly heavily muscled monster of a man kept his face covered in front of even his most trusted street lieutenants. Though Darius never faltered in his main goal of protecting the people of Buffalo, he couldn't deny that he salivated over the thought of the accolades, self-esteem, and promotions he would receive for being the patrolman to put this much-feared mystery leader down.

That is, if the vigilante didn't get to him first. *Yes, that damn vigilante… I'm gonna take his sorry ass down too,* Darius mused to himself with more than a small amount of aplomb.

***

Shortly after midnight on a fairly chilly evening, Patrol Officer Darius McCain pulled up to the curb near The House of Music, a small-time seller of CD's with a somewhat grandiose name. Word on the street had it that the owner of this establishment, Amelia Hiller, wasn't paying the amount of dues demanded by the New York Boys. When the ever-observant patrolman saw the front door seemingly ajar despite the time being several hours after the store had closed for business on a Saturday, he knew that he should investigate.

Unfortunately for Darius, calling for back-up wasn't his first thought. He insisted to himself that this was nothing he couldn't handle himself.

Knowing my fellow patrollers, it would take them an hour to respond to my request in this part of the district. There's at least one all-night Tim Horton's between their regular patrols and Main Street, and I sure as hell can't expect them to resist the temptation to stop there for some high-calorie junk food before coming here.

Besides, it's not like this is the mayor's neighborhood. And it will probably be about two years before the New York Boys become powerful enough to lay claim to even that area of the city. Let's see what I can do to stop it from happening; and prove that an officer of the law working entirely within procedure can do it. The lawman looked at the agape door of the record shop and grinned to himself. *Hmmm, I totally see good probable cause to enter that establishment.*

Having decided to take no chances, Darius had his Glock 22 in hand as he cautiously walked through the door. He could tell that the lock was broken, but he also noticed that the security system Hiller had wisely invested in had for some reason failed to go off. *Someone employed by this store in a management position obviously gave the code to the gang. These fools have connections far and wide. They need to be put down like a pack of rabid dogs.*

The 27-year-old officer walked carefully through the darkened aisles of the store, being careful not to alert any unauthorized individuals of his presence by accidentally knocking over one of the display towers. As his dark eyes scanned the interior of the store he suddenly heard what sounded to him like a crashing sound in the back aisle. This aberrant noise prompted him to move stealthily towards that section of the store.

Sure enough the officer's keen visual acuity caught sight of a young man who appeared to be wearing the distinctive headband and jacket emblem of the New York Boys. And clearly this intruder was in the midst of vandalizing the merchandise.

"Put your hands up where I can see them," Darius ordered with his Glock pointed at the startled gang member. "Consider yourself under arrest."

The rage-countenanced gangbanger slowly complied with the officer's demand, though the look on his face was one of vicious defiance.

Darius couldn't help himself from verbally venting to his target. "You think you can break in here and cause trouble for an honest businesswoman who refuses to pay your intimidation money, you punk?"

The youthful criminal displayed an expression that seemed to imply the patrolman had just asked him an obviously rhetorical question.

Just then, out of the corner of his eye, Darius saw the silhouette of another figure rise up from behind a nearby glass display case while brandishing a firearm. He noticed this movement just in time. Using his well-trained reflexes, the tough young officer swiftly swiveled his gun arm and sent a bullet through the left shoulder of his would-be murderer. The impact of the blast knocked the gangbanger back against a display tower right behind him. This collision was accompanied by a huge spray of blood that decorated the glass counter with what resembled a grisly pattern of crimson Rorschachian blots.

However, this distracted the patrolman just enough to afford the gang member he previously had in his gun sights the opportunity to rush him with a bellow of enraged fury. Darius again turned quickly to face his attacker, but this time he wasn't quite swift enough. The brazen young criminal grabbed the officer's throat with one hand and seized his gun arm with the other by the wrist, turning it away from its target. The full weight and momentum of this heavyset malcontent knocked Darius back against a nearby display table, which sent both the glass counter and the two struggling adversaries crashing to the floor.

Darius was a bit over-weight but still worked out regularly, and he was no weakling. He thus held his own despite the primal ferocity with which his opponent fought to gain the upper hand. The policeman grasped the right ear of the savage criminal on top of him and pulled back on the thin cartilage as hard as he could. The pain experienced by the gang member was immense, which his howl of agony made abundantly clear. Nevertheless, the enraged young ruffian was determined to maintain his grip on Darius's wrist to prevent the officer from using the firearm against him.

"Hold him, Nino!" a young voice shouted from behind them. "I'll blow that pig away!"

Darius's worst fear came to light as he glanced over the shoulder of his attacker and saw the clear image of another gang member holding what appeared to be a Smith & Wesson M&P 9 hand gun in the direction of the dueling men before him. The officer knew that if he managed to pull the gang member called Nino off him, he would instantly become an easy target for his accomplice. *Shit,* he lamented to himself.

No sooner did that expletive cross Darius's mind than an object resembling a small sickle with razor sharp points flew out of the darkness and embedded itself in the gun-wielding thug's hand. Taken by surprise, the skewered criminal yelled out and dropped his firearm to clatter loudly on the hard marble floor.

Less than a second later the gray-attired form of Moonstalker leapt off a nearby display table and delivered a brutal mid-air side kick to the gang member's jaw. A very audible cracking sound was heard at the moment of the blow, and the young criminal fell to the ground like a heap of discarded meat. He didn't get up again.

A moment later, two other gang members rushed from behind the display cases where they were hiding. One of them wielded a large, razor-sharp stiletto blade; the other, another M&P 9 hand gun. In a blur of motion Moonstalker somersaulted out of the line of fire, disappearing into the shadows on the left side of the store. Thus, the bullet intended for him simply ricocheted off the floor and through the glass of the front window. The vigilante could, of course, see clearly in the dark, whereas his opponents had to strain their optic nerves to discern anything in the blackness.

Taking full advantage of his own adversary's distraction, Darius pulled Nino's ear with as much force as he could muster. He felt the rubbery cartilage tear in his hand as the young man screamed in agony. He then wrested his gun arm free and pistol whipped the gangbanger in the side of the head. This served to crack the ferocious criminal's skull and open a gaping, bloody wound that effectively removed him from the fight.

The other armed gang member speedily turned towards the officer and fired his gun. The bullet thankfully missed its intended head shot and embedded into Darius' bullet proof vest, cracking one of his ribs and bruising another. The officer held back a yelp of pain and pushed himself to return fire. His aim wasn't fully accurate due to his injuries, but the bullet did graze the skull of the gangbanger. The violent youth pooled his equally strong will into maintaining his grip on the gun, but he couldn't help first putting his hand over his bleeding right temple while uttering a string of obscenities. He was suffering from a moderate concussion and blurred vision, yet still managed to stay on his feet while positioning himself to once again send a lead projectile into Darius.

That intended shot was ruined when Moonstalker exited the shadows from the right and clubbed the gang member's wrist with a short bo staff. The bone joining his arm to his hand was split in two, and he immediately dropped his firearm. The vigilante then kicked the gun away and followed up the attack with an elbow strike to the criminal's throat, bashing in his trachea and sending him hurling back against a nearby display counter. The heavy-set malcontent landed atop a scattered collection of LL Cool J vintage compilation CD's. A trail of blood could be seen dribbling from his mouth as he lay unmoving upon the many cracked jewel cases that did nothing to cushion his fall.

"You're dead, man!" the final standing gang member exclaimed as he ran towards Moonstalker and attempted to slash his chest with the stiletto.

The dark-clad urban warrior barely moved aside in time to prevent his belly from being sliced open like a gutted fish. He swung his short staff at his attacker's face, cracking the cheekbone like a piece of ice struck with a mallet. The now blindly enraged criminal let loose with a plethora of swears that would make a college frat boy blush. Nevertheless, he remained on his feet and again lunged at his vigilante opponent with the business end of the blade.

This time, though, the gangbanger's severe facial injury and blinded right eye caused his second assault to falter awkwardly. Moonstalker easily evaded this clumsy attack, knocked the blade from his attacker's hand with a blindingly swift sweep of his foot, and culminated the combo by bashing his foe directly on the septum with the end of the hard wood staff. The cartilage of the youth's nose was crushed like a piece of discarded fruit that one stepped on, and torrents of blood spewed from his nasal openings like vermillion geysers. The gang member stopped for a moment, gasped, sneezed out another spurt of blood, and finally lost consciousness before he fell to the floor.

With the gang members now entirely dispatched, Moonstalker stepped into the glare of the street lights shining through the front window of the store. It was enough for Darius to see that the vigilante's charcoal-hued, ninja-like outfit was modified with lightweight exterior padding to withstand the cold of the harsh Buffalo winters, as well as the often chilly spring season. The young warrior then stepped in his direction and helpfully held out a hand to aid the officer back to his feet.

Instead of accepting, the patrolman again fought back against the pain of his injured ribs and pointed his Glock at the vigilante.

"Despite how you saved my life, it changes nothing," Darius uttered with stern conviction. "You're a flagrant violator of the law, and you're under arrest."

"Seriously?" Moonstalker replied in an artificial but effective grating voice. "If you people did your job…"

"I *was* doing my goddamn job when you showed up! Are you too far gone to see that?"

"You would now be 'far gone' yourself if I wouldn't have intervened, cop."

The vigilante slowly withdrew his hand and backed away a step.

Darius then continued his verbal reprimand with his gun held firmly in place. "It's a chance we take. It's part of the job description."

"I take the same risk. And without getting paid for it. Or receiving a single free donut."

"This is about more to me than just money, dammit! I barely earn a living off this job, yet I still take the risk. And those free donuts hardly make up for that, you sarcastic idiot! But do you know why I continue to do it? Because I care about the people in this community!"

Moonstalker could readily discern the sincerity in the officer's voice, but he also felt that it changed nothing. "Considering I do this without being paid at all, do you believe I do it for any reason other than concern for the people in this community?"

"It doesn't matter! You're not authorized! You should have joined the police force legitimately if you wanted to do your part in stopping these criminals!"

"Sorry, but I'm not good with standardized tests. I would have flunked the written exam."

"You son of a bitch, you think you're amusing or something? You're as much a criminal as these gang members, and you're going down with them."

"No. I'm not."

With that pronouncement made, Moonstalker suddenly hurled one of his darkout bombs at the floor in front of him. A "bamfing" sound was heard with the simultaneous manifestation of a gray-ish cloud of billowy smoke that quickly encompassed a third of the store section in which they were situated.

"No, you don't!" Darius shouted as he pulled the trigger and shot directly into the mass of foggy gray smoke.

Within just a few seconds, the billowy cloud dispersed to reveal… nothing. Moonstalker had made his escape, much to the officer's consternation. The fact that he owed this vigilante his life only irked him all the more.

"Damn that bastard," Darius babbled as he forced himself to his feet and prepared to call for back-up. "You are so going down along with the rest of the criminal scum in this city. Count on it."

***

Around the same time that the fracas in The World of Music was ensuing, Father Morrie Harris trod into the darkened, cavernous main chapel of St. Luke's Church. He walked until he was facing the life-size statue of Jesus Christ attached in unsettlingly realistic fashion to the crucifix that adorned the center of the room.

The priest lit several candles to illuminate the contours of the colorless sculpture and knelt reverently in front of it. He looked at the mournful, pain-wracked expression which was expertly carved into the visage of this marble simulation of his personal savior. He noted that this countenance reflected his own mood, and how the legendary sacrifice of the Christ child was perfect symbolism for his own future plans.

"Dear Lord," he said to the being whom that statue iconically represented. "I may be making a mistake in what I plan to do. If so, I will gladly suffer penance when I finally have the honor to enter the gates of Heaven; assuming, of course, that I am even allowed entrance. But I am aware that your ways of giving signs to your followers are many and varied. And I interpret the emergence of the gray-attired warrior as one of these signs. I know that your will is never as simple as many would prefer to believe. Such is the origin of the expression, 'the Lord works in mysterious ways.'

"So please forgive me for what I am about to do in the interest of the community if I should happen to be interpreting your sign incorrectly. I cannot match your perfection, my Lord, and I can only pray that my mortal flaws do not lead me down a path that is ultimately counter to your will. But I am nevertheless prepared to put everything on the line to take the chance. Please grant me the wisdom and foresight to serve the greater good in harmony with your plan for this city. Amen."

With that call for guidance and possible forgiveness completed, Father Harris placed a leather attaché' case he had recently purchased atop the altar. He then produced a key and opened the small lock holding the case closed. His expression was dour but unwavering as he removed the gleaming gray Ruger LC9 hand gun from the case and looked it over carefully, acclimating himself to the feel of its oppressive but powerful weight in his hands.

Chapter 8: Panic at the Disco

As always, Alan Perez sat in the disc jockey booth of the East Side Inferno with an expression of accomplishment and pride. Here he was as much in his element as he was at Master Kai's martial arts dojo. For most of his young life he had hoped to parlay his talent for using the latest technology to create music into a lucrative vocation. This dream drove him as stringently as any other in his life, right up there with sex and the benevolent conquest of the ghetto.

Alan was an alpha male to the core and rising to the top in all his planned endeavors was the surest way to prove this to the world… and to himself. His disc jockey persona of "King Cut" was just as important a component of this goal as was his more recently acquired alter-ego of a certain masked urban guardian.

Moreover, the East Side Inferno was likely the best and most popular location for him to showcase his musical skills to party-inclined young adults native to Buffalo's East Side, with a few from the West spilling in from time to time. It was also one of the best local spots to network with fledgling hip-hop artists hoping to find a DJ for their group, or even the odd traveling talent scout for a major record company.

Then there was the matter of the plethora of young women to be found there, of course. However, since Alan had started dating Shanice he made a personal resolution to only court the attentions of other girls if he happened to be angry at his current significant other.

On this Friday evening the locally popular King Cut relaxed in the DJ booth while playing the beats he put together for a local trio of young female rappers who called themselves the Sweetheart Bitches. Both the young man's ego and his loins were thoroughly stoked by watching the rhythmic movements of the three shapely girl performers to sounds he had created on his own drum machine. The patrons of the club were delighted to show off their moves on the dance floor as the attractive triad rendered their latest paean to black feminism, "Our Time of the Month is Yo' Time to Cook Yo' Own Dinner."

No sooner had the girls finished their song than Alan's best friend Ty Reynolds sauntered over to the window of the booth. As usual, a young woman whom he had just met that night was arm-in-arm with him.

"Yo, Alan, I'd like you to meet the awesome lady I've been getting acquainted with tonight," Ty said with a smug beam. "Rayissa, this is my main man, Alan; Alan, check out Rayissa." The young lothario hoped only Alan noticed that the second part of the above introduction was a wry innuendo.

"Hey," was Alan's friendly return salutation.

"Hey there yourself," Rayissa replied in a sensuous tone.

"Rayissa just so happens to be here with three friends," Ty continued. "So, I was sorta' wondering, exactly how 'together' are you and you-know-who at this point?"

Alan gave an exasperated sigh. *Try to be strong here, dude. At least for now. Keep thinking about Shanice, because you don't want to screw things up with* this *girl.* "Sorry, but Shanice and I are now official."

Rayissa gave Ty a dejected glare, and then turned that glower to Alan before uttering a verbal protest. "Awww, I was hoping you could show us how to use your drum machine in private tonight. My friend Leelee has a dorm room all to herself."

Ty hit Alan with an intense scowl. "Dude! Are you absolutely sure that Shanice hasn't done *something* to piss you off lately? I'm sure if you think hard enough, you'll remember something she did wrong. And it's not like you don't get pissed off easily when you're in one of your moods."

Alan rolled his deeply set brown eyes. *Be* strong, *man! Keep reminding yourself of how hot and totally dope Shanice is.* "Have fun at the dorm without me, Ty."

"My, how far the whipped have fallen," Ty quipped while shaking his head. "Oh well, that just leaves more for me, if you know what I mean."

Alan grinded his teeth. *You better be worth this, Shanice. You sooooo better be worth this.* "Have fun teaching them the drum machine by yourself, man. You don't need me to bring mine, because you have one of your own."

Rayissa rolled her eyes in annoyance, and Ty quietly led her away from the booth window. "Whatever, *niggah*. Later, dude."

"Hey, I had no idea that you have your own drum machine," Rayissa said as she and Ty walked towards the juice bar. "Are you some kind a' DJ too?"

"Huh? Say what?" Ty was confused for about two seconds before realizing that only he had picked up on Alan's salacious allusion. *Smart ass…*

***

Several blocks away, the back lot behind the East Side drugstore was bursting with hidden activity as the solid steel delivery door was unlocked and pulled open by two young men with jacket colors identifying them as members of the New York Boys. The gangbanger duo slavered at the sight of the exposed pharmaceutical treasure trove like a wolf salivates upon spotting its prey.

"This is the shit, man!" one of the gang members said to his shorter and stouter partner. "How did you manage to get the key to the storage door, not to mention the pass code of the security system?"

"With my usual power of persuasion," the shorter man replied with a cracking of his knuckles. "Along with a bottle of Oxycodone as their commission. The rest of this batch is all ours. You have any idea how much just *one* bottle of Lortabs sells for on the streets these days?"

"Probably more than two of my dad's paychecks," the taller youth remarked.

"You shall not profit off of these illicit items," came an unexpected gruff voice from the shadows just outside of the lot.

Both gangbangers turned around with a start. "Who the hell…?"

A darkly-dressed figure strode out of the shadows that enveloped the back portion of the store. It immediately became obvious that the two young gang members were facing a man who wore a black, concealing overcoat. The interloper appeared to have a dark hood covering his entire head, though it was difficult to tell for certain with the waning moon in the sky being the only source of illumination.

"Oh shit, man," the taller gang member said. "It's – it's … Moonstalker!"

Before either of the two criminals could decide what to do next, they both realized that the dark-clad figure's leather-gloved hand was brandishing a firearm. A loud "boom" reverberated across the width of the back lot as a bullet blasted into the abdominal flesh of the first gangbanger like a miniature guided missile. The young man's eviscerated bowels hit the ground a split second before the rest of his body did.

The shorter criminal screamed in horror, only to have a second lead projectile enter his gaping mouth and tear out the back of his head. The inner contents of his skull spattered over the almost-purloined boxes of pharmaceuticals in a spectacular spray of gray and scarlet. A second and a half later his mutilated body gave way to gravity and came crashing down on the boxes of drugs.

With the bloody deed done, the mysterious executioner removed his black hood to reveal the impassive visage of Father Morton Harris. The priest took a quick moment to look over his gory handiwork. Much to his own surprise, the man of the cloth didn't become ill or melancholy at the mess before him.

"Lord, I *pray* that I have interpreted your message correctly," the pastor of St. Luke's said aloud quietly. "Just as the avenging warrior you sent to this city in its time of need wore a dark hood while dispensing your justice, I have elected to do the same. May he inspire others to oppose these human agents of Satan much as he did this humble worshiper of yours."

His task completed, Father Harris turned and casually walked back into the darkened neighborhood streets from which he had emerged. The clergyman correctly surmised that no police cars would arrive on the scene anytime soon, so his stroll back to the church a few blocks distant occurred at a leisurely pace.

***

Alan had just completed playing his personally remixed version of Kid Quick's newest hip-hop hit "I Can't Get Enough of That from You" when his boss, club owner K.T. Jones, approached the booth window.

"Yo, Alan, I ordered a medium-size shipment of that papaya juice your fellow teenyboppers are so fond of lately," the tall businessman said. "So, if I happen to be in the back on the phone or something when it arrives, be a dear and tell the deliveryman where to put it, all right?"

"No *problemo,* chief," the young DJ replied. "Any chance of our getting a shipment of wine coolers or beer after that?"

"Only if the laws happen to change over the next half hour, kid."

"Now you *know* I would be voting for Elijah Manley this year, if I was actually allowed to cast a ballot in the presidential elections."

K.T. grimaced at his younger employee before heading back to the juice bar. "It never hurts to dream, kid."

However, the owner of the East Side Inferno found his smirk replaced by a very prominent frown when he saw five members of the New York Boys enter his establishment. He immediately realized that it was probably too much to hope that they were simply there as customers who loved his tropical fruit mocktails and Alan's funky electronic beats.

Not that he would actually want the likes of them in his club as patrons no matter how much money they may have to spend; especially when one considered what they typically did to "earn" their cash.

Needless to say, K.T. was determined to control his very well-founded fears in deference to his position of responsibility. Accordingly, K.T. adjusted his 1980s style Kangol hat into a more "gangsta" fashion in the hope of toughening his appearance before confronting the gangbangers. He then strove to appear as calm as possible as he approached the dangerous intruders.

"Can I help you gentlemen?" he asked the tall, light-skinned leader of the group.

"Hey look, this club is owned by LL Cool J," a stout but impressively built gang member known as Ganke sniggered. "Do you think you're ba-a-a-d, bro? Ha!"

K.T. gritted his teeth while seeking to maintain his composure. The other three subordinate gang members laughed at Ganke's snide comment, but the leader maintained a deadly serious expression. He was obviously there on important business, not simply to poke fun at the club owner, let alone to sample the papaya mocktail.

"I take it you're K.T., the owner of this place?" the imposing leader enquired.

"I am," K.T. responded with an almost audible gulp.

"Either that, or he's LL's gay ass twin," Ganke remarked just loud enough for K.T. to hear. All his compatriots except for the leader chortled in response to the comment, and one of them high-fived the cruelly sarcastic gangbanger.

"You can call me Shank," the leader stated.

"Unless he wants to call you 'Daddy,' right, boss? Hah!" Ganke flippantly interjected.

"Shut up, porky," Shank said to his cohort. "No need to be dissing the man we're going to be working with."

"Say what?" K.T. said with more than a bit of incredulity.

"You heard me, man," Shank rejoined. "We're here to make a business arrangement with you, considering that you're operating in our territory."

"Erm, exactly what type of 'arrangement' are we talking about here?" K.T. queried rhetorically.

"We need to calculate a 'permission fee' from you, based on your net profits," Shank explained. "You can consider that a new operating expense, a taxation for authorization to operate a business on New York Boys turf."

"Yeah, plus free papaya mocktails for all of us!" Ganke quipped. "Word of that awesome tropical delicacy of yours really gets around, man! Ha ha!"

"Shut up, Ganke," Shank repeated.

"Are you kidding me?" K.T. said in a mounting state of panic. "My club isn't in your territory! That ends at the perimeter of East Mulberry!"

"We've recently expanded our territory," Shank explicated. "Your club is now within the boundary line of our turf. That means your business now has an executive board; and those board members are *us*. And you can consider The Assailant to be the CEO."

"Or your Sugar Daddy, whatever way you wanna look at it, LL Lite!" Ganke snorted, a remark which elicited raucous laughter from his three fellow subordinate gangbangers.

Shank turned to face Ganke. "Do you mind, bruh?" the powerfully built leader said. "I'm trying to conduct business here."

"Aw, c'mon, Shank," Ganke pleaded. "I don't mean no disrespect. Well, at least not to you. It's just that I don't like how this Flavor Flav-looking punk ass bitch is getting so fidgety with you. I think we should teach him a lesson. I think we should make him take a dump and then wipe his ass with his Kangol while I use my cell to camcorder it. We'll make sure to show footage of LL Lite's greatest moment to any other business owner in our turf who gives us any attitude."

"And we can show it at parties just for the entertainment value! Bwah-hah-hah!" a diminutive gang member called Urchin suggested with all due discourtesy. "We can even be generous enough to send a video file to everyone on LL Lite's cell phone address book, hah!"

Shank eyeballed the now visibly trembling club owner, as he seemed to ponder Ganke's suggestion. "Hmmm… that's an idea. Maybe we *should* make an example out of Mr. K.T. here."

"Oh, Christ," the now utterly terrified entrepreneur said while he raised his severely quaking hands. "Look, look, I didn't say that I *wouldn't* do business with you guys. We can work something out!"

"Sorry, Mr. K.T.," Shank retorted with an icy cold demeanor. "Ganke may be a big mouth, but he's got a point here. Now head for the men's restroom. Or for the ladies' restroom, if you prefer; there's no need to be picky in *our* club."

Ganke began bellowing with laughter. "Ooohhh, man, this is gonna be epic! This is gonna be the shit! Pun *totally* intended! Bwah-hah-hahhh!"

"Jesus, Shank!" the panicking K.T. exclaimed. "Don't do this, man! That camcorder footage would be incriminating evidence for the police!"

"Do we *look* like we're scared of the police, dude?" Shank asked defiantly. "Now get moving! Before you *really* get me riled."

"Security!" The thoroughly desperate K.T. hollered at the top of his lungs, praying that his three bouncers would respond and do their job despite what they would be going up against.

Two of those three bouncers had quietly stepped out of the club and took an impromptu late evening "lunch break" as soon as they saw the New York Boys enter the premises. "K.T. doesn't pay us enough for *that shit*," one of them said just before exiting the night club they were hired to safeguard.

However, a third security guard -- a muscular young veteran of the streets named Reggie Diaz -- had refused to leave upon seeing the quintet of gangbangers enter the premises. Though he initially remained wary of approaching them, Reggie eventually found that his conscience and sense of responsibility would not let him abandon his employer at a time when he was needed most. Hence, once the conflagration began on the other end of the club, Reggie responded to his boss's impassioned plea for assistance.

Ty had also noticed the situation, and he meandered over to the DJ booth to let Alan know what was going on. Upon reaching the open window, however, he found that his best friend wasn't present in his usual spot. *Hmmm, it's not like my man Alan to bolt whenever trouble comes along. Not even trouble of this magnitude. Maybe he's in the crapper, or something.*

As it turned out, the young man was partially correct. Alan had indeed fled to the restroom soon after seeing the gang members enter the club. However, his flight to the lavatory was neither to hide nor to relieve himself. Rather, it was to find a secluded location to change garb with practiced speed.

Moonstalker was about to make his presence known at the East Side Inferno.

Chapter 9: A Knight at the Club

Ganke's incessant laughter at the humiliating experience K.T. Jones was about to be subjected to quickly morphed into a scream of shock and pain as a razor-sharp, sickle-shaped ceramic shuriken penetrated his left ear. The projectile's business end skewered clear through the cartilage just above the vicious gangbanger's ear lobe and out through the back of the hardened tissue, where it came to resemble a truly exotic earring.

Spurts of blood from Ganke's perforated flesh spattered across the faces of the other members of Shank's "collection" crew, dotting them like crimson speckles. Shank was the only one of the gang members hit by the hemo-splotches who didn't flinch in startled disgust; rather, his mocha-toned visage took on an expression of extreme rage.

"What the hell, man!" Ganke shouted as he grabbed his punctured ear.

A split second later, another ceramic razor sickle struck a different gang member in the left shoulder, causing him to duplicate his comrade's bellow of shock and pain. Shank reacted with an expert degree of fleetness by drawing his fully automatic 9mm Glock 26 and aiming it in an "at alert" position.

The experienced urban soldier didn't fire a warning or suppressing shot, however, as he understood a random spray of this formidable but difficult to maintain weapon would only risk quickly depleting its ammo and damaging the chamber. If this occurred without hitting an intended target, then no gain would accompany the loss. He was also wary of the possibility of hitting civilians needlessly, as that only brought more police "heat" upon the gang.

As one may have expected, though, Ganke held his bleeding ear with his left hand while drawing a previously concealed Ruger Sigma with his right. The pain-wracked gang member bellowed expletives and fired a round in the general direction he perceived the shuriken to have been hurled from. The .32 caliber projectile struck the wall behind the bar, shattering a bottle of Loganberry fruit juice and causing the two bar tenders to dive for cover.

The rest of the club's patrons began screaming in terror and either rushing towards the doors or crawling under tables. Ty Reynolds made a point to grab his date by the arm and pull her towards one of the back exits, hoping that Alan would remain in the relative safety of the rest rooms. Little did he know…

Shank kicked Ganke in the side of his ribs. "You stupid prick! Don't fire wild and don't waste ammo!"

"The hell with that!" Ganke hollered in defiance. "Some bitch's son threw something in my ear! My *ear*, man!"

A fourth gang member also brandished a pistol, but the still-hidden Moonstalker could tell this was a cheap "Saturday Night Special," most likely of the Davis brand; quick to malfunction and low caliber, but still more than capable of causing a severe injury or even a fatality to himself or one of the patrons.

The fifth of Shank's crew simply pulled a stiletto from his belt, only to have the approaching bouncer Reggie Diaz take advantage of the ensuing chaos by subjecting the knife-wielding gang member to a brutal football-style tackle. The force of the young security guard's full weight knocked the criminal against a bar table, and he dropped his blade upon impact.

"Chino, deal with that!" Shank commanded the fourth gangbanger, not wanting to take his attention from the still unseen source of the shurikens for even a split second.

The member of the New York Boys' "collection crew" who was sickle-skewered in the shoulder was desperately trying to pull the projectile from his flesh, but its slightly curved razor-sharp ceramic point was determined to remain embedded. The youthful criminal could tell he was more likely than not to cause himself grievous tissue damage if he actually did manage to rip out the shuriken on his own rather than leaving the task to a professional surgeon. Nevertheless, pain and panic combined to overcome his sense of reason. When he finally managed to tear the sickle from his shoulder blade with a single desperate yank, an artery was ripped open in the process.

The young malcontent screamed in agony as a small geyser of blood spurted from the now gaping wound. The vermillion shower poured over Shank's left pant leg, leaving a dark rogue stain across its khaki material.

"Alto, you *pendejo*, why did you do that?" the front-runner of the brutal collection crew berated his now gravely injured and useless soldier.

In the meantime, Chino was attempting to carry out his leader's command. He pointed his small pistol at Reggie but couldn't get a clear shot since he was still struggling with the gang member whom he tackled.

"Ricky, get 'out the way!" Chino hollered.

"Can't you see 'Dude' has me in a headlock?" the red-bearded Ricky responded rhetorically as he struggled to break Reggie's iron grip.

The bouncer then noticed something which he reckoned to prove useful to his predicament: A still intact mocktail glass that had fallen from the collapsed table was laying a mere two feet from where the struggle was ensuing. Reggie reached for the transparent chalice with his free hand, which he managed to grasp before either Chino or Ricky could react. After taking a split second to aim, the courageous security guard chucked the glass directly at Chino. It struck him just over his left eye, breaking on impact and causing a small stream of blood to dribble down onto the gangbanger's iris. The resulting sting of ocular pain led to the desired effect.

"You asshole!" Chino yelled as he lost his temper and risked a shot at the bouncer.

As Reggie hoped for, the angle from which he was fighting resulted in the low caliber bullet inadvertently hitting his opponent instead of its intended target. The small projectile deflected off the side of Ricky's abdomen and fractured one of the lower false ribs.

"Shit!" was all Chino could say in response to his costly gaffe.

The now injured and incessantly swearing Ricky greatly relaxed his grip and Reggie pushed his body towards Chino with a mighty heave. The wounded gang member was smashed into his partner like a wrecking ball, and all three young men ended up falling against another table. The trio's combined weight caused the piece of furniture's legs to collapse underneath its frame, and all went crashing to the floor in a messy pile of wood and flesh.

As Ganke continued bleeding down the side of his face, he decided to go for broke in flushing out their hidden opponent. This he attempted by pointing his Ruger at the trembling form of K.T.

"Come out of hiding or I swear I'll kill 'im!" the gang member exclaimed.

"Oh man…" was the only sound that emanated from the terror-stricken club owner, other than the unmistakable noise of K.T. explosively defecating in his pants.

"That's not your call, Ganke!" Shank shouted.

But the pain-enraged young man ignored his feared leader and continued with his ploy. "I don't care, I'll kill 'im, Shank! I'll kill 'im if that asshole doesn't come out of hiding!"

A moment later Ganke screamed as another sickle-shaped ceramic shuriken penetrated his wrist. It seemed to hit at just the right spot to deaden the nerves of his hand without causing his muscles to contract, so that he dropped his piece without involuntarily firing it.

"Enough of this shit!" Shank yelled as he decided to dispense with caution and fire several rounds in the direction he was certain the projectile originated.

A salvo of hot lead smashed several of the daiquiri bottles on the wall of the bar. This resulted in the entire vicinity being showered with streams of fruit juice and slivers of glass. Nothing living was hit.

Nevertheless, Moonstalker was impressed with how well Shank aimed the piece despite the erratic kickback that is typically caused by firing a handgun on fully automatic sans the support of a shoulder stock.

He's clearly a serious threat to myself as well as the civilians here. But Reggie may be an asset not yet fully developed. For now, though, I need to draw Shank's fire away from the civilians until he's out of ammo or that damn piece overheats and malfunctions.

"Are you looking for me?" the vigilante's artificially deepened voice said from a few meters behind Shank.

The lethal collection crew's do-rag wearing front-runner whipped his head around to see Moonstalker's gray-garbed form standing in front of the popcorn machine. Shank reacted in a split second by firing another several rounds, which the vigilante narrowly evaded by leaping behind the bar counter. The fusillade of lead instead struck the front glass pane of the popcorn maker, causing it to shatter and spray transparent shrapnel in every direction. After a few seconds, the barrel of the Glock overheated and ceased firing as a thin trail of smoke wafted from its muzzle.

"Shit," the criminal said quietly as he dropped the now useless piece.

Shank swiftly rolled across the floor and recovered Ganke's discarded Ruger Sigma. He then leaned on one knee as he attempted to use the weapon's rear sight to get a bead on his elusive opponent. Because Ganke's continued agonized shouting as he attempted to remove the sickle embedded in his ear were distracting Shank, the crew leader ended that problem by bringing his elbow down on the rotund gangbanger's face, which broke his jawbone and knocked him unconscious. The deadly street lieutenant did that without taking a bit of his attention away from the area in front of him, which he continued to keenly scope for the slightest sign of his target.

Shank had to count on Ricky and Chino to take care of the sole employee of the club who dared stand up to them. His own focus, for now, obviously had to be the vigilante.

Several feet away, the two aforementioned gang members continued to pound on Reggie. Nevertheless, the stocky bouncer continued to demonstrate impressive resilience by taking everything his two opponents inflicted upon him. He finally ended what seemed to be a vicious impasse by slamming his fist down on Ricky's wounded shoulder. The gangbanger's grip immediately went slack, and Reggie grabbed his limp adversary while attempting to use his body as a living barrier against Chino's assaults.

The small Davis firearm had fallen to the floor, and none of the three young men involved in the melee could see that it lay just a short distance from the smashed table where they were brawling.

However, Ty spotted the chintzy but potentially dangerous weapon from his spot beneath another table about twenty feet away. It was clear none of the other panicking patrons were going to attempt to grab the discarded firearm and use it to help the man fighting on their behalf. Reggie's fellow bouncers had all fled, while K.T. was busy on his knees apparently saying prayers while a dark brown stain formed on the back of his once-immaculate blue jeans. And since Alan never reappeared from the rest room (or so Ty thought), the former's BFF realized he would have to take the initiative himself.

Ty had no sooner started crawling out from the under the table and towards the discarded Davis than his erstwhile date Rayissa began tugging on his arm.

"Tyyy-yyy, where the hell do you think you're going?" she lamented just loud enough for him to hear.

"I have to try and help Reggie," he replied.

"The hell you do!" she said. "That's his job, not yours. K.T. hired him to deal with stuff like this."

"I don't care, he put himself on the line for us," Ty retorted as he yanked his arm free of Rayissa's grip. "I can't do any less for him."

"You're gonna get killed!"

"If I got a choice between getting killed and not being able to live with myself, then I know the one I'm gonna make. Sorry."

***

Shank continued to scan the front of the juice bar counter as carefully as humanly possible. The corner of his eye suddenly caught a slight flurry of movement, and his hand involuntarily moved in front of his face. By doing so he actually managed to catch a third shuriken before one of its two sharp edges could impact on his left eye. One of the sharpened points penetrated halfway into his hand, but the pain and bleeding of this wound was but a minor annoyance to such a seasoned street warrior.

Shank immediately countered by firing another shot from the Ruger in the exact direction from which the sickle was hurled. The bullet nearly struck the face of a female patron who was hiding under a table near the juice bar. She screamed as her cheekbone received numerous cuts from the small shards of wooden shrapnel that were blasted off one of the table's legs.

This has gone far enough! Moonstalker silently declared as he somersaulted out from behind the juice bar counter and side-kicked the shattered chair towards

Shank. The gang enforcer still managed to fire another round, and this one ripped a mean flesh wound across the vigilante's right leg just below his knee. The simultaneously propelled chair struck Shank in the side of his face, a move that snapped back his head and caused him to drop the Ruger.

Much like the injury delivered to the gangbanger by the shuriken, Moonstalker's leg wound was considered a minor annoyance to the nocturnal avenger. He pushed past the pain and rushed towards his momentarily debilitated adversary with a barely visible limp.

Ty scooped the "Saturday Night Special" from the floor and pointed its small rusted barrel at Chino. Though he had no idea how to fire a gun, he figured it couldn't be much more difficult than simply aiming it at its intended target and pulling the trigger. Whether the bullet would have hit its mark or not will never be known, however, since a protracted accumulation of dust in the weapon's nozzle caused it to jam as soon as pulled the trigger. *Awwww, shit…*

When Chino saw what Ty had attempted to do, the gangbanger extricated himself from the pig pile on the floor and lunged at his new target.

"You're so dead, man!" the tall, lanky rogue yelled as he knocked Ty to the floor with a single blow to the chin.

Chino then picked up the malfunctioned Davis by its barrel and prepared to use its handle to bludgeon Ty's skull. The young man reacted more out of desperate terror than anything else when he kicked forward with his right leg.

That proved to be a fortuitous move, since the sole of his foot struck Chino right on the groin. The gangbanger uttered a loud "ooolphh!" and dropped the gun as his hands went over his throbbing testes. He nevertheless struggled to remain on his feet and managed to succeed. But the young tough was in no condition to remain that way when Ty jumped to his feet and barreled into the muscular thug.

However, Chino was a veteran brawler who long ago learned to recover from even such daunting pain with remarkable quickness. Though Ty fought furiously to keep him down, the gang member hurled his physically inferior opponent off him with only a fair amount of effort. As the gang member got to his feet to finish the job with his bare hands, he was suddenly distracted by a tap on the shoulder.

Chino turned to find himself face-to-face with an angrily glaring Reggie, with a bloody and beaten Ricky laying sprawled unconscious on the floor behind them.

"Sorry, but your *compadre* gave up on me, asshole," the bouncer announced just before he delivered a crushing haymaker to Chino's jaw.

Looks like the party just got more interesting, Ty thought to himself as he tried getting back to his feet.

***

Moonstalker ignored the painful flesh wound on his right leg as he used its left counterpart to deliver a side kick to Shank's sternum. The gangbanger flew back against the counter of the juice bar but remained on his feet. He grabbed a glass bottle of ginger ale off the counter and smashed it against the wooden frame to form a makeshift, multi-serrated stabbing weapon. He then bellowed a terrifying war cry as he ran towards the vigilante while slashing with the broken bottle in maniacal fashion.

Moonstalker quickly blocked his face, but the shards of broken glass cut deep into the flesh of his forearm, with one of them breaking off into the vigilante's epidermis. The pain of this attack distracted him just enough for Shank to again penetrate his defenses, this time managing to plunge the bottle's sharp broken edges into his chest. The homemade chainmail-like coating under the front part of Moonstalker's uniform stopped the jagged glass points from piercing deeper than half an inch into his flesh, but it was still far enough to deliver a fairly serious wound.

The vigilante had been aware since the beginning of his crusade that he would sooner or later encounter a non-metahuman foe who was skilled enough to give him a serious fight. That time in his career was "sooner," since Shank appeared to be one of those rare street fighters who was heavily disciplined and a superlatively quick thinker. And the leader of the New York Boys was known to be considerably deadlier than this. The gray-garbed avenger knew he had some difficult work ahead of him should he survive the present encounter.

As the battle continued, Moonstalker's well-honed mental faculties enabled him to block much of the pain and enhance his resolve to win. Shank's next slash with the broken bottle aimed for his opponent's throat, and the vigilante evaded the slashing assault. He then delivered a spear hand thrust to the gang member's armpit, deadening some key nerves which caused him to drop his ersatz slashing weapon.

Much to Moonstalker's surprise, though, Shank remained on his feet and used his free hand to deliver a punch to the right side of the crime fighter's head that cracked his clavicle bone. The gang enforcer managed to stun the dark urban warrior with that blow just long enough so he could grab him by the throat with his one free arm. He then pulled his charcoal-attired adversary to the ground in what was a truly herculean display of strength for a non-metahuman.

Moonstalker was determined not to yield, however. While down he delivered a punishing reverse punch to the front of Shank's left leg, a blow that fractured the bone. Though the street fighter yelled in pain he remained on his feet and retaliated with a grueling rabbit punch to the back of the vigilante's neck. The gray-attired martial artist used every erg of his willpower to resist the urge to pass out as his vision blurred.

He forced himself to shrug off the enveloping darkness and retaliate via a focused hammer fist strike to the front of Shank's sneaker. This blow broke every bone of the gang member's instep and separated the joints of his toes from the rest of the foot.

Shank was subjected to so much pain from his shattered foot that he couldn't resist the temptation to vent by screaming in agony. Moonstalker took advantage of this distraction by grabbing his opponent's lower leg in both arms and twisting the limb in a counterclockwise direction. A sickening wet snap was heard as the cracked leg bone graduated to a compound fracture that jutted clear through the gang member's khaki pants.

Shank bellowed like a canine run over by a car as he fell to the floor. Moonstalker knew that he could take no further chances with this one, so he used his last remaining iota of energy to bring a crushing kick to his enemy's neck. A thin stream of blood trickled from Shank's mouth as his eyes rolled into his head and consciousness departed his battered form.

A moment later, the victorious Moonstalker joined his enemy on the floor as he, too, slumped into unconsciousness.

Chapter 10: The Smoking Gun of the Law

"There is much yet to be done, Little Tiger; the law has changed, and never forget your place in the new order of things."

For just the briefest of moments Master Kai's familiar white-bearded, Oriental visage seemed to be replaced with a distinctly different visage: a much more robustly built Caucasian man of similar years with a considerably thicker cloud-gray beard and a missing eye covered by what appeared to be a leather patch. The second archetypically "wise old man" countenance replaced the first just as the visage's last words were spoken. Moreover, the voice changed in concert, going from Master Kai's familiar soft but firm monotone decorated with a discernible Oriental accent to a quite unfamiliar one that was loud, blustery, and thunderously reverberating, whilst punctuated with an accent very different from the first.

Moonstalker promptly forgot whatever that chimeric vision was meant to convey when he was abruptly thrust back into consciousness, courtesy of a stream of sticky chilled mocktail juice being splashed over his masked face by Ty Reynolds.

The vigilante reacted with his usual fleetness of reflexes as he coughed up some of the sweet-tasting fruit drink while simultaneously grasping Ty's wrist in an unbreakable grip. His index finger and thumb instinctively pressed into sensitive nerves which lay just beneath the young man's epidermis, causing him to drop the glass pitcher. Moonstalker was further knocked back into a conscious state by the loud crashing sound made by the brittle liquid container as it splintered into a thousand splintery shards upon hitting the hard floor.

"Oww!" Ty yelled as the pain centers on his upper arm were compressed. "Easy, dude! I had to wake you up somehow, and there weren't any pitchers of regular water that didn't already get smashed. And I had to wake you because…"

"Yes, I know," Moonstalker interjected as he quickly got his bearings. "The police are coming. I *can* hear the sirens, Mr. Reynolds."

"Of course, you can," Ty said with a loud sigh of relief as the vigilante released his wrist. "But waitaminnit, how'd you know my name?"

"I know everyone's name around here," Moonstalker retorted in his distinctive artificially gravel voice.

Ty bit his lower lip and decided to go for the gold, verbally speaking. "Especially anyone you've been best friends with for years and years, right… *Alan?*"

The young man once again felt the pain of compressed nerve clusters, albeit this time in his lower facial muscles, as Moonstalker clasped the area around Ty's mouth. This move instantly rendered him incapable of further speech, and his eyes appeared to bulge from their sockets with his shock over the lightning-fast movement initiated by his costumed friend.

"Be *quiet,*" Moonstalker said with a terrifyingly firm conviction.

Ty nodded his head in a desperate and nervous manner, which convinced the dark-clad vigilante to release his grip.

"Oww, geez," Ty said as he rubbed the inflamed nerve endings around his mouth. His next words were carefully uttered in a low tone that only the person sitting a few inches from him could possibly hear. "Look, sorry, but I know it's you, man. I've seen Alan in action, and no way would he not have come out of the bathroom by now if he was a separate person from you. I don't think anyone else in here knows you like I do, so I wouldn't worry about…"

"I need to get to my feet," Moonstalker interrupted as the sound of the swiftly approaching police sirens became much louder.

Ty put his shoulder under the urban ninja's arm and helped him regain his footing. He was quickly joined by Reggie Diaz, who had just delivered a T.K.O. to the gangbanger Chino at the culmination of their brief tussle.

"Thank you for the help," said Reggie through a bleeding lip, his right eye nearly swollen shut. "And don't worry about me, the other guy looks a lot worse."

"No need to thank me, it's what I put this uniform on for," Moonstalker noted. "But thank *you* for staying and doing your job."

Reggie nodded his head to indicate "you're welcome."

"We need to get him out the back way," Ty suggested.

"No," Reggie replied. "The police always have the back door covered when they get here. We'll help him to the bathroom. He can get out the same way he came in."

Obviously, the bouncer was unaware of the vigilante's actual means of ingress to the club (he walked through the front door in civilian guise hours earlier!). Instead, he presumed that Alan Perez fled the bar when he wasn't looking. Or so the vigilante *hoped* he had presumed; unlike Ty, the bouncer said nothing to indicate otherwise.

"The bathroom will work just fine," Moonstalker said. "You two delay the police as best you can without making them suspicious."

The vigilante then broke free from Ty's and Reggie's sustaining grip and rushed into the men's room. As Moonstalker plowed through the door he found himself in the very awkward presence of club owner K.T. Jones, who was in the midst of changing his soiled pants.

"Oh god!" the proprietor of the East Side Inferno shouted. "Please, don't… oh my god, oh my god, you're not one of them, you're the one of… I mean, you're *him*…"

"Yes, I'm him," Moonstalker said as he walked towards the window on the far end of the rest room. "Just keep cleaning your undies and stop making noise. I need to get out the back window."

"Um, you won't be able to do that, um, sir…" K.T. stammered. "A few days ago, I had iron bars installed over the glass, because too many people kept sneaking into the club through the bathroom window to avoid the cover charge…"

The businessman's diatribe was cut off a split second later as Moonstalker rushed him and dragged him into the closest stall. K.T.'s stained pants and underwear fell to the floor as the vigilante quietly closed the stall door with his left arm while keeping his right hand gripped firmly over the tall man's mouth.

Moonstalker then glared directly into the terrified club proprietor's eyes as he placed his index finger over the area of his mask where his lips would be, and uttered, "Shhhhh*hhhh*."

K.T. nervously nodded in compliance and went completely mum.

***

Officer Darius McCain was the first of a trio of police officers to enter the establishment, which by now was virtually vacant save for patron Ty Reynolds, employee Reggie Diaz, and a posse of bloodied and unconscious members of the New York Boys. Another group of police were, as Reggie predicted, covering the back entrance of the East Side Inferno, the location of which they were by now aware of.

"Everyone freeze!" Darius bellowed with his Glock pointing in front of him.

His two fellow officers followed suit with their own firearms, determined to take no chances where a report of New York Boy involvement was concerned.

"Easy, Hoss, it's all good!" Ty said while he placed his hands on his head.

"Who are you two and why are you still here?" Darius queried with authority.

"I'm one of the bouncers, Officer," Reggie calmly responded. "My name is Reggie Diaz, and I stayed here to deal with this. The other guy, Ty Reynolds, is a customer who stayed to help out."

Darius demanded to see I.D., and this order was promptly complied with by both young men to the officer's satisfaction (the patrons of this mostly underage teen club were required to have at least a school bus pass on them for that purpose if too young to earn a driver's license, or if they hadn't acquired a non-driver's license). Reggie also offered his employee badge to prove his association with the club. The policeman nodded upon scanning it.

"Where are the rest of the bouncers?" Darius asked while his two fellow officers looked around and checked the anatomical status of the unconscious gang members.

"They left when things got rough," Reggie said.

"So, you mean to tell me that you and this guy, who isn't even a bouncer hired to guard this place, took out all of these gang members?" Darius inquired suspiciously.

"Well, we're pretty bad ass, what else can we say, sir?" Ty replied with a forced smile.

Reggie compelled himself not to slap Ty on the back of his head, while Darius took on an expression making it clear that he was anything but satisfied with that answer.

"He was here, wasn't he?" the officer demanded to know.

Reggie made a point to respond quickly. "If you mean the boss, K.T. Jones, he *was* here, but he had an accident…"

"No, not the club owner; I meant *him*," the young officer firmly clarified. "That goddamned vigilante! You think I don't recognize his handiwork by now? He did this, didn't he?"

Before either Reggie or Ty could decide whether to attempt to lie or not, the answer was given by Officer Cindy Meachum as she finished checking some of the wounds on the incapacitated gangbangers. "It *was* the vigilante. The damage on most of these men was clearly inflicted by someone with extensive training. Not only that, but the puncture wounds made by those crescent shurikens of his are not exactly hard to notice."

"Better yet," Officer Ted Claymore said from across the bar, "look what I just found." He used a pair of tweezers to lift one of the blood-soaked, grayish-black ceramic blades off the floor, where it laid next to the pool of crimson that was congealing around Ganke's unconscious form. "This thug must have ripped the thing from the flesh under and behind his ear. Jesus. No doubt he's going to lose that ear."

Officer Darius's countenance now took on a more severe sense of rage as he turned back to the two young men he was questioning. "I'm going to ask you this just once, and you had better not lie to me: is he still here somewhere in the club?"

"Arrest me if you want, Officer," Reggie said with a strong though polite tone. "But I'm not going to give up Moonstalker. He stopped these assholes from stealing from here again, and he likely saved our lives. I didn't see 'Buffalo's Finest' doing the same."

"Yeah, what - what he said," Ty muttered in a manner that didn't quite conceal his nervousness. But it was nevertheless clear that he too would go to jail before ratting out the vigilante.

Darius gritted his teeth in extreme anger, but nevertheless resisted doing or saying what first came to mind, and he turned to his fellow officers. "If you two can handle securing those pricks for when the ambulances arrive, I'm going to keep looking around. Tell the guys checking the other door that if it's all secure there, I'd like some back up from as many of them as can be spared."

"Will do, but what about those two?" Officer Cindy Meachum asked.

"Take them downtown and book their sorry asses for obstructing justice," he said. "I'll be down there to chat with them later."

"Say what?" Ty said. "'Obstructing justice?' Seriously, man?"

"Ty, shut your mouth and cooperate with the 'heat,'" Reggie admonished. "Don't say shit else until we have a lawyer sitting beside us."

***

Moonstalker stood as still as a mannequin in the bathroom stall, his left arm holding the trembling K.T. against the wall while his right hand covered his mouth, when Officer Darius McCain burst into the rest room with his brandished Glock leading the way.

"Freeze!" The policeman saw nothing and heard nothing. In fact, the silence was so deafening that he considered leaving and continuing his search elsewhere.

That is, until the panic-ridden K.T. suddenly had another loose and very loud bowel movement. *Shit!* was, ironically, all the vigilante could think as he leapt backwards onto the top of the toilet seat to evade being spattered by the exclamation's physical manifestation.

"Hey, what the hell!" Darius shouted just before kicking open the stall with his firearm pointed at the interior.

"Don't shoot, Officer, please don't shoot!" K.T. screeched as he fell to his knees while his colon continued to evacuate its contents onto the floor. "I'm not one of those gangbangers! For God's sake, I'm the owner of the club, the owner!"

Darius was distracted by the sorry sight and horrid stench before him just long enough for Moonstalker to leap from the top of the stall divider and deliver a flying side kick to what he remembered was the policeman's previously injured shoulder. The lawman shouted in pain as he flew back against the wall. The hard-hitting officer managed to take a shot, but the poorly aimed bullet merely bounced off the toilet bowl's porcelain base. K.T. screamed and fell to his knees as Moonstalker turned to run out of the rest room, being more than aware that a combination of the gunshot and K.T.'s bellow of terror would have alerted Darius's fellow officers to the ruckus.

However, Darius proved tougher than the vigilante had imagined. The young patrolman forced himself to resist being overwhelmed by the biting pain of his shoulder wound as he leapt forward and plowed into Moonstalker with surprising strength. He then wrapped his arm around the vigilante's neck and pointed his Glock to his forehead.

"You're under arrest, you son of a bitch!" Darius hollered.

"Let's leave my mother out of this, okay, McCain?" Moonstalker said just before he ducked under the firearm and backed both himself and the policeman up against the wall with pounding force.

The vigilante managed to get a tight grip on the stunned officer's gun wrist and inflicted severe pressure to the limb's sensitive nerve endings. Darius dropped the firearm, but he still managed to slug his would-be prisoner in the side of the jaw with his other fist. The strength of the blow was sufficient to stun Moonstalker in turn, and Darius swiftly wielded his hardwood nightstick.

With it, he delivered one heavy blow to the crime buster's shoulder, and it took every iota of the latter's will not to yell in agony. Instead, the street warrior channeled the pain into an adrenal rush that enabled him to swiftly deliver an elbow strike to the officer's groin. Darius shouted in concert with the mean-spirited blow as he covered his genitals with his free hand while again proving his resilience by immediately swinging the baton with the other.

Moonstalker managed to barely duck the swing, which would have given him a serious concussion had it struck its intended mark. The hooded crusader then side-kicked the officer with a move that finally knocked him off his feet and sent him sprawling across the grime-ridden floor. The blow also caused Darius to drop his nightstick, which his gray-clad opponent caught as it descended towards the floor.

Moonstalker did his best to block out the agonizing pain biting through his right shoulder and the left side of his jawbone while contemplating a means of escape. Another serious monkey wrench was thrown into that plan, however, when two other officers then rushed through the rest room door.

The first one, a short but well-built man, was about to yell "freeze!" only to find himself startled by the sight of the baton-wielding vigilante just an inch in front of him. Moving almost faster than the policeman could see, Moonstalker smashed the officer's gun-holding wrist with the nightstick, quickly disarming him. The vigilante followed up that literal bone-splitting move with a roundhouse kick to the hapless lawman's chin that sent him sprawling into the corner of the bathroom. The officer was so stunned that he slid to the ground and remained there.

However, the policeman directly behind him was a tall, athletic woman whom he recognized from his neighborhood patrol as Officer Ella Farrell. Her intention was obviously to back up her fallen compatriot with her own baton.

Ella wasted not so much as a nano-second going into action at the vigilante before her. Shouting in anger she swung the truncheon at her charcoal-garbed opponent, and Moonstalker just barely managed to block it with his own purloined nightstick. A near-debilitating jolt of pain bit into his seriously bruised clavicle bone, causing the warrior to buckle. The female officer then redoubled her efforts and continued a vicious series of swings with her baton. Moonstalker deflected two more of them with the nightstick in his possession, and then delivered a reverse punch to the policewoman's mouth.

Though Ella's bottom lip was split in half, the well-trained and highly athletic officer withstood the blow and delivered a punch of her own to her vigilante opponent. This haymaker to the face took Moonstalker off-guard and sent him crashing through the glass of the window at the end of the bathroom, where he banged the back of his skull against the iron bars behind it. The hardened officer then rushed towards her opponent and swung her baton at him again.

Moonstalker blocked the oncoming strike with his forearm, which caused a small fracture to his ulna and severe bruising to his flexor muscles despite the padding under his sleeve. The vigilante realized the likely extent of the injuries inflicted upon his arm, and despite his resilience he had taken too much damage by this point; he needed to end this fight and escape the premises if he had any hope of continuing his career as a masked crime fighter, let alone keeping out of juvie.

Upon being beaten down to the ground by the policewoman, Moonstalker initiated a wide leg sweep that knocked her left foot out from under her. As Ella struggled to retain her balance, the vigilante delivered a turning kick to her lower abdomen. That sent her into the wall situated to the side of him, and before she could fully recover, he struck the Amazonian officer in the diaphragm with the end of the nightstick. The woman fell to the ground and began vomiting on the floor.

The ninja-like warrior then struck Ella on the back of her neck, knowing there was a nerve cluster there that would cause her to lose consciousness without wreaking any serious damage to her upper vertebrae. Provided he hit it just right, that is. Thankfully, his desperate risk paid off, and the tough-as-nails cop went down in a non-permanent fashion.

As Moonstalker pushed himself back to his feet, he gave a quick bow to honor the warrior prowess of Darius McCain and Ella Farrell. As he turned around, however, he found himself confronted by the just recovered Officer Darius. The policeman was again on his feet regardless of the streams of blood dripping out of both his nostrils and lips was nevertheless on his feet, his baton raised above his head in a threatening manner.

Despite the respect he's earned, I'm really starting to hate that guy.

"It's over, vigilante," Darius said. "Assume the position or I'll be too happy to break you like a bad habit."

"You're a fool, McCain," Moonstalker said. "But you're a brave fool and a good man. So, I hope you'll one day forgive me for this."

With the draw speed reminiscent of one of the greatest of the Old West's gunslingers, the vigilante whipped a tiny blowgun in front of his mouth. He then exhaled a small hardwood dart that penetrated just a fraction of an inch into the skin of Darius's forehead.

"What the f…" was all the policeman managed to utter before his eyes rolled into his head and he collapsed to the floor.

"Sleep well, McCain," Moonstalker said as he pocketed the blowgun and turned towards the exit to the rest room.

Thank you for showing me how to brew that concoction out of a few herbs, Matoi. Everything I ever learned in that dojo is now paying off handsomely.

***

"Look, man, I just want a little taste, that's all," Juno said to the young man known on the streets as Chief, who was tantalizingly holding a syringe filled with liquid heroin just a few inches out of reach from her emaciated arm.

Juno was a middle-aged addict who was well known in this area for her willingness to give just about anything in return for even a small fix. Chief was a 19-year-old Caucasian member of the New York Boys who took his street name after the fact that he was often told his dark black hair, which he frequently wore in a ponytail, made him resemble a Native American. The muscular young gangbanger enjoyed teasing the woman in this manner.

"I'll give you anything for a little taste, Chief," the disheveled woman pleaded through a quivering mouth full of rotting teeth.

"Okay, here you go," Chief said as he moved the syringe closer. He then laughed uproariously when she grasped for the container holding the precious substance, only to have him callously move the needle out of reach.

"Stop it, please, this is killing me," she whimpered through tearing eyes. "I told you I'd give you anything you want."

"Bitch, you can't give me anything that I couldn't easily get from an attractive young thing," Chief grinned, a single gold tooth glimmering under a corner streetlight off Apple Street. "Since I went and joined the gang, every chick on my block wants to be all up on this. I don't want that nasty-ass infected mouth of yours anywhere near any part of me."

"Please, Chief, please, I never begged for nuthin' before…"

"Ha ha, that's not what I heard! Tell you what, I'll give you a little taste of this if you beg me like a dog."

"Okay, okay, I'm begging you…"

"No, no, I meant begging like a *real dog*! Walk back and forth on the curb on all fours, barking like a dog while wagging your ass around. After all, that's what a bitch is, a scurvy female dog like you. Beg for me, bitch!"

Despite the tears in her eyes and the shakiness of her limbs, Juno began doing as she was ordered without hesitation. The decrepit woman coughed up days old phlegm as her attempts to imitate the vocalizations of a canine to Chief's satisfaction wreaked havoc on her parched throat. Her emaciated wrists and knees were filled with agonizing pain, but she pooled the last vestiges of willpower she had towards earning the fix. Nothing was worth more to her than that, and her dignity and self-respect were things she sacrificed for her habit long ago.

"That's a good doggie," Chief said after a long bout of laughter.

"Can I have it now?" Juno asked in barely audible fashion as the waves of pain sailing throughout her body further strained her now severely inflamed throat.

"No," Chief said, lifting the syringe higher in the air. "First you gotta get up on your knees, bend your hands in front of you like paws, and stick that tongue of yours out while you pant just like a dog desperate to get scraps from the table. Ha!"

"Please, Chief, I'm hurting…"

"Do it or you don't get a single drop of this shit!"

"My, but you certainly are one cruel young man," came an unfamiliar voice from behind them. "Did you leave your soul behind the moment you joined that gang and decided to prey on your neighbors? Or had it departed your mortal coil long before that?"

Chief turned around to see the figure of a man wrapped in a dark garment who stood just within an alley at the edge of the corner. He was unaware that it was a fully armed and incognito Father Merlin "Merle" Harris.

"Who the hell are you supposed to be, man?" Chief asked.

"I'm a man who is here to clean up these streets, so God's flock may go about their daily lives without being assailed by those who follow the path of Satan," Harris replied in a stone cold voice.

"Seriously?" Chief queried incredulously.

"*Very* seriously," the priest answered as his piece became visible in the streetlight.

"Oh geez, man," were the last words Chief uttered before Harris pulled the trigger and sent a hot lead projectile into the young gangbanger's shoulder.

The wounded young malcontent immediately fell to the ground and dropped the syringe, which shattered and leaked its liquid contents onto the curb. Juno screamed in terror, not because a man was just shot in front of her, but because her prized heroin was now soaking into the ground.

"Not my stuff, not my stuff!" she bellowed as she bent down and attempted to lick its rapidly evaporating drops from the cold cement.

Father Harris displayed none of the sympathy he so often showed the numerous parishioners of his congregation who sought his council over problems like this through the decades. "My apologies, ma'am, but had you avoided the weakness which led you to that addiction in the first place, then perhaps you wouldn't have ended up at the mercy of people like this. Think about that the next time you trade your human dignity for a fix. Now go to the local rehab clinic for help!"

As the priest-become-vigilante turned to disappear back into the alley from which he emerged, he didn't see the still conscious Chief slip a "Saturday Night Special" from his jacket pocket and point it at Harris's back.

The priest turned and brandished his weapon again when he heard a smashing sound that was immediately followed by Chief's scream of agony. It was then he saw the illuminated profile of a large man wearing a ski mask and clad in a dark apron to conceal the lighter clothes underneath, who was standing above the body of Chief. The mysterious Samaritan held a baseball bat whose business end was covered in blood.

That blood obviously belonged to Chief, whose right temple was smashed in. Father Harris had failed to hear that above Juno's continued crying over the loss of her liquid treasure.

"Ya'll need to watch your back, Father Harris," the dark figure said in the rough voice of an older man whom the disciple of God was quite familiar with. "Or at least have me watch it for you, huh?"

"How did you…?"

"Aw come on there, Father, I knew it was you, I've heard your voice in the parish every Sunday for years now," the new arrival said as he removed the ski mask to reveal the bald pate and bushy salt and pepper mustache of deli owner Fred Gifford.

"Did you have to announce that in front of the lady, Fred?"

"Oh, don't worry none 'bout her, Father. Old Juno is so sick right now that she's not thinking of nothin' besides where she'll get her next fix. Believe you me, it's not 'cause of the cold that she's laying there shivering right now."

"Are you following the path of the Moonstalker too, Fred?"

"Damn straight I am, Father, even if not for those spiritual reasons you probly are. But we're on the same team. I spotted this little prick at the corner doing his thing, and I came here to do my thing to him; then lo and behold you came outta the alley and did that thing before I could. Glad I got a piece of him myself, though, after what these hooligans have done to me and a whole lotta good people around here."

"Do you not consider yourself 'good' any longer, Fred?"

"Now that I did this, Father, I really dunno. But it sure as hell *felt* good – pardon me for saying 'hell' in front of you -- and I'll gladly do this again, so no *really* good people have to. Maybe you're just the man to talk to about this here thing. Can we go somewhere less public to rap about this?"

Father Harris smiled. "We can indeed, Fred. Welcome to the path."

Chapter 11: Kindred Spirits

Two police officers who had previously been assigned to watch the back entrance to the East Side Inferno strode into the front door. They believed the club was more or less secured now, as the unconscious bodies of the New York Boys who had attempted to collect "protection money" from owner K.T. Jones were now in custody.

Not only that, but Officers Meachum and Claymore had arrested two additional young men; one a bouncer, the other a patron, on obstruction charges at Officer Darius McCain's insistence. Officer McCain was said to be searching the premises for the presence of Moonstalker, and Officers Farrell and Eagan had previously been sent to aid him in that task.

"It's pretty quiet in here," noted Gollock, the first new cop to enter the club, to his partner, a young woman named Reed. "I thought McCain was supposed to be in here. Usually his big mouth can be heard anywhere in any joint he may be in, even if he's on the opposite side of the place."

As if on cue, a bruised, bloody, and groggy Officer Darius burst out of the men's room, and hollered at the top of his lungs, "Did you see him?"

"Geez, what happened to you, McCain?" Gollock, asked. "Did you slip on someone's piss in the crapper and land on your face or something?"

"Shut up, Gollock!" Darius exclaimed. "That vigilante! Moonstalker! He did a number on me, Farrell, and Eagen in there, and then he retreated from the bathroom."

"He took out all *three* of you?" Reed queried. "Seriously, McCain?"

"You heard me, Reed!" he shouted to the burly woman in blue. "Did either of you see him slip out? He was injured, so he couldn't have gotten far!"

"I'm sorry, McCain, but we saw nothing when we walked in here," Reed replied. "You need to get your ass to the hospital now, because you look like you spent an hour on the bottom of the mosh pit. And since Farrell and Eagan haven't even come out of there yet, I doubt they look much better."

"No! I'm not letting that bastard get away!" Darius declared as he used every iota of his considerable will to force his bruised body and wobbly legs to carry him to the front entrance.

The lawman kicked the front door open with his Glock brandished in front of him, and he looked in every conceivable direction. The throbbing pain in his skull, ribs, and left leg were fully ignored, as was the remaining after effects of the potent drug Moonstalker filled his bloodstream with.

"Where did he go?" Darius shouted to no one in particular.

Another officer on the scene, a middle-aged cop named Elliot, ran out from the club's back alley upon hearing Darius's screech, and seeing the noticeably trembling form of the younger officer, he ran to his side.

"McCain, is that you?" Elliot said.

"It's not my goddamned twin brother, Elliot!" Darius spat in reply. "Did you see Moonstalker leave the club? He was here!"

"No, I was at the back entrance, where I was assigned," Elliot answered. "But you need to get checked out by a doctor right now, because you look like any second you might…"

Elliot didn't finish his sentence before Darius's eyes rolled into his head and the intrepid lawman fell to the concrete like the slab of human meat he now was. Needless to say, Officer Darius McCain had once again bid adieu to consciousness.

"Jesus, McCain!" Elliot yelled as he ran up to the fallen officer and checked his vitals. "Thank God, you got a pulse, but geez are you a mess! How did you even manage to walk out of there, man?"

It was then that Elliot got over the initial shock, realized he was now talking only to himself, and did what he had to do. The officer quickly grabbed his two-way, 700-megahertz radio and called for paramedics.

In the meantime, back in the club Reed and Gollock were momentarily startled when the door to the men's room burst open again. This time it wasn't a police officer that emerged, but the lanky form of club owner K.T. Jones. Nevertheless, the tension combined with the suddenness of K.T.'s exit from the bathroom caused the two officers to point their firearms at him. Startled by the terrifying sight of twin Glocks pointed at him, the club owner screamed in terror and once again discharged the contents of his bowels into the jeans he had just spent a half hour cleaning.

"Awww shit!" K.T. exclaimed.

"That's certainly the operative word for it, man!" Gollock replied. "My god, that's disgusting!"

A second later, the door to the men's room again burst open. This time, the statuesque form of Officer Ella Farrell emerged, her face bruised and bloody, and still having difficulty staying on her feet due to the blow she took to the back of her neck. Like Darius before her, though, she was determined to remain on her feet.

"Where's that vigilante?" Ella inquired angrily. "I'm gonna kick his ass, then use my nightstick on it like a plunger!"

***

Several blocks away and more minutes later, a brawny but run-of-the-mill mugger held an elderly man up against a street light at the intersection of Mulberry and Virginia Street. The large man raised his fist in a menacing manner and made it quite clear he would bring it to bear on the older man's facial bones if the elder gentleman refused to give up whatever cash he may have had on his person.

Suddenly, a ceramic, sickle-shaped object deflected off the street light's metallic frame, missing the mugger's face by a mere two inches.

"Ooohhh, shit!" the criminal screamed. "It's Moonstalker! Man, I didn't do a thing to the old guy! I just mistook him for some dude who owed me money, but I'm outta here now, okay?"

And within seconds, the hefty man had retreated up Mulberry Street, to vanish into the darkness. His would-be elderly victim, while still somewhat shaken up, peered into the shadowy back alley from just across the street where he believed the shuriken that drove off his attacker had originated. He saw the barest outline of a gray-attired figure standing amidst the shadows, and he immediately perceived that the individual who just saved him from a severe, potentially fatal beating was injured.

The older man limped over to the figure, one of his legs clearly lagging behind the other in terms of locomotive capacity. When he was within two feet of the entrance to the side road, the vigilante was clearly tottering on the verge of collapse. He barely managed to stop himself from keeling over by grasping and leaning onto the edge of the building that framed the right side of the alley.

"You're hurt," the grateful senior citizen observed aloud. "Let me help."

"You... need to get home," Moonstalker said through teeth gritted behind his mask. "I should have hit that thug in his lower jaw... with the shuriken. Missed by... inches. I'm in worse shape than I... thought. Took every last bit I had... to get away from the club... unseen. I may not be able to protect you... again."

"Nonsense, young man," replied the gentleman he saved. "My name is Eli Matthews, and I'm a veteran with years of training in combat medicine. Let me

87

get you back to my home, it's just across the way there on Locust. I'll tend to your wounds."

"My... parents will be worried... if I don't get home."

"Your parents? Jesus! How young are you?"

"Never mind that. I need to get in without them... noticing."

"Even if you did manage that, young man, they'll sure as hell notice the shape you're in soon enough. And I'm guessing you didn't tell them about your evening activities in this uniform. So, in your condition, it's either my place or the emergency room. Let me know now, because if you pass out, I won't be able to carry you. Then the choice will be out of your hands; I'll have to use my cell phone to call an ambulance. And if I have to do that, your nightly jig will be up."

Moonstalker took note of all the pain he was suffering and blood he was losing. He couldn't help but notice that his well-honed mental faculties were barely keeping him conscious and mobile. He had to face facts that any stubbornness on his part would either cost him his life, or his secret identity. Hence, the decision he promptly made to Eli.

"Your... house."

"Good decision, young man. Now lean on my shoulder, we can cut through the alley there, and that leads into my yard. We can get into my house through the back door. I doubt anyone will see us, as not many folks are stupid enough to be outside at this time of night. Well, other than myself, obviously."

***

"So, before we start, can I ask which of you is gonna be the 'good' cop, and which one the 'bad' cop?" Ty Reynolds asked Officers Cindy Meachum and Ted Claymore, who were presiding over the interrogation of both himself and Reggie Diaz. "The lady officer is sort of hot, so I'm hoping she'll be the 'good' cop, right?"

"I'm about to become a 'bad' cop in the worst way you can imagine if you don't cut the shit and show some respect for both me and the situation you're now in, young man," Meachum said in an ominous tone.

"I think my friend here is just nervous," Reggie interceded, "since this is the first time he's ever been interrogated after acting bravely as a civilian forced into a gang-related attempt at robbery and torture. When is our lawyer getting here, Officers?"

"Your lawyer will get here as soon as one becomes available and is assigned to your case," Claymore said. "I'm presuming neither of you are in a position to afford one on your own, so you'll have to wait a bit."

"Was that a dig at our economic position in society, Officer?" Ty wryly asked.

"Stop being paranoid, kid," Meachum rejoined.

"Considering the better service we'd now be getting if we could afford a big shot lawyer, I'd say my friend has a point," Reggie noted aloud. "Now, before my friend says another stupid thing, we can just sit here all night in total silence until our assigned lawyer walks through that door."

"Yup," Ty agreed. "Do you officers happen to have a deck of cards handy? I'm partial to Pinochle, so maybe you should check to see if you have one of those decks in the armory, or wherever you keep the cards."

"Enough, Ty," Reggie said while elbowing him hard in the side.

"Yes, that is *'enough,'* Ty," Meachum reiterated. "I've about had it with your mouth…"

Just then, the door to the interrogation room opened, and an attractive young female dressed in a "power suit" and carrying an attaché case walked in. She had a flawless mocha skin tone, long black hair pulled back into a pony tail, and piercing dark eyes.

"My name is Marita Espinoza, and I'm the lawyer for these two young men," the young woman in the high-powered attire said. "I'm taking their cases pro bono, and I'd like to know what the charges are."

"Whoa *whoa*," Ty stammered upon seeing the attractive attorney, just loud enough for Reggie to hear.

The muscular bouncer elbowed him again. "Show some respect," he whispered. "This woman is here to help us."

"Who says I don't respect her just 'cause I think she's hot as freakin' magma?"

The two youths were startled when Officer Meachum slammed her nightstick on the table a few inches from where they sat. "That will be quite enough, you two! Now let's listen to what your lawyer has to say without all the comments."

"Why are you taking our case pro bono, if I may ask, Ms. Espinoza?" Reggie queried.

"Let's just say your employer called and asked for this favor," Marita replied. "He's an old friend, and I owe him a few."

"Nice to see K.T. is good for something other than coming up with funky ass mocktail concoctions and shitting in his pants," Ty said softly.

"Shut up, Ty, before I belt you," Reggie demanded with a tone full of annoyance.

"Now, I reiterate my first question," Marita addressed to the officers. "What are the charges?"

"Our partner at the scene of the East Side Inferno incident said they were guilty of obstructing justice," Claymore explained.

"And how is that?" Marita asked. "Details, please."

Claymore continued. "It seems that Moonstalker vigilante made another illegal assault on gang members, these ones being present in the club at the time. Our partner, Officer Darius McCain, suspected he was still there when we arrived, hidden somewhere in the club. When asked, your clients refused to tell us where he was, saying they wouldn't give him up because they believe the vigilante saved their lives with his illegal assault on the gang members."

"He *did* save our lives, 'Softy'," Ty said under this breath. "He certainly saved K.T.'s ass, even if he couldn't save the jeans and boxers that were covering it."

"Please be silent and let me do the talking," Marita told her errant client. "You're Tyrone Reynolds, correct?"

"I sure am," Ty replied with a wide toothy smile. "I can give you my cell number as proof."

"And you're Reginald Diaz?" she asked her other client while shrugging off Ty's comment.

"I am," Reggie clarified.

"May I remind you officers that Mr. Reynolds is a minor, and neither of you bothered to call his parents. Mr. Diaz is a few years past the legal age of adulthood, but there is no proof that he, like Mr. Reynolds, were actually aware that the vigilante was hidden anywhere on the premises. Officer McCain seems to have just assumed that based on how they responded to his inquiry."

"Exactly, because neither of them denied knowing the whereabouts of the vigilante when Officer McCain asked them!" Meachum exclaimed. "They both said they weren't going to give him up! That clearly implies they knew the vigilante was there but refused to cooperate with the arrest of an individual who was violating the law."

"But they didn't *confirm* that they knew," Marita said while raising her index finger to emphasize her point. "They had just had a harrowing experience, where they were assaulted by dangerous gang members. In fact, their boss informed me that both acted quite heroically, standing up to defend him and his patrons, and risking their own lives in the process. That was actually Mr. Diaz's job, which he stuck to while his fellow bouncers fled the establishment. Mr. Reynolds stood up to help despite having no obligation to do so, and with no motivation other than doing the right thing. I'm certain Mr. Jones, the club owner, will not fail to make this clear to the press when they inevitably interview him."

"Being heroes doesn't mean they can obstruct the efforts of police officers searching for a law-breaking vigilante!" Meachum bleated loudly. "Everyone is subject to the law, no matter what they do or how they act in any given situation. And you know this, Ms. Espinoza!"

"Let me repeat the facts at hand, Officer Meachum," Marita said, emphasizing each point by tapping the table with the index finger of her right hand. "One of my clients is a minor, whose parents were not called here before you started questioning him. My other client put his own life on the line while carrying out his job. Neither of them explicitly admitted to knowing where the vigilante was, and from what I understand, there was no proof the vigilante was even still present on the premises as your partner seemed to have assumed.

"Both of my clients were in a state of fatigue and possible trauma after their selfless acts in defending others, only to find themselves harassed by a police officer who was himself injured at the time, and who may have been acting improperly due to a combination of a desperate personal agenda against this vigilante and the injuries he received himself. Yes, my clients were being indignant with an officer of the law, but I think this is quite understandable under such extenuating circumstances."

"Our partner at the scene, Officer McCain, actually received these injuries from the vigilante, not the gang members!" Meachum hollered. "He had every right to be indignant himself when questioning your clients."

"That doesn't nullify any of my previous points," Marita retorted. "Now, do you officers want to push this further? I think it may be the judgment of Officer McCain that will be called into question here by the press, and that will likely lead to a full investigation of the matter. Your unquestioned complicity in charging these young men, one of them a minor, both of them heroes, with obstructing justice sans any real evidence that the vigilante was even actually present at the club when Officer McCain confronted them will also be unlikely to go over well, either in a court of law or in the press."

Meachum and Claymore looked at each other for a moment, each seeming to silently reach an agreement on everything.

"No charges will be filed," Meachum said with forced civility. "This was a rough night for everyone involved, and mistakes were made all around. These young men are free to go."

"Thank you, officers," Marita said as she motioned to her two clients to leave the interrogation room immediately.

"I totally owe you dinner for this," Ty told his lawyer while watching her strut down the hall of the police station. "Just tell me when, and I'll show you where."

"Thank you for the help, Ms. Espinoza," Reggie said, making a point to interrupt Ty. "And please do thank K.T. for us, as I have no idea when he plans to re-open the club."

"You're welcome, Mr. Diaz," she responded. "K.T. is very shaken up right now, but he should be fine after a bit of recuperation time, though he'll have to consult a physician to know for certain. Unless you should need me again for anything related to this case, be well, Mr. Diaz, Mr. Reynolds."

"You can call me Ty," the young man called out to the quickly departing legal eagle. "All my friends and lovers do!"

"Will you shut up, Ty!" Reggie roared.

***

The juxtaposed images of Master Kai and the mysterious one-eyed bearded man with the thunderous voice cascaded across Alan Perez's mindscape, their joint message repeating like an extended vinyl record whose needle kept perpetually "skipping." This repetitive psychic montage seemed to continue for a perceived eternity until the young man awakened from a deep sleep on an unfamiliar bed.

He noticed that the top portion of his uniform was removed, and his injured arm was patched up professionally. His fractured shoulder was likewise taped up, and he seemed to have been well stabilized. Then a stunning realization hit him. *My mask! Is it still on?*

The young man hastily moved his right arm up to check his face, until the pain of the injured limb reminded him of his brawl with the police officers in the East Side Inferno restroom. Startled by the intensity of the pain, he yelped and stopped its movement midway. He then cautiously continued his hand's move towards his face. It was at that point he realized his mask had indeed been removed. *Aw, shit.*

"I see you're awake now," came the gentle voice of Eli Matthews, who was standing in the doorway of his own bedroom. "I'm glad you woke up again, otherwise I'd have slept on the couch for no good reason."

"Why did you remove my mask?" Alan asked, as he forced himself to sit up despite the severe pain of doing so.

"At ease, young man. You don't want to rip open anything I stitched shut, nor do you want to pull any bone out of place that I spent the better part of the night putting back where it belonged."

Eli noticed that his erstwhile young patient took a deep breath and did his best to relax despite the intense emotions building within. After all, there was no denying the unassuming older man patched him up professionally, thereby sparing him a trip to the emergency room and therefore assuring that only one person saw his true face that evening.

"Now, to answer your question. I had to make sure your airway was cleared and that you had no damage to your throat. Even with a mask as porous as the one you wear, it could still have impeded your breathing to a fatal extent if you had a collapsed lung, damaged windpipe, or even just a deviated septum. In case you haven't guessed, I was a front-lines medic in the Vietnam War, so I'm a specialist in combat medicine. I'm also a retired physician's assistant, and I've kept up the skills by volunteering at the Veteran's Hospital and at the emergency room at ECMC."

"So I see." Alan then endured the pain of turning his head from side to side as he endeavored to take in the entirety of his environment, even if it did momentarily seem friendly.

"Yes, you're lucky that I happened to be the guy whose life you saved from that mugger, considering the condition you were in when it happened. That's another reason I patched you up. Not only was it the least I could do considering what you risked for me, but I wanted to be able to thank you properly."

Alan let out an exasperated sigh, and replied, almost under his breath, "Yeah. Thank you too."

"Are you thankful enough that you won't kill me for seeing your real face?"

Alan couldn't help smiling at Eli's sarcasm, and he found himself starting to like this man.

"Yes, consider yourself safe. If you did all this for me, then I think I can trust you not to make a sketch of my face and hand it over to the police or the newspapers. And you're old enough that it's likely you wouldn't know how to upload a pic to the Internet anyway."

"Um, yeah, though I'm actually quite adroit with navigating the online world, thank you very much. But I'm glad you're going to spare my life. I really didn't want my good for nothing daughter to collect on any life insurance just yet. No doubt she took a policy out on me and has been impatiently waiting for my demise ever since. If not for you, she would probably not only be collecting right now, but would have sent that mugger a few thousand dollars out of gratitude."

"You just gotta love family, huh?"

"Yes, love for family tends to be unconditional like that, no matter what. Other people in our lives must earn the respect that family members don't, which is why I again want to thank you in all seriousness. No one has watched my back like that since my days in the war, and I totally hated those days."

"No problem."

"Good, good. Now you get some rest, let those wounds heal up and the stiches settle, and I'll go make you some soup to get your strength back up."

Just as Eli turned to exit the room, Alan held out his right hand and spoke to him again. "By the way, Eli... my name is Alan. Alan Perez. Nice to meet you."

The older retired medic gently took the younger man's hand and shook it, impressed that he didn't visibly wince at the pain even such a soft grip must have caused him just then.

"It's an honor to meet you, Alan."

***

An attractive young woman of about eighteen or nineteen was casually walking up the much-feared nighttime boulevard of Fulton Street on Buffalo's East Side. Her long, straight dark brown hair was held up in a ponytail courtesy of a hot pink scrunchie, and she wore a comfortable blue hoodie that was unzipped just enough to make it clear that underneath it she had on a tight sleeveless white crop top which exposed most of her belly as well as ample cleavage. The girl's tan skin tone and dark eyes suggested a Latina heritage. Her light blue jeans hugged her lower extremities tightly, and all of this revealed a very fit figure that many professional models would be envious of.

The young woman was walking up the darkened street towards the infamous Perry Projects subsidized housing area, where the New York Boys were known to have a major base of operations. It seemed quite likely she lived in that housing unit, and she appeared oblivious to the barely lit alleys and dilapidated apartment complexes surrounding her.

"That young lady must want to be assaulted or somethin', Father," Fred Gifford told Merle Harris from within the shadowed alley where they hid. "Either that, or she's totally on somethin' that craps up her senses. It's just too damn easy to get all sorts of drugs in this neighborhood."

"The latter is a likely possibility," Merle replied while quickly pulling the brim of his antique dark gray fedora hat down over his eyes to better obscure his features. "As I highly doubt a young woman like Dee Dee Garcia, who grew up on these streets, would normally be inclined to walk alone, and dressed like that, anywhere near this neighborhood."

"You know who this girl is?"

"I do. In years past she and her family attended my services on a regular basis. Her older sister recently suffered a serious tragedy due to being lax on her moral fortitude and buying drugs from these gang members. She became dependent on them for that and formed… immoral relationships with several of those men to pay for her habit. I was truly hoping Little Dee Dee wouldn't make the same mistake."

"Dear Jesus…"

"It's ironic that you should invoke the Lord's name in reference to her situation, Mr. Gifford, as it seems Dee Dee's sister Teesha abandoned Jesus for the path she took. As a result, her sins led her directly to an overdose."

"Let's not be fast to judge, Father. I respect your spiritual beliefs as much as the next good Christian, but it's not easy 'round here to completely avoid gettin' into really bad stuff."

"Perhaps not, Mr. Gifford, but temptation is a part of life, and while God forgives those who stray from the righteous path, it's our responsibility to remain resolute…"

"Yeah, yeah, Father, but enough right now, we need to keep our eyes on that girl and make sure she gets home okay."

Fred was unable to finish his admonishment of Father Merle before young Dee Dee, who was by that point two blocks away from where the men were sequestered, was suddenly grabbed and pulled into one of the alleyways between the tenement buildings. The scant illumination of a nearby street light revealed the silhouettes of two large, husky men as the culprits who assaulted her.

"Father, we need to be moving!" Fred shouted. "Some hoodlums just done snatched that girl!"

The two older men were not in poor shape, and in fact each were quite tough in their own way. But they were not fast sprinters, and their stamina wasn't what it used to be. Nevertheless, they pushed themselves to their limits to reach the alleyway near the corner of Fulton and Perry Street before too much harm could befall the young woman. They realized how futile their efforts would likely be when agonized screams and what sounded like the shredding of both clothing and flesh could be heard emanating from the entrance to the alley.

"Father, we gotta move faster!" Fred hollered as he ran up Fulton with his baseball bat raised and ready for an all-out battle.

"I'm moving as fast as these weathered legs will carry me!" Merle retorted as he brandished his firearm.

Another scream of mortal pain reverberated from the alley just before the two men reached it with their weapons prepared. As the nearby street light made the first few feet into the dark passageway visible, the two vigilantes became extremely disheartened as they saw puddles of blood at their feet.

"Dear Lord, why couldn't we have been faster?" Father Merle yelled at the One he worshiped and looked to for spiritual strength.

"Father, lookit that!" Fred cried while pointing to the source of the blood.

Instead of finding the mutilated body of hapless Little Dee Dee, which they both expected to see, they instead beheld the kneeling and profusely bleeding form of what was clearly one of the two large men who grabbed her. His gut was slit open vertically from one side to the other just above the belly button. Viscous blood was streaming from the wound, and a visible portion of his pink viscera was exposed as he squeezed the eviscerated flesh together in a frantic effort to keep his bowels from falling out. He screamed in horrific pain while blood spurted from his mouth as if a mini-pressure hose was sequestered in his gullet.

Several feet back in the shadowy lane, the two vigilantes observed a seemingly berserk Dee Dee Garcia brutally slashing her other attacker to pieces with repeated swipes of what appeared to be a long, sharpened steak knife. The man was wobbling in obvious shock as her final slash went across his eyes, a move which slit open both of his ophthalmic lenses. The huge brawny man fell to the filthy concrete with a loud wet thudding sound, his quivering body carved open in numerous places.

"You killed my sister, you *cabron*! You killed my sister!" was what Fred and Merle could hear the enraged young woman repeatedly shrieking.

Dee Dee culminated the savage attack by plunging the knife into the fallen man's protruding stomach. She then began exhaling heavily as the torrents of adrenalin racing through her system began leveling out.

"You can calm down now, young lady," came Father Merle's calm voice from a few feet behind her.

Dee Dee turned around quickly, her blood-soaked fists raised to defend herself. But something about the sight of the incognito priest made her stop.

"Do you recognize my voice, Little Dee Dee?" the man of the cloth asked her.

"Ya'll need to put a lid on things!" Fred warned.

"No, my friend, I do not," Father Merle replied with continued calm. "In fact, I must not."

The priest removed his low-brimmed hat and revealed himself entirely to the nearly hyperventilating young woman.

"Father Harris?" she said. "Is… is that… you?"

"It is, Dee Dee," the priest quietly replied.

"Oh damn, now you went and done it," Fred complained.

"Please be silent and let me deal with this my way, Mr. Gifford," Merle told his friend with a firm raising of his index finger.

"Well, we need to do somethin' 'bout this man whose stomach she gutted like some fish," Fred insisted. "He's still sittin' there in shock and in lots of pain, and he may have brought all of that onto himself, but I still don't wanna see no man suffer like that."

"You're correct, my friend," Merle concurred while raising his piece. "He needs to be put out of his misery."

"Wait now, Father…"

But Fred's plea was drowned out by the sound of Father Merle's firearm being discharged a few inches from the disemboweled man's head. After a handful of gray matter exploded from the would-be-rapist's skull, the heavy-set criminal slumped forward, his incessant quivering ceasing after a few seconds.

"Aw, Jesus Christ, Father!"

"Don't take the Lord's name in vain, Mr. Gifford," Merle said with a louder and more authoritative tone.

The man of the cloth shifted his attention back to Dee Dee, who was trembling at the realization of her own actions. She didn't even seem to notice Father Merle's bloody act of mercy killing a moment before. The young woman then turned to the priest with an incensed expression on her lovely caramel-toned countenance.

"Father Harris, I will not beg God for forgiveness," the adolescent girl said with firm conviction reverberating through her slight Spanish accent. "I respect you and I love Jesus enough, but men like this hurt my sister. She never hurt anybody, but men of this sort hurt innocent people all the time. They deserved this. And if He wouldn't strike them down, then I will! And if you try to stop me…"

"Perish the thought, young lady," the priest said with a smile and the most soothing voice he could muster. "When my associate and I first saw you walking these streets, I thought maybe you had strayed from God's holy path, but you didn't. Instead, you stepped directly on the right path, by becoming one of the Lord's modern crusaders against evil on Earth."

"Really?" Dee Dee asked while calming down as the priest's reassuring words told her exactly what she needed to hear. "You're not gonna call me a sinner or anything like that? Because if you do…"

"Oh, I'm not, dear child," Father Merle said with a continued wide beam on his face as he stepped over a puddle of blood to approach the young woman and rest two reassuring hands on each of her shoulders. "To the contrary, I'm bringing you into our special fold."

"Father, this ain't a good idea," Fred rebutted. "The things we get into…"

"Are things that *I'm* going to be getting into now too," Dee Dee said in a no-nonsense tone, as if daring the man to object. "If that Moonstalker dude can do it, then so can I. These may not have been members of the gang, but they were *pendejo* scumbags just the same. And I'm gonna get the leader of the New York Boys myself! I don't care how tough that *puta* is supposed to be, he's *dead*!"

***

Within a few minutes, Eli was able to serve his unexpected patient a large bowl of microwaved minestrone broth.

"I'm guessing you loved the soup, considering how fast you just devoured it," Eli said with a pleased smile.

"Food is fuel for healing," Alan replied. "Especially vegetable-heavy broth like this. I needed some of it to bolster the fast healing I'm going to initiate with my meditative techniques."

"Hmmm, looks like you could teach a few things down at the ER too. You've already taught me plenty despite your age, and I've only known you a few short hours. Speaking of that, I must say that you look very young. Forgive me for putting it this way, but do your parents know you do this kind of thing?"

Alan closed his eyes tightly as another realization hit him with the force of a speeding SUV. "Awwww, man! My parents! I can't *believe* I forgot! How long was I out?"

"Actually, you've been out all night; it's now just past 10 AM. You were hurt bad enough that I administered a little sedative, so you would rest a bit easier. Sorry if it was a school night, but you were in no condition to go anyway."

"I'm not worried about that. I miss school often enough, and the truant officer is more than happy to cover for me. It's my parents! They must be totally freaking out that I didn't come home last night. The police must be out looking for me!"

"That's not good, Alan. Now that I know for certain you're a minor, I can be in deeper shit than you, with the current hysteria being what it is."

"Maybe not. Listen, do you happen to know if my cell phone I had hidden in a pocket on my uniform is intact?"

"I believe so."

"Then bring it to me now."

"Look, Alan, maybe we'd better…"

"Maybe what you had *better* do is listen to me, Eli. Despite the age difference, you're not in charge of me. Neither are my parents, though they like to think they are and I need to let them believe it's true some of the time. Bring me my cell now. Please."

Eli was no meek individual, but he was not about to argue with this particular young guest. There was something heavily authoritative about him, a potential to lead others that was both impressive and unsettling. Within seconds, the host of the home retrieved the top of Alan's uniform, and the cell phone proved fully operational thanks to the padding stitched into the hidden pockets.

Alan quickly typed in the pass code to access his phone's mini-desktop and sent a quick text to his girlfriend Shanice: "Hay babez r u thare??? [heart emoji]"

Within a few seconds, the young woman responded: "Alan!! Baby!!! XOXO Why arent u in school? Your rents called me sick w/ worry! Where did u stay last night???"

Alan's next response: "cant explane over txt need rilly HUGE faver & need it NOW k??"

Shanice's final message: "OK OK. What do u need me to do?"

Shanice strongly suspected that she would end up regretting this latest favor for her boyfriend. But as she was already beginning to fall deeply in love with this unpredictable young man, she also knew she would end up fulfilling his latest crazy request anyway.

And regret it she most certainly would.

Chapter 12: Trial by Tribulations

Shanice Morris felt like nothing less than a disingenuous jerk as she hid in the girl's restroom stall while punching in the numbers of Alan Perez's home phone on her cell. She wanted Alan's parents to like her, as she really and truly cared about their son. However, she knew once they caught on to the fact that she was routinely lying to cover for their son's more mysterious activities, the opinion they would ultimately form of her would be less than stellar, to say the least.

This is the price you pay if you want a guy like Alan, she kept reminding herself. *And a hottie like him is certainly worth it, right?*

"Shanice?" came Mrs. Lenore Perez's voice through her cell as she read the caller I.D. "Have you heard anything from…?"

"Yes, Mrs. Perez!" Shanice quickly interjected. "Alan is okay, so please don't panic, but he was hit by a car while crossing the street with me last night."

"What? Why in Heaven's name didn't you tell us when I called you before?"

"He insisted that I didn't, because he didn't want you to worry. So, he told me to bring him to my Uncle Eli's house. My unc is a retired physician's assistant with training in…"

"Shanice! You lied to us?"

"I didn't want to, Mrs. Perez, you know how much I like you and want you and your husband to like me. But I really care about Alan, and you also know how he can pressure you into doing what he wants…"

"Enough about that! Give me your Uncle Eli's number *now!*"

"Well, I don't have it, but…"

"He's your uncle and you *don't* have his number stored in your cell's address book? *Seriously?*"

"I'm not super-close to him, but Alan met him at a family function. And because of his skills at patching up injuries…"

"You're 'not super-close to him' yet you entrusted our son to his care just because he asked you to? When he was injured and possibly not in his right mind?"

"He wasn't unconscious or incoherent or anything like that. As I said, you know he can be really persuasive and guilt-trippy, and…"

"Yes, I do know that. Now I'm going to show you and my son how persuasive *I* can be. Give me your uncle's address right this instant or you will never again be welcome in our house. Is that clear, young lady?"

Shanice sighed and forced back tears before whispering, "255 Mulberry."

"We're all going to sit down and have a long talk soon, Shanice. And don't let me find out you lied about anything else, now or in the future, or we'll never be talking again."

Lenore then ended the call before Shanice could say anything else.

"Damn you, Alan," the tear-struck young woman said quietly to herself. She then quickly dialed his cell.

"Yeah?" he answered within two rings.

"Alan, I told your mom what you wanted me to, but she is really *really* pissed, and she told me to give her Eli's address."

"And you gave it to her?"

"Well, I didn't have any other choice. She said I wouldn't be welcome in your house anymore if I lied for you again. It's bad enough you put me in this position in the first place…"

"Don't worry about that right now! Did you tell her I was hit by a car and that Eli is your uncle and about his medical training like I said?"

"Yes, I did, but she's probably on her way over there now, so…"

"Alright, let me go deal with this, okay? I'll talk to you later."

"Okay, I love you…" She never finished the words before Alan ended the call, as he was determined to immediately get prepared for his mother's imminent arrival and not waste a single second exchanging further niceties with Shanice.

"Damn you twice, Alan," Shanice spoke aloud to herself again, her eyes once more swelling with tears. "I love you, Alan, but sometimes I totally hate you."

After the pretty young woman had composed herself and re-applied a touch of make-up in the bathroom mirror, she exited to find the intimidating personage of Tony Kirkland leaning on the wall right next to the door, his gang colors fully visible on his jacket and bandana.

"Hey, babe, funny you should cross my path, huh?" he said with a cold smirk.

"You were waiting for me out here?" Shanice replied. "How did you know I walked in there?"

"It's my job to know everything in our turf, babe. You look like you've been crying. Is that little boy you're dating giving you some hard times?"

"That's none of your business, Tony. Now, I gotta get to class, okay?"

As she attempted to walk past him, the young gang member grabbed her arm and held it in a tight grip.

"Did I say we were done talking?"

"No, but *I* said we were done talking. Now please let go of my arm."

"Do you know how far up in the organization I am now?"

"You mean that gang? I don't care to know."

"Well, you and everybody else needs to know. And since you're special to me, I'll let you be the first to know something really cool: after tonight, I'm going to be the right hand of the man in charge."

Shanice had no idea if this was true or not, but the truth of it mattered less than nothing to her. The only fact that was of any concern to her was how much Tony and that gang terrified her. And such would be the case even if he was destined to forever remain on the lowest tier of whatever their ranking system happened to be.

"Good for you, Tony. Now let me go, I'm off to class…"

Her attempt to break her arm away from the tall and well-built basketball player proved futile, as he simply tightened his grip and pulled her up against the wall.

"I'm not done talking to you, Shanice. I wanted to make you an offer to become part of what we're building here. We're gonna be running the entire East Side in just a few months. We already have the Fruit Belt and Fulton, and we'll have all of McKinley by the end of this month. And you could have a big chunk of all of that if you were my girl instead of going out with that loser."

"He's *not* a loser just because he isn't a member of some violent street gang. And don't you mean, if I was the sweetheart of *anyone* in that gang who happened to want me for a few minutes at a time? I know how things work for the girls who 'join' those gangs."

Tony chuckled icily. "No, no, babe, that's not how it would work if I was second-in-command of the war council. I would have you all to myself."

"That sounds almost as bad as the other way. The answer is *no*. That's final, and I'm telling you to *let me go now*."

Tony's countenance was suddenly taken over by a look of pure maliciousness that fully darkened his usually attractive features and chilled Shanice worse than any of the less pleasant expressions Alan would display even when he was in one of his infamous moods. Her boyfriend may have scared her from time to time, but never like this. She also found herself wishing Alan was at school right now rather than recovering from injuries at Eli's home.

Before Tony could react any further to Shanice's defiance, one of the school security guards happened to pass the entrance to the corridor and spotted the two from several feet away.

"Hey, shouldn't you both be in class now?" he asked from across the hall.

Tony took what seemed like an eternity to force himself out of the state of mind he was in and restore a semblance of normalcy to his facial expression (it was actually just a few seconds, but to Shanice's perception, it may as well have been years). He then turned to face the guard.

"Not a problem, man," Tony said in a convincingly affable tone. "I was just telling Shanice something. I'm off now, I wouldn't want to miss wood shop."

Just before walking away, Tony turned to Shanice with the same malevolent mien as before and whispered a single word just loud enough for her to hear: "Later."

The young woman took several deep breathes, as if to forestall a panic attack, and then quickly trod off in the opposite direction, where she knew the security guard would be. This wasn't a good morning for Shanice Morris on many levels.

***

Alan Perez felt well enough to sit up and explain to Eli the scene which was soon about to ensue at his home.

"Your mom, huh?" the older man said. "I'll do my best to assuage her concerns, but I want you to know up front how much I hate lying to people, Alan."

"You don't have to like it, Eli. You just have to understand that sometimes it has to be done."

"Alright, while we're looking forward to your irate mom showing up here to give us both a major telling off, there is something else I figured you might want to see. Something went down on Masten Avenue this morning, and it's already uploaded to the MetahumanCarnage4Ever channel on YouTube. And yes, I know all about what YouTube and social media are, so please don't start on me about all that again, okay?"

Alan merely smirked slightly as Eli brought his computer notebook over to him and played the video footage of the disaster that had occurred just several hours ago in the immediate area of Buffalo Historical School, a combined middle and high school.

The video began with Centurion, a teen costumed metahuman who had recently begun an ill-famed career on Buffalo's West Side, battling a similarly powered being whom the channel owner identified as Light-Lord. Alan watched with a combination of fascination and indignation as he viewed these entities trading blows and devastating beams of projected energy that wreaked severe havoc on both each other and the infrastructure of the school; not to mention the homes, trees, and vehicles in the surrounding neighborhood.

"Jesus, look at the glowing rays of energy those guys are tearing everything apart with!" Eli lamented. "You may run around in a costume too, but you're not one of those metahumans who turn entire houses to rubble when they get to doing their thing. I'm telling you, Alan, I'm actually glad you were in my care when that was going down. Otherwise, you probably would have ended up in the thick of it, considering it's not that far from your usual stomping grounds."

"You're probably right about my getting involved in it, Eli, but you're probably wrong that I wouldn't have been able to handle myself. I may not have metahuman powers, but the costumed pricks who have these powers rely far too much on them. They know nothing of skill, stealth, or strategy. They think if you have the power to blast off the front portion of a house with an energy beam or lift an SUV over your head, that you don't need any type of training, thinking ability, or finesse. Big mistake."

"Okay, I see your point there, but I can't find myself believing that you would have made it out of that mess intact. Fighting gangbangers, armed robbers, and muggers may be dangerous enough, but those threats are nothing compared to what we're watching here, young man. Once you get better, I strongly suggest you stick to opposing common criminals rather than metahuman threats. You're just not suited for that."

"You'd be surprised what I'm suited for, Eli. And I'm telling you based on my observations of this video and recent news reports that this Centurion is an imbecile who would be nothing without those powers. Just look at him go at that Light-Lord maniac; he went down at least twice already, and the slack was picked up by those people armed with the taser pistols, whoever the hell they are. But they obviously aren't metahuman, just well-trained and equipped, which goes to prove my point."

"Yeah, and look how well they're doing against that glowing guy whose tossing out laser beams from his hands like pellets from a BB gun! As you can see from the end of the footage, even though that Centurion cat went down more than once, he still ended up winning in the end."

"Maybe, but only after the whole neighborhood was totally thrashed, including the school's parking lot. And those soldiers or whoever they were – and I can tell you they aren't part of the BPD – were a big help even if they didn't give the finishing blows. If they could jump into the thick of something like that and make an important contribution towards taking a metahuman down, then so can I."

"Quite possibly, Alan, but I think it's important to pick your fights, and to know the difference between confidence and bravado."

"I agree. So, make sure you know the difference, Eli."

The salt-and-pepper-haired gentleman sighed in frustration but couldn't help smiling afterwards. Alan shared the grin with him. That was just before a loud knocking was heard at the door.

"Do we need to even guess who that is?" Eli said.

"It's probably not the Avon lady," Alan replied. "Let her in and let's get this drama dealt with. Afterwards, we have some important things to put into effect."

***

Later that evening, the much-dreaded leader of the New York Boys, a young man known only by his street name Assailant, stood facing an obviously nervous Shank, who had been extricated from the hospital for this very purpose.

The Lord of Queen City East's most powerful street gang stood a full five inches taller than his already lofty main subordinate. A sleeveless leather jacket revealed a truly impressive set of muscles bulging through tan skin. The Assailant's right arm had a burning tower expertly tattooed on it, an obvious symbol that no one in the gang, including Shank himself, had the nerve to ask about.

Like the growing number of costumed crime fighters and criminals who had begun to appear across the globe in the wake of the first few Warp Events, Assailant was inspired to wear a red and black full-head mask that not only concealed his true visage, but also gave him even more of a psychological edge by making him resemble nothing less than some vile executioner or sadistic dominator.

The master of most he surveyed stood in front of his makeshift throne, regally towering over Shank with his massive arms folded. His deep, dark eyes seemed to penetrate all the way through Shank's very essence of being, as if the smaller man was beholding some sort of metaphysical judge and jury melded together and personified as a single being. The subordinate gangbanger nevertheless did his best to keep his composure for as long as he could.

"You got your little suntanned ass handed to you," Assailant rumbled out in a deep, scratchy voice punctuated with a strong Latino accent. "And not by Moonstalker, but by one of the club's regular bouncers."

"He was a good fighter, boss," Shank replied defensively. "And we were already caught by surprise when that vigilante…"

"No excuses!" Shank couldn't help jumping at the ferocity of Assailant's exclamation, nor could the rest of the gang members who stood behind them to watch   the   proceedings. "I expect my people to be able to handle anything this city may throw at them."

"Boss, everyone makes mistakes. And it's not like it's something I do often…"

"It's something you need to do *never*! Now we have one business owner in our expanded turf who isn't paying us their operating fee. How many others will start thinking they don't have to pay either? How many other security guards and bouncers will start standing up to you as long as that Moonstalker *cabron* is running around the territory?"

"We'll deal with him, boss. I swear that *pendejo* is as good as having a stake up his ass."

"We will deal with him, yes. But you won't be with us when we do."

"What do you mean, boss?"

Assailant turned around, looked into the crowd of observers standing directly behind his war council advisors, and extended an index finger towards one particular individual. And that individual was Tony Kirkland.

"Please approach the throne, *amigo*."

The young man hastened to rush to the designated area and stood beside Assailant, who also towered over the six-foot-tall basketball player moonlighting as a gang member.

"You see, Shank, Tony has been sharing some interesting opinions with me lately," Assailant continued. "The main one being a few reasons he thinks he would be a better right hand to me than you could ever be."

Tony smiled at Shank, whose expression took on one of intense rage. "Boss, you can't be serious about this! That little bitch with a dick is a newbie. He's just taking advantage of this single screw-up of mine to make himself look like some kinda hard ass! But his ass is softer than a scoop of jello."

Tony smiled. "How do you know that, Shank? Have you felt on it lately?"

Shank raised his fist and took a step forward. "I'm gonna feel your face with *this*, asswipe!"

Assailant stood in between his two subordinates, and neither dared advance so much as a fraction of an inch further.

"You are retarded, Shank!" Tony declared. "You're an import from New York City, you don't know shit about how Buffalo works! But I do, and it should be me running the collection operations here."

"Yeah, I'm from The City!" Shank retorted. "And I grew up in the gang life, and our leaders were the *real* shit! Not like these Mickey Mouse clubs you call gangs over here!"

Assailant gritted his teeth. "Maybe I should remind you, Shank, that I'm from Buffalo, not New York. We call ourselves the 'New York Boys' to make our level of bad-assery clear."

Shank began noticeably trembling at the realization that he had inadvertently insulted the most dangerous leader he had ever served (which was saying something). "I didn't mean you aren't the real deal, boss! That's why I'm working for you, and no one in New York anymore. I was impressed enough by you that I came to live and work here."

"Lying little bitch," Tony said. "I heard you left because you owed money to the Brooklyn Knights."

"You're the one who's lying!" Shank exclaimed. "You don't care anything about this gang! You only care about how much juice you can get out of wearing these colors, so you can hook any girl from that filthy ass high school you can't even graduate from! You wouldn't even be there at all if you weren't good at throwing a rubber ball through a hoop!"

Tony moved to lunge at his rival, only to be easily stopped by one of his leader's single bulky arms.

"You boys don't fight without my permission!" the gang leader shouted. "But don't worry, you're about to receive it. Shank, after your epic *jodido*, you need to prove you have what it takes to be my right hand. That earns Tony the chance to take your position from you. And I'm granting you the opportunity to prove your worthiness for a second chance by defending your position."

"You're talkin' about a trial by combat, boss?" Shank inquired.

Assailant's grin was clear despite his mask. "Absolutely."

"Let's do it now," the current right hand of the New York Boys insisted.

Tony smiled eagerly in response. "For once I agree with this bitch. And by the way, boss, will this be to the death?"

Assailant once again beamed, only this time accompanied by a cackle of malevolent glee. "It would be rather pointless if it wasn't."

***

Shank and Tony Kirkland now faced each other in the center of a demarcated ring, both of them holding a razor-sharp stiletto. The circle was on a concrete floor in the basement section of the main building encompassing the Perry Projects subsidized housing tenements. There was just enough light to see the proceedings, as only one bulb was placed in the chandelier fixture attached to the ceiling. About forty members of the New York Boys stood just outside of the ring, forming the perimeter of the circle which the two combatants were bound to stay within for the duration of the battle.

The four individuals who had accompanied Shank on the ill-fated debt collection to the East Side Inferno stood several feet away from the circle and off to the side, each well aware that the end result of the coming trial by combat would determine their fate as well. This group included Ganke, whose right ear was still heavily bandaged and soaked with crimson splotches due to the wounds of the mutilated slab of cartilage continuing to split open.

Directly in front of the circle, standing a few inches within its perimeter, was the lethal Assailant, acting as the master of ceremonies of this brutal contest. He stood towering over everyone else in the room, his physical presence matching his exalted status. His grayish eyes glared through his fearsome Luchador-like mask and locked on the two young men who were about to endeavor to take the other's life, all for his pleasure. The leader of the New York Boys wanted to gush with pride over being the overseer of such a contest, but he knew better than to show emotion in this situation.

"Here's the deal," the Assailant said through an iron voice punctuated with his distinct Spanish accent. "Each of you will try to kill the other. Simple enough deal, eh? Or do I actually need to explain it to you?"

Several of the surrounding members of the circle began laughing but ceased immediately after Assailant slapped his palms together to signal "silence."

"I know exactly what to do, boss," Shank said with a face void of expression.

"Soon as you give the word, boss," Tony said with an obvious smile. "I don't want to miss *South Park* tonight, so I'm all for getting this over and done with."

"I killed Shankey!" one of the guys in the circle screeched in a forcefully shrill voice.

That flippant remark was followed by riotous laughs throughout the men comprising the circle. This time Assailant stopped the frivolity by pulling a .45 out of a holster attached to the left leg of his khaki pants and blasting a hole in the wall directly behind his men.

"One more interruption, and I'll make a point to aim for someone's balls at random, ¿entendido?"

The sudden absolute silence made the huge basement seem like a mortuary, which strongly suggested that everyone in the room did indeed understand. The self-declared master of the Queen City's East Side then raised his two enormous hands and slapped them together again.

"Do it, boys."

With the green light given, Shank wasted no time taking the offensive. He leapt forward like a predatory demon straight out the gates of Hell and slashed his blade at Tony's eyes. The athlete-turned-gangbanger proved his great flexibility and reflexes by bending backwards fast enough to dodge the full fury of the stiletto's deadly business end. All it managed to do was cut deep into the bridge of his nose, but the pain and blood that seeped from the small but potent wound was quite severe.

Tony wasted not a split second in retaliating, which he did by delivering a quick thrust towards his opponent's mid-section. Shank leapt backwards just in time to evade what would have been both an extremely damaging and embarrassing blow to his manhood. Unfortunately for Tony, Shank had long learned to be wise to such moves.

Before the basketball player in gang colors could fully recover his momentum from that failed maneuver, his adversary stepped forward and kicked him in his nose, a brutal blow that broke the cartilage right beneath where it was cut at the beginning of the battle. Tony jumped back thanks to a surge of adrenalin, though blood spewed out of his nostrils like twin crimson gushers.

Shank, determined to promptly end the battle in his favor, was quick to press this advantage. Allowing himself to entirely surrender to his primal instincts, the powerfully built young man raised his blade and rushed his enemy like a determined bull charging a matador.

However, Tony was much more resilient than Shank gave him credit for. The lanky athlete had been through much in his young life, and he was not one to go down or lose without offering serious resistance. Despite the salty tears welling in his eyes due to the pain of his cracked septum, Tony moved in, dodged Shank's rushing attack, and delivered a punishing haymaker to his opponent's lower jaw. The force and speed of the robust basketball player's blow caught Shank unawares, and the lower row of his front teeth were pushed almost completely through his bottom lip. The taste of blood filled the craw of the Assailant's right-hand man like a mouthful of liquid iron.

As Shank recoiled from the blow, nearly dropping his blade as blood flowed from his perforated flesh, Tony bit back his own continued pain and ran towards his foe. The Riverfield High student cut the shorter but burlier gangbanger across his chest, slicing clear through cloth and over an inch into his flesh.

Shank was intent to remain standing, however, and he slashed his blade wildly, slicing open the flesh of Tony's right forearm. The athletic urban warrior moved back just enough to avoid having a major artery severed before immediately countering with a thrust of his own blade. However, Tony managed to get the razor tip of his stiletto past Shank's guard, puncturing clear through his trachea.

Shank began gagging on his own blood while experiencing the debilitating sensation of his throat caving in. Tony swiftly prodded his blade forward again, this time penetrating deeply into his opponent's right eye. The delicate gelatinous organ fairly exploded in milky and cerise-colored fluid as Shank fell to the hard cement floor after emitting a single agonized scream. His body convulsed for a few seconds as more blood spurted from the various new orifices Tony managed to carve onto his body.

The newly dethroned second-in-command of Buffalo's most fearsome gang then ceased twitching altogether, the only further movement on his body being a final stream of blood that dribbled out of his gaping mouth.

The victor of this ruthless contest stumbled due to his wounds, but he forced himself to remain on his feet. Upon seeing the horribly damaged corpse of the rival he vowed to take down, an overwhelming sensation of euphoria seemed to flow through every cell in his body. Tony Kirkland raised the still-dripping weapon above his head and roared the loudest victory scream he could muster.

The gang members in the surrounding circle began cheering and hooting loudly.

"He kiillleeddd Shaankeeyy!" the same individual who said it before repeated in his distinct exaggerated voice.

"You da man, Tony!" another of them shouted.

"Yes, it would seem Tony is now 'the man,'" Assailant concurred, his steady stance and folded arms having changed in no discernible way. "My *right-hand man*, to be exact."

"I told you, boss!" Tony screeched, still unsteady on his feet due to his injuries. "I told you I could take him!"

"Yes, you did," Assailant replied rather icily. "But don't' get cocky, because if you screw up like our now departed Shank did, I'm sure one of my other more ambitious war council members will want the same shot at you."

"Let them try!" was all Tony had left to say before two men from the circle stepped in and helped their new superior officer into the next room for his wounds to be tended to and crudely sewn shut.

"Okay, I declare everything to be settled," Assailant said. "You can all leave and enjoy some *caliente*."

As the crowd began dispersing, the masked gang leader pointed his muscular index finger at Ganke and his four compatriots.

"Not you guys," he said in his commanding dark voice. "You too were at the East Side Inferno, and like our departed *comarada*, you failed to collect a required operating fee from the owner. Now it's time to discuss how you can avoid becoming a job for the janitor to clean up, like Shank!"

***

Father Merle Harris sat in the quiet evening chapel before the stature of Jesus nailed to the cross, an enduring symbol of one person's ultimate sacrifice for the greater good. The melancholy pastor couldn't help wondering if he was living up to what Christ's sacrifice meant to him, and whether or not he was living up to the example set by the Lord's son… or if he was betraying it. He leaned on his knees in a position of reverence before the statue and all it represented to him and so many others for two thousand years, his rosaries in one hand and his firearm in the other, as if both were different tools towards a united purpose.

"My Lord Jesus Christ, am I doing the right thing? Am I doing your work, or have I fallen under the influence of Satan? Please give me guidance, for I cannot go to any of my fellow clergy over this matter. I have only you, and I cannot do with silence as a response. I need to know. Please do not let me stray from the path or falter before temptation. More importantly, please do not let me cause the others who now follow my lead to stray from that same path because of me. My own soul is one thing, but I cannot abide by turning the souls of others under my guidance into the hands of Satan."

The priest closed his eyes tightly with his hands over his face as he meditated for several minutes, begging Jesus for a sign, or something – anything – other than just silence. Father Harris knew he had to work through this himself, but he needed counsel. And he needed it from the highest voice in the spiritual hierarchy which he dedicated his life and soul to.

A moment later, the tune of "Amazing Grace" could be heard stemming from his cell phone as it vibrated in his robe pocket. Knowing it must be a matter of great importance if anyone called him at this time of the night, he made a point to answer it. The call was from Fred Gifford.

"Father, have you heard?" Fred's grating voice queried through the mini-speakers of the device.

"No, I haven't, Fred," Merle replied, "I haven't been watching the news for some hours now. I have been in the chapel doing some work."

"Well... those bastards... sorry, those *ruffians* in the New York Boys have done struck again. They raided Mr. Hefler's drug store, since I guess he decided to hold out payin' them any 'protection' cash. The man and his wife were... look, even I'm havin' trouble sayin' what was done to them. It was horrible. I thought you might want to know."

Father Merle Harris sat silently for just a few seconds. "Yes, Fred, I... needed to hear this. After I complete Dee Dee's firearm training tomorrow, and we say our prayers, I want you to meet us back here at 7 PM, no matter the weather conditions. Is that understood?"

"Yeah, man, of course it is. I'll see you there."

Father Harris then ended the call and looked back up at the statue of the mortally wounded son of God looming above him, its disheartened countenance biting into the core of his being like never before.

"Thank you, my Lord, for giving me the sign I asked for. Thy will shall be done."

***

As Fred ended the call on his end, he turned to the young Dee Dee, who sat on a chair behind the cashier counter of his corner store.

"Do you think we're doing the right thing, Dee?" he asked her.

"Damn straight we are!" the girl decreed as she swiped several strings of hair from her left eye. "After what those punks did to my sister and would have done to me if I wasn't able to defend myself. And what they've done to so many other people who have families.

"I mean, look what they just did to poor Mr. Hefler! Right in front of his wife! And what they did to her afterwards! Are we supposed to just ignore this and not take our streets back? Are we supposed to rely on the police, who're too often hamstrung by all these rules and regulations, not to mention stretched thinner than a strand of angel hair and half the time being paid off by the same people they're supposed to be protecting us from?"

Fred drooped forward noticeably as he sat on the counter itself several feet away. "Yeah, I hear you, girl. This same thing got me really pissed off, 'specially after what they did to me and my store, which is all I've ever had to live on."

The pretty young woman stood up and raised her arms in the air. "Well, then what's the gripe, man?"

The older gentleman looked down again, his bald head reflecting off the dim lighting. "It's just… what we've been doing. We've done some nasty things, and Father Harris has been… killing. Without remorse, and then sayin' God's been tellin' him to do it."

"I don't care who's telling him to do it, even if he's just confusing his own conscience for the word of God. He's a religious guy, and he can interpret those 'inner voices' any way he wants. The point is, he's training me how to use a gun, and other stuff too. We have to defend ourselves, our property, our fam, and we can't rely on the cops for that. And we shouldn't be forced to rely on the cops for protection in the first place! Moonstalker showed us the way, and his way is the only one getting results."

Fred thought about the young woman's words for several moments and was greeted with flashback sequences of the local thugs coming into his precious store and shoplifting, loitering, congregating there as if to send the message to its proprietor that *they* owned the store, not him. And this was before things escalated and the New York Boys began sending "debt collectors" to demand portions of his hard-earned cash in exchange for the continued integrity of his skeletal structure.

He saw how stretched thin the police were and even the honest ones couldn't offer him the type of protection he required. Moreover, acquiring a firearm for self-defense is all but impossible to come by legally in a "blue" state like New

York, and a sophisticated alarm system was beyond his price range. Hence, Fred Gifford understood Dee Dee's points quite well. He was just a decent, hard-working man for his entire life, and he couldn't be certain if their way of going about things was the correct way. All he knew was that it *felt* right, but he also knew from much hard experience that feelings weren't always the best thing to go by.

Excuse me for havin' trouble believin' that wacky priest when he goes and says God done told him so… but what about when my own gut is tellin' me the same thing? Is what I wanna believe getting in the way of what I should be believin'?

"Well, my cell phone watch tells me we gotta meet the priest at the church in about an hour. He'll probably make us say twelve Hail Mary's if we're late."

Dee Dee snickered and jumped up from the chair. "Let's go! I got me some firearms training before we head out to deal with those guys who did that messed up shit to Mr. Hefler!"

END PART 1

Part 2: Who Rules the Streets?

Chapter 13: Strength of Numbers

Lenore Perez's larynx was clearly straining as she admonished her son in the home of Eli Matthews. "My dear god, Alan, I can't believe you didn't call me and your dad right away! Or that you didn't go to the hospital after something like this happened!"

"Mom, calm down, I'm going to be all right," Alan said while endeavoring to hide how much pain his combo of fractured bones and skin lacerations were causing him. "I just didn't want to burden you and Dad with this in the middle of the night when I could handle it myself."

"Burden us? Handle it yourself? For Christ's sake, you said you were hit by a car! And honestly, Alan, I think you're lying to me!"

"What are you talking about, Mom?"

"You lied to me before! You had that girlfriend of yours lie for you!"

"Please get to the point, Mom."

Alan focused his mental control on holding back the temptation to grit his teeth and sweat profusely from the pain he was in, lest he worry his mother all the more. He was well aware, however, that this dispute needed to end quickly, as he wasn't sure he could long endure the stress of a protracted argument.

Lenore continued her interrogation. "Did you really get hit by a car? Or did you get into another scuffle with that street gang?"

"Seriously, Mom?"

"Yes, *seriously*, Alan! You think I don't know what someone looks like after they've been beaten up? Your dad was recently beaten by those little punks! For God's sake, I can see their knuckle marks on your face."

"Mom, you need to get home, okay? You're letting your paranoia run wild."

"It's not paranoia, and you know it! And I'm not leaving here without you!"

Alan glared at his parent with a gaze whose sheer emotional intensity looked as if it could burn a hole in a steel wall. "Mom, I'll be fine, and I'll be home in a few hours. Go. Please."

The now thoroughly nerve-wracked woman turned to Eli Matthews as he stood to the side of the comfortable parlor couch where Alan was lying.

"Mr. Matthews, I'm going to ask you something, and I want you to tell me the truth. Because if you don't, and I find out, then God help you. I swear to God almighty I'll have you arrested."

"Mrs. Perez, I understand you're upset, but…" was all Eli managed to utter before being interrupted with Lenore's big question.

"Did my son really get hit by a car? Or did he get into an altercation with that street gang again? Don't you dare lie to me, because I've had more than enough of that lately, and I *know* you know the truth!"

Eli's pale brown eyes looked over the faces of both mother and son and saw the two glaring at him with the unspoken demand that he say what each expected of him. He was loath to defy either, as doing so would each carry its own set of potentially severe consequences. What was a man to do while caught between the proverbial rock and a hard place like this?

"Mrs. Perez, I swear to you, on the Holy Bible, that I didn't see your son get into any sort of scuffle with them gang members," Eli said with a slight tremor in his voice. "This is what happened, honestly and truly: I was attacked by a mugger, and your son walked out of an ally and threw something at the scoundrel and scared him away. He did that despite the bad shape he was in. I owed him a lot, so seeing as I have this medical training, I took him home and helped fix him up."

Lenore maintained a strong stare at the older man. "His girlfriend Shanice told me you're her uncle. And that she called you to come and pick Alan up."

"I told her to say that, Mom," Alan quickly interjected. "He isn't really Shanice's uncle, but he is a good Samaritan who helped me because I scarred off a mugger who was about to hurt him. So, lay off him; you have no right to be pissed at Eli. You should thank him instead of hassling him like this."

"Why didn't he call your dad and I immediately?"

"Before I passed out, I insisted he didn't bring me to a hospital, because I don't like them, and I told him I wouldn't cooperate with him if he tried. So instead, he helped me to his house, which was just down the street. I ended up passing out before I could give him my number."

"Damn it, he could have looked through your wallet!"

"He couldn't, Mom, it was taken from me."

"So, you did get beaten up?"

Alan looked his mother directly in the eyes and sighed. "Yes, Mom. I got mugged, okay? It was a bunch of them, and they took me off-guard."

"Alan, I don't know if I can believe you. I do believe Mr. Matthews is telling the truth, though; he sounds very sincere. Mr. Matthews, I'm so sorry I blew up at you like that. I'm just very upset, and this son of mine…"

"I understand, Mrs. Perez," Eli replied with a smile. "I'm a parent too, and I've been there with my own flock. And please, call me Eli."

"Okay, Eli. And please do call me Lenore." She clasped her eyelids shut in exasperation for a second, as if struggling to think of what to say or do next. The older bespectacled woman then turned to her son. "Alan, come home later today when you're feeling up to it. Your dad and I are going to have more words with you, and with that girlfriend of yours, when you do get home. Call me when you need to get picked up."

"No worries about transportation, Lenore," Eli said. "I'll drive him home when he's up to leaving. I'll make sure his bandages are changed and dressed properly before he does, and then you and your husband can take it from there. I agree he should have a doctor look him over. I can assure you he has no internal bleeding or anything like that."

"Alright, thank you again for helping my son like you did," Lenore replied with a courteous tone. "And I'm sorry you had to get in the middle of all this."

Eli smiled again. "If not for your son, I may not be alive now to get in the middle of *anything*. It was an honor to help him after what he did for me. Think nothing else of it."

Lenore Perez then took off for home, and Alan struggled to get himself to a sitting position on the couch.

"That was slick how you covered for me," Eli said.

"And it was equally slick how you told the truth without giving me away," Alan replied. "I owe you another one, Eli."

"Let's just get those wounds of yours dressed."

"Fine. Then I need to get back in a meditation mode to expedite the healing process. I also need to get some of Matoi's herbal meds from Dell and Janice. You can take me home after I get a few hours of that in."

***

Over the following weeks, Alan Perez spent a frequent number of hours in meditative trance -- including while he slept -- in addition to imbibing herbal-based beverages introduced to him at Master Kai's Dojo by Matoi, which supplements his psychic healing routines via invigorating each of his organ systems. During that time, his fractured bones and epidermal tears healed with a speed that would impress any doctor or professional athlete.

Alan also made a point to continue training at the dojo, with his injuries taken into full consideration by Master Kai's top instructors, Dell Boyd and Janice Rosenberg. His muscles were rubbed with special salves created from a variety of exotic but almost forgotten herbal tinctures that further enhanced the process of repairing torn muscle and lacerated skin.

Just before those weeks of convalescence had ended, Alan performed a roundhouse kick that shattered a fifty-pound cinderblock, and a spearhand thrust which broke a nearly two-inch-thick oak plank in two. Sensei Rosenburg commended him.

"I think I'm up for returning to 'work' now," Alan said with confidence.

"Just about," Dell answered the thinly disguised interrogative. "Just be sure to continue taking the herbal supplements over the next couple of weeks as well as performing the meditative exercises. And yes, see your regular doctor and chiropractor as well. Master Kai is friends and colleagues with both of them, so they'll give you full cooperation while following the Master's instructions."

"I'll do all of that. But speaking of the Master, why has he been absent for the past few months?"

"You know that Janice and I can't provide you, or any other student, with the answer to that right now, Alan."

"I'm his top student, and before you know it, I'll be running this place along with you and Janice."

"No doubt, Alan. But until then… we have to follow protocol to the letter. You know how the Master is about that."

"Have you at least received word from him?"

"We did. And to be his charming and traditional self, Master Kai wrote it by hand while using   a feather quill pen, on a crumpled sheet of parchment. And his signature was in Japanese characters, of course."

"That's the Master for you!"

"Sure is. He was a bit ambiguous about how things are going over there, but he did say that the entire world is in some type of cosmic alignment with forces we wouldn't quite understand. Because of that, he needs to be where he is now and nowhere else, and you need to continue doing what you've been doing above and beyond all else."

Alan took on a sarcastic smirk. "Sensei, am I the type of warrior to let something like homework get in the way of what I'm doing for the world?"

"You certainly aren't! That's why we back up your decision totally. Master Kai said he's foreseen this since the day he first took you on as a student."

"And I appreciate that, not to mention everything the Master and his staff at this dojo have done for me over the years. I swear I'll do all of you proud. But I'm wondering if where the Master is right now, and what he's doing, has anything to do with that weird ass vision I had when I was out from the injuries I sustained at the East Side Inferno."

"A vision?"

"I didn't tell you already?"

Dell shook his head.

"Hmm, I thought I did. Anyway, what I remember of it was seeing the Master's face floating above me in a cloud of billowy mist or something. I then clearly heard his voice telling me 'the time of change is now' or something like that, over and over again, until his face was replaced by some big older guy with a bushy gray beard, one eye, a hood, and a really scary ass voice. That new guy was saying the exact same things."

"One eye? As in, he was like a cyclops?"

"No, not a single eye in the middle of his forehead. He was missing one of his two eyes, with the empty eye socket covered by a gray cap, or a gray eye patch like the one worn by that spy character Samuel L. Jackson plays in all the Marvel movies."

"Now I get what you mean! I believe I know *who* you're describing too. Oh wow."

"Sensei, who, exactly, did it sound like I was describing in my vision?"

"Alan, you won't believe me. I'm going to call Janice in here, and I think we should all sit and talk."

***

An incognito Father Merle Harris stood within a pitch dark alleyway on South Park Avenue, his deep gray trench coat and low brim antique fedora neatly concealing his form and facial features.

Also inside the entrenched area between two tenement buildings were Fred Gifford, whose long dark coat, ski mask, and black leather gloves effectively concealed his identity as he beat down on a captured member of the New York Boys with his now trademarked aluminum baseball bat.

Dee Dee Garcia stood behind the injured gang member, who was unable to walk due to a brutal compound fracture protruding through the lower portion of his denim jeans. The tough young street urchin held the young man's throat with a tightly wound strand of severed telephone cable wire. A flesh-colored, generic strap-on mask molded to resemble Gem Delgado, the princess character from an eponymous popular children's show, was concealing her face; her long lustrous hair was tied up in a ponytail directly atop her head, a style she never wore in her civilian life. Her body was covered in a dark red pullover hoodie and black exercise pants.

The young gangbanger with the broken leg gagged as Dee Dee pulled the phone wire even tighter around his already severely bruised trachea while Fred raised his bat in a threatening manner. The criminal youth had blood flowing out of each nostril as the disguised Father Merle walked up to him.

"You will partially repent from your sins if you tell us exactly where the New York Boys make the poison they distribute to the streets," the priest said in a cold tone which belied his usual affable voice.

That change was not lost on Fred Gifford. *Jesus, Father Merle seems like he becomes a whole different man when he puts on that get-up. The change with his voice spooks me somethin' fierce.*

The always-angry Dee Dee also noted the change, though she felt quite differently about it. *Ha! I love it when Father puts on his vigilante voice. It hypes me up and puts the fear of God into these* enredaderas *like none of his sermons can.*

"I don' know what ya'll mean, *niggah*," the gangbanger said through bruised lips. "I'm part of the war council, so I don't narc. All I know is you're a dead mutha…"

Before the gang member could finish the obscenity, Father Merle drew his .22 and shot the young man in his good leg. The explosive sound marked by the bullet's departure from the gun turret was lessened by the presence of a makeshift silencer. The young tough screamed bloody agony as the small lead projectile tore through both denim and ligaments.

Fred gritted his teeth, forcing himself to stay silent.

Dee Dee simply said, "Whoa, man" under her breath.

"Shame on you!" Father Merle exclaimed. "You compound your sins with both defiance and profanity! Princess, cover his mouth and stop his screaming!"

Dee Dee quickly unwrapped the telephone wire from the young man's throat, tugged it around his open mouth, and pulled the back of it tightly, greatly squelching the gangbanger's bellow of agony.

"You now have two limbs left," Father Merle said as he moved his face closer to the gang member, his voice taking on an even more icy tenor. "After that, you have a jawbone, numerous teeth, and a tongue to receive the pain of your penance. I'm going to ask my comrade here to remove the wire from your mouth. When she does, you tell me where the rest of that collection agent team who hurt Mr. Hefler and his wife are located. Anything else comes out of that swear-hole of yours, and the wrath of God will continue until either you tell us what we need to know, or there is nothing left of you to absolve for your sins. Choose wisely."

Fred quietly closed his eyes. *Fred Calvin Gifford II, just what do you got yourself involved in here? I know this little punk deserves a lot of heavy shit, but is this the right way to deliver it? And I'm too damn far into this now to just… stop.*

Dee Dee admonished herself as well, but over different conditions. *Calm down, and breathe quietly, girl. Don't make it too obvious how much this is exciting you; how much… fun this is. You're doing it for your sissy, not for your own sweet self.*

"Princess, remove the wire," Father Merle quietly ordered Dee Dee. "He now has another chance to make good on his penance."

Dee Dee did as commanded, and the gangbanger drew several desperate exhalations before licking his lips and struggling to speak again. The criminal street soldier coughed several times before he could form coherent words through his badly injured larynx.

"South… South Row…" he said before exploding into another coughing fit.

"That would be the South Row of the Commodore Perry Projects, am I correct?" the priest-turned-gang-smasher queried.

The young gangbanger nodded his head with his eyes squeezed shut, attempting to force himself not to continue screaming due to the severe pain emanating from his mutilated legs and deviated septum. Not that much of a sound could have been made from his throat at any rate.

"Only 59 of those 300 old housing units are occupied by legitimate tenants," the priest continued. "Tell us which ones we're looking for. Then, may God have mercy on your soul by showing you a better path, one that will lead to your absolution."

Fred gritted his teeth again. *I wish Merle would just tell that guy to force himself to say a few Our Father's and Hail Mary's so I can call him an ambulance and we can get the hell outta here and go do what we gotta do… before I end up changing my mind.*

***

Alan Perez was practicing kata moves in his room, now nearly three months since he last put on the Moonstalker uniform. He was determined to heal as quickly as possible. And with a combination of rest, standard medical treatment, conditioning at the dojo, and a blend of extensive meditative techniques and rare herbal curatives to speed the process along, he now stood prepared to put the costume on again in just a few days.

His appearances at school were furtive during this time, as he was well aware he needed to avoid being seen there in an injured state as much as possible. Alan had learned to pick his fights carefully and was in no shape to challenge Tony Kirkland at this time, especially with the rumors that he had recently become the second-in-command of the New York Boys' war council.

Thanks to a note he talked his doctor into writing for him and the arrangement of his various teachers and staff members at North Park with whom he was on good terms, he remained reasonably "caught up" with his studies. He sat in on some classes via Skype video and completed the bulk of required assignments over email, just enough to keep him from falling hopelessly behind.

Alan already knew he would be in his rightful graduating class of regardless of how much work he turned in or didn't turn in, though he had to put forth some modicum of effort to make things look legitimate. A combination of friends in high offices at the school and a system that couldn't afford to let too many students fail their grades lest the state government step in and take over would make that general high school diploma almost certain for him, provided he avoided doing something so terrible that he had to be expelled.

He kept his urge to go into action as Moonstalker in check before he was fully healed by noting in the papers, the news, and online media outlets that a trio of other vigilantes – using the monikers Fist of God, Princess Pummel, and Breaker – had been keeping the New York Boys and other criminals effectively at bay for him. Alan was intrigued by the trend he had started, and he knew that sooner or later he needed to gain control over the situation lest others with cross purposes formed rival power bases to himself. Little did he know such a procedure would begin taking place that very evening.

As Alan continued practicing katas, his cell phone rang, with its classic hip hop tune from Sir-Mix-A lot letting him know it was his closest friend and now confidante of his secret identity, Ty Reynolds. The young man skillfully somersaulted over to his bed and swiped up the phone.

"What's up, Black?" he asked.

"I thought you might want to know that word on the street has it those other vigilantes you've been keeping track of are making a big move tonight," Ty informed him.

"Really? Do you know where?"

"Well, it's only rumors, and all I heard was that it involves something going down in the 'South' of the city. Not much, but maybe it's something?"

Alan thought for a moment before abruptly speaking again. "Okay, that's all I need to know. Thank you for keeping me informed. I have to go now."

"If you're going back into the costume tonight, make sure to be careful, man."

"Yes, Mother. I'll get back to you later."

"And if the chick vigilante is there, see if she's single and might want to…"

"I have to go, Ty. Later, dude."

"So, you're gonna hog her yourself, huh? Man, you really suck…"

Ty's words were cut off as Alan ended the call. He then hurled his cell phone on his bed mattress and opened the bedroom's closet door to access the false section he built to hide his specialized costume and paraphernalia.

***

The Fist of God (a.k.a., Father Merle Harris) stood before the line of a few hundred dilapidated, boarded up, and supposedly abandoned flat-roofed homes which made up the infamous "South Row" of the Perry Projects, an impoverished stain on the Queen City that desecrates the view visible from vehicles driving on the I-90 of the Niagara Thruway. These buildings were built prior to World War II, and most were in horrendously shabby condition due to an inability of the city to acquire enough federal funds to either tear them down or renovate them. Some of the residents described the South Row as resembling a ghost town in the middle of the inner city.

Yet due to a fluke of the antiquated system used to heat the low-rent apartments lining Perry Street and South Park Avenue in the area of the city known as the First Ward, all of these abandoned homes still receive heating during the cold months of the year. The cost of this heating system falls on the residents in more ways than just the financial, since two of these buildings serve as major crack manufacturing units for the New York Boys.

"Are you sure he didn't steer us wrong?" Breaker (a.k.a., Fred Gifford) asked. "All of these houses are still boarded up."

"They just want to make them look abandoned," Princess Pummel (a.k.a., Dee Dee Garcia) noted. "The big boss, who calls himself Assailant, operates in one of the big tenement buildings on the other side of the projects, but no one knows exactly which one; plus he has other safe houses on the East Side. These two South Row houses are drug manufacturing factories for him, run by some sleazy prick with funky eyes called Skid.

"I always figured this was going on here, but I didn't know for sure, or which houses, until we just 'persuaded' that punk to do his civic duty by telling us. The gang pays the Buffalo Municipal Housing Authority to overlook these houses. If any funky sounds are reported by the tenants, the Housing Authority just tells them it's squatters and they'll 'look into it soon,' blah blah blah."

"And the 'debt collectors' who hurt Mr. Hefler and his wife act as security for these two crack houses when they're not collecting money?" Breaker queried.

"It's what that ruffian told us," the Fist of God said, "and he was in no situation to risk lying."

"So which one do we make our entrance in?" was Breaker's next question.

"I say the second one on the left," the priest answered.

"For any reason in particular?" Princess Pummel inquired.

"It just *feels* right," Fist of God said as he brandished his .22 and walked towards the sealed front entrance.

The man of the cloth blasted a hole through the door knob with his piece and then kicked the front entrance open. As their involuntary informant had reported, a small but efficient chemistry lab was set up on a large metal table with several people working around it. Two gang members who also acted as debt collectors were guarding it, and each one pulled an Uzi.

However, they weren't as fast as Father Merle's alter-ego, who blew a hole in each of their guts before they could spray him and his two compatriots-in-vigilantism with hot lead. Both men fell to the floor with their hands grasping their bleeding lower abdomens, desperately hoping to keep their viscera where it belonged.

Another gang member came running out of a side room with a stiletto in hand. Before he could reach the Fist of God, however, Breaker hollered and slammed him across both legs with his bat, causing the thug to drop his blade and fall to the ground. Princess Pummel then let loose a loud scream of rage and ran towards the fallen criminal, kicking him in the face as hard as she could and smashing his nose.

"You vile miscreants will pay for what you've done to this city!" the disguised priest decreed. "Repent now or meet Jesus sooner than you may have wanted."

"Fist, the one on the end has a cell phone in his hand!" Princess Pummel warned. "He must have called for reinforcements from the other house!"

"Oh, great," Breaker griped aloud.

Just then three other gang members rushed through the compromised front door. The trio were led by none other than Skid himself, who was revealed as a somewhat diminutive albino with muscular arms, a head of curly white hair, and pinkish eyes. All three of these men wielded Uzi's.

"Skid, it's those vigilantes!" one of the other men yelled.

"I can see that, you dick!" Skid retorted as he raised his fully automatic firearm in his heavily-tattooed arms. "I'm gonna cut them in half!"

Before Skid could depress the trigger, however, a sickle-shaped ceramic blade embedded itself in the back of his neck. The bright-eyed albino gasped and dropped his Uzi.

The other two reinforcements quickly turned around to face whoever had attacked from behind, hoping and praying it wasn't whom they thought. Their prayers would prove unanswered in ironic fashion while the Fist of God held his piece at the ready as a gray-soled boot kicked one of the gangbangers in the face before he could lift his Uzi. The force of the blow pulverized his nose and sent him flying backwards, his blood-covered face hitting the floor right in front of Princess Pummel.

"Oh my god oh my god, cool!" she yelled.

The remaining armed gangbanger, in a state of confusion and panic, raised his Uzi and looked into the darkness where he knew his opponent was hidden. Before he could press the trigger, however, he was struck in the jaw by a devastating haymaker courtesy of a different individual; this one wasn't wearing a ninja-esque outfit like Moonstalker, but instead wore a flowing black coat, matching black pants, and a bandana covering much of his face excepting the holes for the proper orifices.

The blow this latest unwelcome delivered was enough to send the young gang member reeling back against the wall. The firearm-wielding youth still managed to hold onto his Uzi, but this changed after the individual who decked him followed up with a sock to the solar plexus. That punch caused the gangbanger to keel over and vomit on his shoes; and a second blow to the jaw sent him to the floor unmoving.

The first figure, whose form was hidden in the room's darkness turned to someone standing behind him just outside and said, "Now."

The walls of the small flat-roofed house shook as the one right next to it was hit by an explosion just small enough to demolish the interior of the structure and cause its remaining roof and walls to cave in.

"What the Holy Hell?" Breaker shouted.

"Yes," the Fist of God said with a wide beam as the dark figure walked into the living room and became fully illuminated by the few battery-operated lamps present. "Yes!"

"Oh, wow," Princess Pummel said with more than a hint of awe. "It's… *him*. It's really him."

Moonstalker stepped fully into the room to confront the three vigilantes whom he inspired for the first time. Behind him was Reggie Diaz, his bandana-wearing ally, now using the handle Street Wolf. Joining them a second later was Eli Matthews, the man whose expertise in demolitions from his days in the Army was responsible for the destruction of the other crack house; he wore a dark hoodie pulled over his head to conceal much of his appearance, his face obscured by a domino mask held on by old-fashioned spirit gum. His street name was now Sky High.

"Yes, it's me," Moonstalker answered calmly. "My partner Sky High is about to do the same thing to this house, doing for free what the city government won't pay anyone a cent to do. So, we need to get out of here, leave those chemist fools outside for the police to deal with… and then you three will come with me. We need to talk."

"Of course," the priest said with another beam. "I'm the Fist of God, and these…"

"Yeah, I know," Moonstalker replied. "I read the papers and watched the video uploads on YouTube. But we need to leave now."

"Certainly," the still beaming vigilante pastor agreed. He then turned to Breaker and Princess Pummel. "Listen to the young man. He's God's hammer on Earth, and we're his accompanying tools."

"We're a bunch of tools all right," Breaker said just under his breath.

Street Wolf turned to Moonstalker and quietly said, "*Seriously*, Boss?"

"Yeah, it seems so," the masked urban warrior replied to his student.

***

The next morning, Shanice Morris walked down the now semi-empty corridors of Riverfield High following dismissal from the final class of the day, heading for the door exits into the schoolyard. She spent the last several weeks wishing that Alan would return to school full time and was pleased he was on the mend and planning to return the very next day.

In the meantime, she carried some books for him and intended to drop them off at his house, happy to have any excuse to visit there despite how much he scared and infuriated her at times. She was just beginning to get on better terms with his parents, even though neither of them fully trusted her, and she was frankly unable to blame them after what she pulled at Alan's request.

As Shanice reached the short hallway leading to the door she suddenly found her passage blocked by none other than Tony Kirkland, flanked on his right and left by two fellow students whom he had recently recruited for the New York Boys. The girl gulped audibly in fear but was determined to keep up a bold front.

"Hey, sweet thang," Tony said in deliberate exaggerated slang. "Where's that boyfriend of yours? Still recovering from the car accident, or just afraid to face me now that I'm the right hand to the big man?"

"He's coming along fine, Tony," she replied. "He'll be back tomorrow, and he's not afraid of you. You're just a punk."

"No soft little punk would ever have made it to the position of right hand and second-in-command of the New York Boys' war council. I'm *something* now, and your man is *nothing*. I gave you long enough to think about things, so I'd like to know now if you're still going to stay with him instead of me."

Shanice glared at the imposing presence of Tony Kirkland, her fear now overcome by anger. "I don't find anything impressive about you or that gang, or anyone else who hurts innocent people for money."

"A lot of people have jobs where they do that, babe. If you want to amount to something in this world, then you need to be on top. Speaking of which, how'd you like to let me be on top of *you* next?"

The other two gangbangers flanking him began to laugh, but Tony put up his right hand to signal silence, something he saw Assailant do often enough. They immediately went quiet, and he reveled in the feeling of power this gave him.

Shanice was now even more angry. "You're a pig, and I don't think so. Now step aside, please, or I'll call over a security guard."

Tony glowered at the pretty young woman for a moment, as if considering taking on the challenge. But the athlete-turned-gangbanger had a better idea. He stepped aside as requested and positioned both his hands in a mock gentleman gesture indicating she was free to pass.

Shanice then brushed past him and exited the building.

"You want us to go after her?" Billy, the gang member lackey on his right, asked him.

"No need for that," Tony replied. "We'll have plenty of time to deal with her, that boyfriend of hers, and every other damned fool in this place tomorrow."

"What do you mean, Tony?" Gary, the minion to his left and a longtime friend, inquired.

"Now that I'm the right hand of the New York Boys, I got lots of decision-making power," Tony answered. "And I just decided that tomorrow we're going to take this school."

"Tony, that's crazy," Gary said. "No way Assailant authorizes that! This isn't a private business, it's a government building, and if we occupy it, it'll bring the cops down on us for sure."

"The New York Boys are going to *be* the government soon!" Tony insisted. "I think the big boss should be proud that his right hand took the first step towards making that happen. If not, then, well… fuck him."

Chapter 14: The Dojo

The vigilante trio known as the Fist of God, Princess Pummel, and Breaker reverently followed Moonstalker, Street Hawk, and Sky High into Master Kai's Dojo. The martial arts training center appeared modest and just a bit decrepit from the outside, where it was flanked to its left by Mr. Izo's Pottery shop. This exterior appearance was deliberately designed to deceive, however. The inside revealed a spacious training facility that was mostly known for the affordable courses in Tai Chi and basic self-defense that primarily served a few dozen kids from low income families and a modest number of adults with equally modest earnings, respectively.

It was from mostly this pool of younger students whom Master Kai had instructed his main trainers, Dell Boyd and Janice Rosenberg, to alert him to any of the few who showed unusual potential. Master Kai would then carefully vet each one, and from that number, fewer still would be chosen to receive the type of special training Alan Perez was given. That special training was completely free of obligation (at least of the financial sort) and provided by staff members that the regular students never met; with the exception of Matoi, whom they knew only from her handling fee transactions at the front desk and occasionally making treats for the students.

The dojo was adorned by large swaths of wallpaper scribed with proverbs written in English underneath their original Japanese or Chinese characters, and various weapons hung on the walls by means of metal hooks. Pictures of the staff with certificates of their various accomplishments directly underneath them were also to be seen. Also present were the standard paraphernalia of blue mats on the floor and rows of benches where parents and prospective students could sit and watch classes; or, where students could be sent for disciplinary "time out" sessions or to recover from minor injuries, whatever the case happened to be.

The major eye-catcher upon entering the dojo, however, was the life size marble statue of Master Kai, said to be sculpted from a friend who owed him a large debt back in Asia. The agate effigy stood several feet to the right of the front entrance and was an amazing constructed likeness of the Master; the arms were folded in a meditative pose, its realistically rendered eyes impassively beholding all that occurred within the dojo's walls.

Alan Perez wasn't unsettled by much in this world, but the statue's eyes were one of those few disquieting exceptions, as he felt they duplicated the usual emotionless calm and penetrating gaze of Master Kai's just a bit too accurately for his comfort. It made him feel as if the Master was *always* watching him when he was in the main training chamber, even when the man was known to be visiting his homeland thousands of miles away.

Four high quality bronze braziers of about five feet in height – generous gifts from others who had known Master Kai in Asia – whose saucers were filled with flammable charcoal, were another impressive sight in the large training area. To most of the regular students and their parents, these braziers were mere decorations, as there was never any reason to light them during ordinary business hours.

After having made sure that no one noticed his entourage enter the darkened dojo, Moonstalker signaled to Street Wolf to lock the door and light a flame in a nearby brazier. This provided the interior of the edifice sufficient illumination for everyone present to see each other, but not enough light to gain the notice of anyone in the neighborhood who may happen to look out their windows or stroll by the dojo.

"You got quite the place here, um, Moonstalker," Breaker finally broke the silence by opining aloud.

"Yea, it's totally awesome as," Princess Pummel said.

"It is an honor for you to bring us into your sacred place like this," the Fist noted.

Moonstalker looked at the three vigilantes whom he inspired, with Street Hawk standing to his left and Sky High to his right, as if they were securing his person.

"And it's an equal honor to know that my actions inspired the three of you to take up the mission," the imposing young vigilante said. "But you can't keep operating in the haphazard fashion like you have been, with no actual training. All of you have natural skill and potential in various techniques, but you need training to fully develop them. It's a miracle you all made it as far as you did earlier this evening at the Perry Projects' South Row. Still, if my me and my boys here hadn't shown up at that house when we did, you would probably all be dead now."

"So, then you went and followed us?" Breaker inquired.

"Yes, I did," Moonstalker replied firmly.

"Where were you for the past few months?" Princess asked. "You seemed to just do a total fade-out after that throw down with the New York Boys at the East Side Inferno." She then pulled off her Gem Delgado facemask and smiled. "Yup, I watch the news!"

Moonstalker was completely taken by Dee Dee Garcia's lovely facial features, and the contours of her shapely body hadn't escaped his observations either.

"Very astute of you to notice," the acting master of the dojo said in a less serious tone. "I must say it's going to be a pleasure training you."

Having picked up his obvious hint, Princess Pummel's mouth formed a half-frown as she responded with, "Not too much pleasure though, stud. You may be cool and impressive and all that, but keep in mind that I'm not into boys."

"Woo, I heard that," Breaker said with a grin. "This girl is for real."

She playfully tapped the older man on his arm and said, "You know it, man."

Moonstalker was thankful his full head mask concealed the startled expression on his face. Being turned down like that was a rarity in his experience, and needless to say he didn't enjoy the embarrassment he felt over being overtly rejected, let alone in front of others.

"Surely these types of thoughts are not appropriate here," the Fist of God interjected. "Pardon me for saying this, Moonstalker, but with all due respect you should be above such things." The justice-dispensing priest then turned to the Princess. "And you, young lady, should really keep those preferences of yours to yourself, because…"

"Let's get something straight here, Father Harris," Moonstalker interrupted with a strong hint of annoyance in his voice.

His identification of the Fist's true identity elicited a dumbstruck expression on the pastor of St. Luke's Church.

"Yes, I know who you really are," Moonstalker continued. "It's my job to know everything on these streets. Now, as I was saying, let's get something clear from the get-go. I respect the Catholic faith, but this is not church, it's my home. You don't set the rules or tell me or anyone else how to behave here. That's *my* job. I may be a Catholic, but I'm not a holy man, so I'm not pious and I don't practice abstinence, and you will deal with that if you want to work with me. Is that clear?"

"Well, yes, and I meant no offense," the fedora-wearing clergyman replied. "However, it's obvious to all of us that you're quite young, much like the Princess here, so maybe you should…"

"Maybe *you* should stop right there, and never go there again, Father Harris," Moonstalker interjected. "No matter my age, I call the shots in this group, and no one else. You're here as a valued student and comrade-in-arms, but *not* as a chaperone, mentor, or 'guardian' figure. I have a mentor and teacher who I acknowledge as master, and you're most certainly not him. He's also not here right now, which leaves me in charge of this dojo. You're free to follow me in the mission, but you won't be leading the unit any longer. Is that clear? Or do I show you the door right here, right now?"

The Fist of God pulled his fedora up to expose his eyes and seemed to think for a quick moment before replying. "Yes. It's clear." *Now I know why God brought me into Moonstalker's life. The boy needs guidance and some manners, and I'm just the one to teach them to him since this 'Master Kai' is gone. Now is not the time, however. I am going to have to make it subtle, at least at first.*

It was then Breaker's turn to look startled. *Geez, did that kid just put the old pontiff in his place? I didn't think anyone could do that after what the priest went and turned into once he got started on that "mission" of his.*

After the gray-clad vigilante received the Fist's apparent complicity, he turned his attention back to the entire entourage. "Princess, I'll answer your question later. Right now, I want to tell all of you what the deal is. Each of you has potential, and I'm going to train you in ways that cater to the specific strengths and weapons you've each displayed a propensity for. Anyone who has unusual potential will learn quickly under the methodology Master Kai perfected."

"Yo, can I ask a question?" Breaker said with a raised hand. Moonstalker nodded his permission. "The thing is, me and the priest ain't exactly spring chickens. Isn't it, like, a bit late in the game for us to start up something like this?"

"No," the vigilante replied. "It's preferable to start as young as possible, yes, but the journey can start at any point in one's life. Because of the potential you and Father Harris have shown, I expect you two to learn as quickly under my tutelage as any younger person. For example, you've shown some good upper body strength, and a knack for using large bludgeoning weapons. Princess Pummel is really good at stealth, and with the use of slashing weapons. And Father Harris has some rather amazing aim when it comes to firing projectiles, apparently natural. Which brings me to another important point."

Moonstalker turned to the Fist of God again. "Even though I'm also new to the 'super hero' thing, and haven't fully decided on my M.O. yet, I'm not a wanton killer. I may be as ruthless as they come in dishing out pain and broken bones, and I may even take a life if I think it's absolutely necessary; but I do not pre-emptively set out to do that. So, we're going to have to replace that .22 of yours with something that inflicts pain and damage, but no fatalities."

"Are you serious?" the Fist asked. "With respect, these criminal ruffians are too dangerous for me to deal with using a B.B. gun."

Moonstalker was quick with a retort. "But your ability, with a bit of training, can be extended to include the use of crossbow guns and blow guns. And firearms can be modified to fire projectiles that aren't lethal but cause enough damage with a single hit to keep a thug down for the count. Rubber bullets can be a lot more effective than you think."

"Hmm," was all the priest could say.

"Can you answer my question now?" Princess pluckily insisted.

"That girl has got the nerve," Breaker said quietly with another grin.

Though Moonstalker was somewhat annoyed by the pretentiousness of Princess Pummel, he nevertheless could not help having respect for her obvious displays of guts, independence, and -- though he would never admit it -- her ability and temerity to refute his charms.

"Yes, I'll do that now," he said through slightly gritted teeth. "To be totally honest, as good as I am, I'm still a rookie when it comes to urban warfare on this scale, especially fighting it on my own. I also didn't use my full arsenal, preferring to do a combination of hand-to-hand and stealth, while using my sickle shurikens for long-range strikes. That went fine for a while, but ultimately it wasn't enough. I received… some major injuries during the fracas at the East Side Inferno, and I wouldn't have made it out of that situation alive if not for Street Hawk and Sky High."

"Wow," Princess said quietly.

"I told you this game is dangerous, girl," Breaker said. "Those New York Boys ain't the Boy Scouts."

"Exactly," Moonstalker concurred. "That's why you all need to take this battle very seriously if you want to be a part of it, and why you need both training and back-up. You'll all provide the last one for me."

"Coolness," Princess said with a smile.

"God sent you to save us," the Fist added. "And I believe He sent us to assist you. We will be the right hand you need."

"You know it!" Breaker added approvingly. However, he found himself secretly hoping that Moonstalker could rein in Father Merle Harris's excesses without falling victim to the same temptations himself.

"Also," Moonstalker added, "from this point onwards, I'm going everywhere equipped with my full arsenal. I modified my uniform to hold more hidden pockets. That will allow me to carry as much as I might need, at least for a single night out. And my darkout bombs and explosive nitro-pellets are small enough that I can fit dozens of them in hidden pockets stitched into my pants and coat."

Breaker's eyes seemed to pop from their sockets for a second. *Did he just say explosives? And do I even want to know what "darkout" bombs are? I mean, they're bombs of some sort, right? Maybe this cat will turn out to be like Father Merle after all, only worse. I sure got my fingers crossed hopin' he doesn't.*

Moonstalker continued his spiel about his sartorial improvements, as if hoping to sound more imposing to his new crew. "Not only that, but my uniform itself can easily be concealed in my backpack, stuffed into my gym gear so that the best security search of my duffel bag won't uncover it or anything stored inside of it. And of course, my collapsible shurikans and kamas can likewise be hidden in disguised pockets sewn into my jeans. Making such concealment in ordinary apparel was something the Master taught his special students for years."

"Wow," Princess Pummel simply repeated.

"What she said," Breaker chimed in.

The Fist of God nodded his head.

"Okay, then training starts here this coming Friday, at 4 PM sharp," Moonstalker said. "Don't tell me you have better things to do, because there *is* nothing better than this. Before we adjourn, I'm going to show you the back entrance, which is the only way I ever want you to enter or leave this dojo."

After that final matter was taken care of, the vigilante sent his crew home, as it was by now quite late and he had to prepare for his first day back to school in the morning. Little was he aware that the greatest and most harrowing battle of his rookie career was going to occur there.

Interlude: The Calm Before the Siege

The following morning was a pleasant day in late April, and the last remaining vestiges of snow were melting in favor of the spring season. Though this agreeable morning was destined to end most disagreeably for the students of Riverfield High, none of them were aware of what was in store for them that day; thus, many of them were happy to enjoy the morning by walking to school if they lived close enough.

Shanice Morris greeted this beautiful morning by making a point to wake up early enough to bus down to Alan Perez's home an hour before it was time to leave for school. She wanted to make the day he returned to Riverfield High special by having the two of them arrive there together, hand-in-hand as a proud couple. She also wanted this to send a strong message to both Tony Kirkland and each of the many other girls who likely had designs on Alan.

The young woman made this early morning excursion despite knowing that her boyfriend's parents would also be awake, and she was still uncomfortable in their presence as a result of the lies Alan had talked her into making for him. She was painfully aware Lenore and Bradford Perez would be quick to remind her of this infraction against their trust to further discourage her from ever doing it again. Despite the differences between them and their son, it was still quite clear to her where Alan got his stubbornness and relentlessness of purpose from.

"You two watch out for each other," Bradford said graciously just as his son and his girlfriend were preparing to leave for school. "And young lady, if anything goes wrong, you call us right away on your cell, and don't let this son of mine convince you to do otherwise."

"I will, Mr. Bradford," Shanice said with every intention of being sincere, but still feeling shame and embarrassment for having them convinced she was untrustworthy.

"Dad, ease up," Alan said. "She had good intentions for doing what she did, and it was all because I insisted it was for the best. So please let it go."

"Alan, lying to us for any reason when it comes to your well-being is not in anyone's best interests!" Lenore exclaimed. "Your father and I want Shanice to know we mean business."

The lovely caramel-skinned young woman continued to look down while trying to take solace by reminding herself of three things: this ordeal would end in a few minutes; she actually deserved it; and that it was all worth it to still have Alan as her significant other. She therefore kept her mouth shut and squelched her anxiety by twirling her black braided hair around her right index finger.

"Mom, she's heard this plenty already," Alan rebutted. "Constantly lecturing her like this is only going to make her feel more horrible, and she already feels horrible enough. She apologized, and she stood by me these past few months while I recovered from my injuries. Let it go, or I'll just have to spend less time around the house."

"Alan, it's okay, I understand why they're still upset," Shanice interjected, still twirling her hair around her index finger.

"No, it's not okay," Alan insisted. "They've told you this enough already. It's time to let it go because all it does at this point is antagonize us."

"You just remember what we said, young lady," Bradford stated firmly. "If you do that, then everything will be fine."

"I will, Mr. Bradford," Shanice assured him.

"And you better mean that, Shanice," Lenore said.

"Yes, yes, she does mean it, Mom," Alan retorted as he took Shanice by the hand and led her out the door. "Goodbye, Mom."

"If you need a ride home for any reason, just call us, okay?" Bradford said.

"I'll be *fine*, Dad," was Alan's final words as he shut the door behind him.

"Geez, those two!" the young man said once he and Shanice were off of his front porch and headed for the bus stop at the corner. "I'm sorry I had you come over this morning. I should have met you at your house instead."

"Alan, it's really okay," Shanice said as she gently squeezed his hand. "Your parents are really pretty cool, and even though they nag you they really do mean well."

"Yes, I know, but they have to let me live my own life."

"It's not like you don't actually give them good reason to worry, you know."

"But it's still my choices, and even if they aren't always the best choices, they're still mine to make. So, I'm willing to live with the consequences for any one of them."

"The thing is, Alan, your parents, me, and everyone else who cares about you has to live with those consequences too."

"Are you going to start now? This is supposed to be a special day for us."

"I'm on your side, Alan. I just see their side too, because I care about you also. I know you're going to make your own choices, and that's how it should be, but keep in mind that you're not the only person affected by them. This isn't only about you."

"I don't need *two* mothers, Shanice!"

The young woman released his hand and looked directly into his eyes, which stood a few inches above hers.

"Alan Garrett Perez, you listen to me. People who care about you are not going to apologize for it. Maybe we do go overboard sometimes, but it's only because we care, not because we want to annoy or inconvenience you. It really hurts us when you treat that concern as if it's a bad thing. It really hurts *me*."

Tears of frustration started pouring down Shanice's stunning face, and she began to cry profusely. Alan's first instinct was to tell her to cease being a "drama queen," but seeing her get like this over him quickly caused the young man to respond very differently. Instead of saying anything harsh, he simply embraced her and held her tightly.

"It's okay, babe, I'm sorry. I didn't mean to behave like that. I'm just… really pig-headed sometimes."

Shanice looked up at her paramour with tear-soaked eyes. "Only *sometimes?*"

Alan frowned. "Okay, maybe… a bit more often than just sometimes. I'm sorry."

"It's okay, sweetie." She pulled a piece of toilet paper off the roll she had in her purse and began wiping her eyes. "Oooh, craps, I shouldn't have started crying. Now my eyeliner is running. I must look horrible."

"You look fine, babe. Only a little is running, and you can easily re-apply it once we get on the bus. Believe me, you're fine."

"Honestly?"

Alan gave her a very sincere smile. "Yes, honestly."

He then embraced her again and kept his arms around her for the full thirteen minutes it took for the bus to arrive. Considering what was to come later that day, the young vigilante would be glad he got the chance to spend these tender moments with Shanice while he still could.

Chapter 15: The Siege Begins

Shanice Morris couldn't help feeling a hefty degree of pride as she approached the less than regal façade of Riverfield High holding hands with Alan Perez. Many of the girls who wanted him but failed to catch his eye glared at her with seething envy. She fancied she could actually hear their thoughts, consisting of things like, "what makes *her* so special?"

The young lady had no answer to such a question, but she knew that right now, despite all the difficulties a relationship with Alan Perez entailed, she *did* feel special. She also knew there was even more to him than the princely personage he presented to his peers and teachers alike. That air of mystery – which she found simultaneously chilling and intriguing – stoked her strong feelings for him all the more.

As the couple walked towards the front entrance, they were suddenly blocked by Tony Kirkland, who stepped out from behind a pillar which had concealed his presence. Once again, he was flanked by two fellow members of the New York Boys who served as his personal bodyguards.

"So, the great Alan Perez is back to school," Tony said in a sneering fashion. "Welcome back, dude. Guess what I've accomplished since you were gone?"

The tall athletic young man answered the question by opening his school jacket so the colors and symbol of the New York Boys, concealed underneath, became visible to his rival for Shanice's affections.

"Nice, Tony," Alan said with an ironic jeer. "I see being a terror on the basketball court isn't enough for you anymore. You have to be a terror on the streets, too."

"Yeah, and don't you forget it, bruh," Tony replied while pointing his index finger a few inches from Alan's face.

"Since we're comparing notes," Alan said, "look what I accomplished even before you got those colors." He lifted his arm, displaying the fact he was holding

Shanice's hand to the gangbanger, thus sending a clear message that he knew his rival would consider the emotional equivalent of a wasp sting on the buttocks.

"Isn't that a cool bit of bling she's wearing?" Alan asked while pointing to an emerald signet ring on Shanice's right ring finger. "That's a promise ring I got her. Doesn't its color go well with her eyes?" His face then displayed a very sardonic beam.

Shanice was glad Alan showed such pride in being with her, but she couldn't help dreading where this interaction was going. *Alan, please don't provoke him. I know you're tough as leather, but Tony is a tough athlete and a gangbanger, and he's backed up by two hoodlums.*

One of the two proverbial hoodlums, a heavy-set boy named Phil, began to step forward, but Tony stopped him with a quick raising of his right hand.

"Now, now, Phil, we're all friends here, right?" Tony said with bitter irony. "A little harmless competition never hurt anyone, right? Let's move aside now and let the nice couple into the school. They both need to get an education today."

Tony's men did as requested, and the couple moved past them and inside the doorway. Alan found himself instinctually entering a state of mental preparedness.

Kirkland has something planned. Good. That means this is the day I get to deal with him. But I need to make sure Shanice, and all other innocents, are out of the crossfire when it goes down.

Tony turned to Phil and his other personal bodyguard, Joshua, as soon as the door swung fully closed.

"Now that Perez and Shanice are inside, you can contact the rest of the boys and tell them we're ready to rumble. There's about fifty other students inside already, at least a few teachers and security guards, and probably at least one janitor. We'll take this building easily, since there's over seventy men who agreed to follow me here. Most of the ones who are armed need to engage the pigs as soon as they get here, to keep them busy and prevent them from getting inside the school. By the time the SWAT teams arrive, the building will be ours. It'll take us about twenty minutes to claim it completely.

"But remember… Perez and Shanice are both *mine*."

***

After about ten minutes had passed, Tony stepped into the school with Phil and Joshua alongside him. As they did so, a security guard noticed their attire under the unzipped school jackets and began walking towards them.

"Hey, you!" the guard shouted. "Didn't I tell you three the other day that you're not supposed to wear gang colors in the school? I let it go because you're an important member of the school's basketball team, Tony, but this time I have to put my foot down."

"Aw, don't go through the trouble of doing that, Bing," Tony said. "I'll put my foot down for you."

The tall, well-built right hand of the New York Boys slammed his right foot down on one of Bing's knees. The powerful blow made a loud cracking noise and less than a second later the security guard had fallen to the floor, his agonized screams echoing down the hallway.

Tony then quickly grabbed a trophy mounted on a nearby display and bludgeoned Bing several times on the face with the object's hard metal base, reducing his visage to a mass of pulped flesh and cartilage. He looked at the tip of his blood-soaked makeshift weapon and smiled. He then pressed a single virtual key on his cell phone to dial a pre-entered number.

"Come on in, boys, the party has started! Woohoo and all that shit!"

With that word given, the trio stepped aside to allow no less than forty gang members to rush through the doors and begin enacting what may best be called a school invasion. The one in front, whose street name was Puma, held an Uzi; the rest were armed with weapons such as stilettos, pipes, and chains. About two dozen additional gang members, all holding firearms of various sorts, gathered in front of the building and prepared for the police to arrive.

All students who were fortunate enough to have not yet entered the school wisely turned away from the building once they spotted what was ensuing on the outside. Tony was certainly aware those students would flood the police station with panic-stricken calls, and he was well-prepared for that. He would have a few dozen hostages within the next several minutes, all of whom he intended to become permanent residents of the building. The second-in-command of the gang's war council was certain he would go down in history as the greatest thing to ever happen to the New York Boys, and a legend among all future street gangs who would beautify an urban landscape with their presence.

***

Assailant, the much-feared leader of the New York Boys, was having breakfast in his Perry Street sanctuary when his cell phone began emitting one of the late Tupac Shakur's more ominous beats. The powerful monstrosity of a man knew it had to be truly important if any of his men or women dared interrupt his morning repast with gang business rather than bringing the matter to one of his lieutenants, so he immediately took the call. To say what he heard was extremely displeasing to him would be an understatement of epic proportions.

"I find myself actually *hoping* that you're lying to me, Fungi," he said to one of his main informants with no attempt to control the rage in his tone, a linguistic habit which always caused his slight Spanish accent to temporarily become more pronounced.

"I'm afraid not, Boss," Fungi confirmed over the cell. "Your new right hand took it upon his ass to initiate a takeover of Riverfield High. And reliable rumor has it that it's all to get back at one fellow student there who got the girl he wanted."

"How dare that *hijo de puta* make such a move without getting it cleared by me first! This is going to bring the gang into direct conflict with the pigs! We weren't prepared for something this big yet!"

"Well, that's love for ya, Boss."

"Shut up, *estúpido*! This is serious shit that has the potential to deal a fatal blow to the entire gang! I need you to tell me a way I can get into the school. No doubt Kirkland will have the doors allowing access to every entry point chained, but he'll be smart enough to have an armed posse surrounding the front and back entrances to keep the police busy while he does what he plans to do inside the building. That will work to my advantage too. I'm going to deal with this *puta* personally. And if this incident attracts that vigilante... all the better."

"I got a map of the school right here, Boss. I'll figure a way for you to get in unseen in about five minutes, tops. You wouldn't believe some of the secret entrances to that school I found. I'll bet you my last ounce of coke that not even any of the students or employees know about all of them. Yup, I'm that good."

"Just tell me, goddammit! You can pat yourself on the back later, if you still have a hand to do it with!"

***

The one remaining security guard, a man named Kyle Hendricks, fought hard, but was quickly overwhelmed by force of numbers. His final thought before being beaten into oblivion was satisfaction over the fact that he knocked a tooth out of one of the invading gangbangers and gave a swollen eye to another before they brought him down. Unfortunately, however, those two injured parties took vengeance on his unconscious body by punching and stomping on it mercilessly for several minutes after all the rest had moved on to other victims.

Several students screamed in terror as they were unexpectedly accosted by a horde of New York Boys, whose colors and jacket symbol they instantly recognized. Because of their well-earned reputation, even the students who were athletes or naturally good fighters gave in when they were ordered to stand against lockers or lay on the floor with their hands over their heads. One of them, a large and tough-as-nails basketball player named Nate Green, considered pounding on the two gang members who had told him to stand against the locker and remain silent after they turned their attention to a pair of students who had just exited a classroom in front of them.

Nate ultimately decided against it, since there were two of them to his one, and they had a knife and chain between them. Further, he didn't know if he could count on these other two students to help him if need be. But he would wait for an opportunity...

Alan and Shanice were on another corridor, in front of the latter's locker, when all the screaming began. They noticed a social studies teacher rush out of his room and head towards the commotion.

"Alan, what's going on?" Shanice asked her boyfriend. "Is that screaming I hear?"

"It's started," was his simple reply.

"What's started?"

"We have a school invasion on our hands. Follow me to the science lab down the corridor, now!"

"No! This can't be true..."

"Shanice, I need you to stay strong and not break down. And I need you to do as I say, without hesitation! Your life depends on it, and so does mine!"

Without another word, the girl held back her terror with a powerful surge of will and followed her boyfriend down the corridor as fast as they could both move. Upon finding the science lab, they saw it was unoccupied by any teacher or custodian, and Alan motioned for her to follow him in there.

"Listen to me, Shanice! I want you to get under that table and don't move until this is over! And don't get out of there for any reason! Do you hear me?"

"Yes, but what are you gonna do?"

"I'm going to do what I always do! Now get under there!"

Too terrified to offer resistance and knowing from past experience that Alan seemed to know what he was doing in extreme crisis situations like this, Shanice crawled under the small metal table. Her boyfriend had clearly chosen that particular table since it was very difficult to see her under its great bulk if one didn't make a point to look. He then picked up several chemical flasks and swiftly poured a few liquids from different containers within, causing a severe fizzling effect to occur in the beakers.

"What are you doing, Alan?"

"I'm putting some of the chemistry lessons I learned from Matoi at the dojo and Mr. McCall right here in the lab to good use. I'm making some corrosive acids."

Before Shanice could ask him the reason why he was taking even a minute to make acid in the chem lab, Alan grabbed a copper wire from a cabinet. With record speed, he tied the acid-filled flasks to a clock attached to the wall directly above the door, while tying the other end of the wire to the door knob.

"I'm going to lock the door to the lab, but if any of those gang members force the lock, it'll give them a hot shower that they'll never forget."

"How... how do you have a key to the door?"

"I told you, I have friends in high places in this school. And it's not hard to get a key copied. Anyway, I need to give you something."

Alan carried a final flask filled with the homemade corrosive over to Shanice and handed it to her.

"Hold onto this. Just in case those punks force the door open, and one or more of them still decides to come in here after they see their friends get the burn. If they do find you, throw this acid on them; aim for their faces if you can. Then run outside the door. Look for whatever exit you can find after that, even if you have to break a window with one of the fire extinguishers. But do not leave for any reason unless that happens. Do you hear me?"

"Yes, I hear you, but..."

"Just listen! And stop shaking, before you spill some of that corrosive on your hands. It's very powerful stuff! I have to go now."

Shanice gently grabbed her boyfriend's wrist to halt his departure for a moment.

"Alan... please be careful. I love you."

"You know I will, babe. And... I love you too."

Alan quickly gave her a passionate kiss and headed for the door to the lab, knowing he had at most a minute to both carefully exit the door in a way that didn't trigger the acid trap and then lock it. He managed to get that done, also in record time.

Next, he rushed down the corridor which would put him a step ahead of the rapidly approaching gang members as they scoured every inch of the school. He also said a quick silent prayer to himself that they would assume the lab was unoccupied when they found the door locked and leave it alone.

It was unfortunate how often Alan's prayers went unanswered, however.

Chapter 16: Alan vs. Tony

By now, the police had arrived on the scene, where they were quickly engaged by the contingent of New York Boys who were surrounding the front and back entrance of the school. Their goal was to at least to give the interior force a chance to fully take the building and secure hostages before a SWAT team was deployed. Among the officers to respond was a now-recovered-from-their-injuries Darius McCain and the Amazon-like Ella Farrell, both of whom were dealing with the back entrance to the building in the schoolyard. Standing alongside them was rookie Officer Don Cohen.

The three law enforcers stood among a small troop of fellow police who hid behind their cars while exchanging gunfire with the gang members who either brazenly stood in the open schoolyard or hid behind corners of the building while shooting.

"Ella, I'm going in," Darius told his uber-tall and powerfully built fellow officer. "I want you and Don to follow me and back me up."

"Seriously, Darius?" Ella replied. "There's more punks in that schoolyard than flies on a hunk of dog shit!"

"Then we cut through the bastards!" was Darius's response. "The crew behind us can provide the cover we need. If the gang is doing something this big, then it's possible the leader will be there. And even if he isn't, I'm betting this attracts Moonstalker. He made an appearance at the Perry Projects this week, so he's recovered from the beating he took at the East Side Inferno months ago!"

"Darius, he's never been known to appear in the daytime before," Don reminded him. "It's just a few hours after sunrise now."

"I know," Darius said, "but I'm guessing something this big will likely cause him to make an exception to his nocturnal ways. So, we're going in. Or at least I am. Follow or don't, it's your choice."

Darius began rushing towards the back entrance to the school, firing and hitting two gangbangers guarding that entrance in the process.

Don turned to Ella. "Well? You've got the seniority now. What do you say we do?"

Ella thought for just a second before answering. "Our orders are to get past those punks and enter the school as soon as possible, preferably before they can get a hostage situation fully set up. So, I say that as reckless as Darius is, he still has the right idea. Let's go!"

Ella and Don then followed their headstrong fellow officer into the melee. The police hiding behind their cars quickly intensified their gunfire to cover the three officers rushing directly into the siege, trying to provide a pathway for them.

Despite the seeming odds, Darius managed to reach the door while the two officers following him, along with his fellow officers behind their vehicles, provided sufficient cover. Any gangbanger who turned and attempted to shoot Darius down were themselves taken down, either by Ella, Don, or the officers sequestered behind their cars. The gang members realized they needed to keep the larger number of police behind the vehicles at bay, so they had to trust their comrades within the school to be able to handle a mere trio of law-mongers.

Darius blasted one last gang member guarding the door, sending a lead projectile clear through his gut and out the small of his back. He leapt over the expanding puddle of blood pouring out of the young criminal's now opened lower abdomen and pointed his firearm at the door. Since the officer knew it would be padlocked, he fired three shots to blast the deadbolt to pieces, after which he sent the door flying open with a single strong kick.

"Darius, wait up, dude!" thundered Ella's voice from behind him.

Darius took a quick second to check and saw that Ella and Don had indeed followed him. He held the door for them as they fired off a few more shots to fend off any gang members who may have tried to take them out, just as their fellow officers behind the cars continued to do the same. The two ran inside the school behind Darius with their Glocks positioned for fire.

It was then that Puma leapt out from a corridor down the hallway with his Uzi pointed at the three officers.

"Die, pigs!" he shouted as he depressed the trigger and sprayed the interior of the front entrance with hot lead.

"Shit! Get out of Dodge!" Don hollered as the triad of officers fell to the floor to evade the fusillade of bullets.

The trio clung to the floor as the deadly lead salvo put numerous holes in the walls and door. The projectiles shattered the glass-covered portraits of previous graduating classes, along with the casing where a prestigious sports trophy acquired in days long past had been proudly displayed. The officers waited a few seconds for the staccato barrage to end, after which they could see the Uzi had overheated.

"Aw, c'mon!" Puma yelled in frustration while slapping the gun.

Ella then jumped to her feet and let off a shot, hitting the spike-haired gangbanger just to the right of his groin area. The perforated thug released a loud but brief scream and fell to the ground as a torrent of blood spewed from the gaping hole in his lower body.

"Whoa! Good shot, Farrell!" Don said as he stood up again.

By that time, Darius was also on his feet. "Don't congratulate anyone yet, Cohen. We still can't be sure…"

Before Darius could finish the sentence, his face and upper torso were spattered with Officer Don Cohen's blood and brain matter as a bullet penetrated the temple of his fellow law enforcer. The latter opened his mouth and let out what sounded like a light gasp followed by an oral expulsion of blood before his now lifeless body collapsed to the hard floor.

Darius's well-trained reflexes caused him to turn and fire a shot in the direction the lethal bullet came from without requiring a single thought. His volley found its mark on a hugely obese gang member who was hidden behind a nearby corridor to also guard the door. It hit the big man in the stomach, and the impact knocked the felon back into the wall a few inches behind him.

However, this rotund criminal was clearly made of seriously stern stuff, as he still managed to keep his grip on his .22. He forced himself to raising his firearm again, but couldn't do so quicker than Darius.

Unfortunately, all Darius's gun did was emit a hollow clicking sound. It was out of ammo.

"Shit!"

Ella quickly raised her own firearm, but it released a similar noise.

"Darius, I'm out too!"

Officer Darius McCain dropped his Glock and swiftly unsheathed his nightstick. Raising it above his head he hurled it as quickly and as hard as he could at the gaping wound of the uber-portly gangbanger. It struck the bloody abdominal hole head-on, causing the gang member to yelp in pain and drop his gun.

Darius then ran towards his opponent and kicked him as hard as he could in the face, smashing his septum into a glob of twisted gristle. Without wasting a second the officer recovered his nightstick and bashed the gang member over the head twice, splitting his skull and knocking him out. He then grabbed the fat man's .22 and checked its chamber.

"Son of a bitch," Darius griped. "This cheap .22 broke after the first shot. All that trouble for nothing. I'm totally out of ammo, and this thug's piece is now useless."

Ella stood above the bleeding body of her fallen comrade. "Cohen is dead, Darius. He's dead."

"I know, but we have to hold it together and get these bastards, Farrell. We can mourn Donny later, and acknowledge how he died doing his job. But for now, we need to clean this school of the rest of those scum."

"How, Darius? We're both completely out of ammo."

"We use our nightsticks. It's that simple."

"Won't the rest of them have guns?"

"That's not the typical M.O. of a gang in these situations. Most of them with guns are outside guarding the front and back of the building to keep as many cops out of here as possible. That way the inside crew can secure hostages and gain the upper hand before a SWAT team is on the scene. This pair with firearms were likely the only two they spared to guard the inside of the back entrance. There may be two more armed goons at the front entrance, though."

Ella looked at the fallen body of Don Cohen once more, and she shut her eyes tightly. The tall woman then unsheathed her own nightstick, and her countenance took on a determined expression.

"Let's go get those mothers."

***

Alan Perez used his superlative stealth training in tandem with his intimate knowledge of the school building to evade any roaming gang members as he sought a place to change into his Moonstalker uniform. The costume was hidden in his duffel bag, which was around his arm.

He was sitting on a ledge above a top flight of stairs, preparing to change, until he heard some voices approaching, one of which was quite familiar. Luck finally seemed on his side as Tony Kirkland and his two bodyguards Phil and Joshua walked by the stairway, not spotting the well-hidden Alan.

"Perez and Shanice are somewhere in the school," the concealed Alan heard Tony say. "We need to find them. They're probably hiding somewhere. When we locate them, you two hold Shanice while I take care of that half-spic ass-rammer."

Alan gritted his teeth in abject rage. He found himself torn between changing into his Moonstalker garb right away or sneaking down and dealing with Tony in his civilian identity, the latter of which felt much more satisfying to his ego.

"After you're done taking care of Perez," Joshua asked, "you'll let us get a piece of the girl after you get first dibs, right, man?"

Tony hit his guard in the stomach, a mighty blow that sent him sprawling back against the wall. "Hell no! She's mine! Mine! You don't touch her! Is that clear, you gangly little bitch?"

Joshua was utterly terrified at the unbridled fury he saw coursing through his superior officer's eyes. "Okay, okay, man, I'm sorry I asked. She's yours, I get it."

Tony forced himself not to wade into his guard any further and took several deep breathes before the look of murderous rage on his face subsided.

"Apology… accepted. Now get up and help me look for them."

"Yeah, okay, Boss," Joshua nervously said while he held his stomach and struggled back to his feet.

As the trio began moving down the corridor where the art center was located, they all turned around as they heard the door to the main art room open behind them. Alan Perez stepped out rather nonchalantly.

"Are you by any chance looking for me, Tony?" he asked.

The expression of fuming fury appeared on Tony's face once more, and both Phil and Joshua instinctually took a step backwards.

"Perez!"

"Good recognition skills, Kirkland. So, do you need your two fellow punks to help you? Or are you man enough to take me on yourself?"

"Boss…?" Phil began querying.

"Both of you search the hall for the girl," the ego-challenged Tony responded. "I'll deal with this prick."

With that order given, Tony's guards turned and resumed the search for Shanice as Alan stepped back into the art room. Tony followed him in.

"I've been waiting for this moment," the right hand of the New York Boys said as he clenched his fists and prepared to thrash his rival into oblivion.

"You're not the only one," Alan replied.

Tony rushed forward with a shriek of rage, only to find himself driven back against a paint canvas courtesy of a side kick to the sternum that was delivered faster than he could react. The canvas was too light to support the impact of the gang member, and the two went crashing down together. In the process, Tony's jacket was doused with several colors of oil-based paint.

"It looks like your jacket is no longer regulation," Alan said. "From this moment you can belong to any number of different gangs, since you're wearing *all* their colors now."

Tony howled in anger once more and jumped back to his feet in an instant. Alan couldn't help being impressed by his recovery speed, so he made a point not to underestimate his adversary despite how much fun he wanted to have with this donnybrook.

The second-in-command of Buffalo's toughest street gang threw several fast punches at his opponent, all intended to ruin his handsome face. But Alan expertly blocked each of them and retaliated with a reverse punch to Tony's throat. The gangbanger gagged and put his hands over his neck. After that, Alan spun around to deliver a roundhouse kick to the side of his face, a blow that sent his foe smashing through a second canvas held up by four wooden legs. This time, before Tony could recover, Alan ran over to him and dropped a hammer fist to his temple, causing him to completely lose consciousness.

"Like shooting fish in a barrel, only easier," Alan said as he wiped flecks of paint off his hands with a rag he found on a nearby table.

Just after that moment he heard Phil's voice yell outside the door, "Boss? Tony? Are you okay? Are you done with him yet?"

Upon hearing that, Alan dropped to the floor and quickly rolled behind the table where he had hidden his duffel bag. He quickly unzipped it, located his costume, and utilized the fruits of his constant practicing as he donned his Moonstalker raiment over the light clothing he wore within seconds.

Phil walked into the main art room, with Joshua close behind him. "Tony, the girl isn't anywhere on this floor. Did you finish off Perez...?"

Phil's mouth froze as he and Joshua beheld the unconscious body of their boss, covered in paint and bleeding out the nose.

"No way..." was all Joshua managed to utter before he was struck in the side of his head by one of Moonstalker's hard plastic batons. His mouth remained gaping but silent as the sudden concussion silenced his voice and sent him falling to the floor in short order.

"What the hell?" Phil exclaimed as the coal-garbed vigilante extended the razor-sharp nylon kama blade concealed within the baton, and with a single swift movement sliced him directly over his eyes.

The gang member cried in agony as streams of salt-saturated blood poured into his eyes, causing him to cover them with his hands in attempt to alleviate the stinging pain. Moonstalker then side-kicked his blinded adversary in the diaphragm, which sent him hurtling back several feet. Phil's skull cracked when his flight was halted by the lab's sink, and he slid to the floor unconscious.

"More fish in a barrel," Moonstalker said to himself as he retracted the kama blade with another twist of his arm.

***

Tony Kirkland returned to consciousness roughly fifteen minutes after he was sent to the realm of dreams by Alan Perez. The dreams he had during that brief interval of unconsciousness were neither pleasant nor flattering, to say the least.

The fallen right hand of the New York Boys forced his aching body to a standing position and felt around his chest area for broken or cracked ribs. One was clearly broken, with possibly two others cracked considering the biting pain he felt when he pressed his fingers into them. The young street tough then rolled his tongue around his mouth, checking for broken or loosened teeth. He found two that were knocked loose, likely by that brutal round house kick he received.

How in the hell could Perez fight like that? He seemed like a total wuss to me! I heard rumors he trained at a martial arts school, but I thought that stuff was all bullshit. Well, I won't be caught off-guard next time.

Tony then utilized his formidable resilience to summon the strength to walk towards the door leading out of the main art room, determined to find Alan and deliver an expensive amount of payback. He was still a bit frazzled as he approached the door, and thus barely seemed to notice the still unconscious bodies of Phil and Joshua strewn about the room not far from the exit.

As Tony stepped out the door, however, he was suddenly grasped by a single hand of enormous size, one that squeezed his esophagus with a grip like a vice. When he saw the arm it was attached to, he noticed it was bristling with muscle and decorated with several tattoos, including a skull & crossbones and a tiny emblem of New York City. Tony began choking copiously as the person whom that massive arm belonged to lifted him into the air with little noticeable effort.

"I trusted you as my right hand, and what do you do?" came a deep, horribly familiar voice with a hint of a Spanish accent. "You started thinking you owned the New York Boys. And you go and do this, you *idiota*."

"Assailant," Tony barely managed to articulate through his closed throat.

"I'm pleased you still recognize the boss you betrayed, Kirkland. You thought you would become a bigger man than me by doing this, didn't you? But there is no one and no thing bigger than me in this city. Not you, not the chief of police, not that vigilante… no one!"

Assailant then hurled his failed right hand man towards the wall on the opposite end of the corridor. Tony hit with such force that the plaster was smashed off the surface in a five-foot circumference that ironically and comically resembled a flash wave often used in comic books to suggest the impact of a punch. The displaced second-in-command hardly found it humorous, however, nor did he even notice the shape his body made in the shattered wall plaster; he simply felt his two cracked ribs break completely, and the one already fractured being pushed out of place to puncture a lung. He coughed up a chunk of blood and some other, more disgusting-looking substance he couldn't identify as he hit the floor.

The last thing Tony Kirkland saw before again losing consciousness a few seconds later was the somewhat blurred image of the Assailant approaching him with both fists clenched. It was merciful that he wasn't conscious for what came next.

Chapter 17: Moonstalker vs. Assailant

A group of six gang members were dragging the beaten form of social studies teacher Malev Johnson across the floor, towards an area they had placed the similarly beaten music teacher Donna Fitzsimmons, woodshop teacher Darryl Larson, and custodian Frank Kennedy. The other three school employees were laying half-conscious and bleeding in the same corner of the music room, right underneath the 40-year-old piano that every student dreaded hearing Mrs. Fitzsimmons play.

As the school invaders dragged the brutalized form of the man the students knew as Mr. Johnson to the door one of the gangbangers suddenly bellowed in pain when a ceramic shuriken embedded itself in the right side of his face.

"What in the hell?" a lanky young gang member with purple-tinted hair said as he looked in the direction of the side corridor where the shuriken was hurled from. He turned just in time to see the tip of a gray baton as it smashed into the bridge of his nose. His cartilage was crushed like a crumpled piece of paper, and the blow sent him sprawling to the floor. The ruffian lost consciousness while soaking in a pool of his own blood.

"Geezus hell! It's the vigilante dude!" one of the four remaining gang members screamed down the hallway, knowing that others in his invasion crew located just around the next corridor would hear and run to assist.

Moonstalker wanted to take these remaining four out before the reinforcements would arrive a few moments later. Remembering his vow to use his full arsenal this time, the gray-garbed vigilante hurled one of his marble-sized darkout bombs at the floor. The thin but sturdy plastic capsule broke upon impact and released a surprisingly fast-growing cloud of black billowy mist that quickly enveloped the immediate area.

The four gang members still standing were confused and unable to see through the unexpected cloud of smoke, which surrounded them and their immediate vicinity much too fast for them to react to. Unlike this hapless quartet, Moonstalker could see their outlines quite well, however, courtesy of his developed night vision. He then proceeded to dive into the cloud with both of his batons at the ready.

All that could be heard outside the billowy blog of blackness was the sound of crunching bone and screams of agony as the vigilante quickly smashed select body parts on three of his opponents, sending them to the ground with injuries just grievous enough to effectively remove them from the fight.

As for the remaining adversary, he was hollering and blindly slashing a stiletto amidst the darkness of the cloud to no avail while Moonstalker dropped to the floor and knocked him off his feet with a fast leg sweep. The young man hit the floor on his back quite hard, and the impact forced the wind out of his lungs. The coal-attired crime fighter then followed up the move with an elbow strike to the throat of his foe, causing him to lose consciousness from the pain of a severely bruised trachea.

Moonstalker jumped to his feet just as the dark cloud of concentrated ash and soot finally expired and wafted out of existence. By that time, he saw a group of five other gang members rushing towards him from one direction, while seven others ran towards him equally fast from the opposite corridor. Each of them held blades or metal truncheons, and he knew that even he would be hard pressed to handle this many armed opponents without the cover of darkness and emerge completely unscathed. He absolutely refused to make another rookie mistake like the one he made months ago at the East Side Inferno.

The vigilante decided to continue utilizing his arsenal to the fullest. To that end he quickly grabbed a marble-sized nitro-pellet from a hidden and padded pocket. He hurled the pellet towards the wall just to the side of the seven-strong group of gangbangers to his left. The expertly and carefully constructed pellet released a small but potent explosion upon impact with the wall, the force of which caught the advancing group directly.

The blast wave shattered their ear drums, while the plaster blown off the wall acted as scraps of mini-shrapnel that penetrated major portions of their exposed skin. Each of them fell to the ground bleeding profusely from the ears and several points on their faces and extremities where bits of plaster shrapnel had penetrated. None of them would be fighting again this day.

As the five-strong group from the opposite corridor was almost upon him, Moonstalker surprised them by hurling another darkout bomb at the floor in front of him. Once again, the casing broke upon impact and released another billowy cloud of darkened ash that quickly surrounded the attacking gangbangers. Two of them stabbed each other while lunging about blindly in the darkened cloud, thereby partially doing the vigilante's job for him.

The urban avenger quickly waded into the cloud while wielding a single baton, the other having been returned to its sheath in his pant leg. With a swift two-part move the gray-attired vigilante smashed the skull of one of his opponents with the bludgeon just before spinning around and striking the other in the Adam's apple. Needless to say, both were permanently expiated from the invasion force.

Within moments, the dark cloud dissipated, and the remaining gang member found himself facing the fearsome-looking figure of Moonstalker. The crime fighter looked like a demon of the night in his distinct ninja-like garb, and this despite his standing close to windows which exposed him to broad daylight.

"Oh, Jesus! Please don't hurt me, man!" the young gang member pleaded. "I surrender, okay?"

"Request not granted," Moonstalker replied before delivering a palm heel strike to his enemy's nose that split the cartilage between each nostril.

A geyser of blood erupted from the gangbanger's nasal openings as his body hit the ground. Suffice it to say, he didn't rise again.

Moonstalker then turned and ran down a flight of stairs leading to the first floor, towards a huge ruckus he heard taking place there. Whatever may have been going on down there was someplace he figured that he needed to be.

***

After Moonstalker descended the final flight of stairs, he turned to see Officers Darius McCain and Ella Farrell fiercely and bravely fighting a large group of gangbangers. There were clearly too many for the two lawmen to overcome. Nevertheless, they were holding their own, effectively thrashing several of their opposition with nothing more than a combo of their nightsticks, training, and sheer determination.

Before the officers could be completely overwhelmed by the numbers, a charcoal-clad figure suddenly leapt through the air and broke a gang member's jaw with a flying kick to the lower chin. The vigilante then quickly unsheathed his twin batons, extended the kama blades with a quick twist of his wrists, and dropped to his knees while simultaneously shoving a blade into the foot of two different gangbangers. As the pair dropped their weapons and screamed upon their feet being skewered, Moonstalker swiftly stood up and smashed his elbows into each of their noses, sending them both down for the count.

The two beleaguered police officers were quick to notice this additional presence in their midst.

"Is this brawl taken, or can I join in too?" Moonstalker said.

"Him!" Darius exclaimed. "I knew it! After we deal with these punks, I'm taking you down too!"

"You better keep your attention focused on 'those punks' in the meantime," the vigilante warned the officer after one of the gang members delivered a punch to the lawman's stomach that sent him keeling over.

Ella was quick to respond to her fellow officer's plight, and she grabbed the much shorter gang member by the throat and hurled him up against the wall. Two others then tackled her, only to find the extremely tall woman a force to be reckoned with. She struck one of them on the shoulder repeatedly with her elbow, which quickly forced him to his knees; the other she divested of consciousness by smashing him over the head with her nightstick. The powerful policewoman then turned and kicked the other in the lower jaw, a blow which sent him sprawling across the floor with several broken teeth evacuating his mouth.

Unfortunately, too many gang members remained in the melee. One of them managed to slash Ella across the back with a switch blade, a move which tore through both her uniform and her skin.

The gangbanger then lifted the blade and prepared to bring it down directly into Ella's spine. However, Darius had recovered by then and he struck the gangbanger between the neck and shoulder with his nightstick before the criminal could carry out the intended move. That blow cracked the young malcontent's collarbone, and the sudden intense pain caused him to lose consciousness.

Darius ran to Ella's side to tend her wounds while Moonstalker somersaulted between the two police officers to stand as a buffer between them and the advancing crowd of New York Boys. The vigilante threw another darkout bomb to the floor, and he and the crowd of gang members quickly disappeared within a billowy dark cloud.

"Farrell, are you okay?" Darius asked his partner.

"That bastard cut me good, but I'm not out of this fight," Ella answered. "Let's get 'em!"

"There's still too many of them, and now we got that vigilante to contend with on top of it all. I have no idea how long it'll be until a SWAT team arrives to plow through that armed crowd outside."

In the time it took for that exchange, the billowy cloud of darkness dissipated to reveal Moonstalker standing above a mass of seriously beaten gang members. He retracted the curved blades in his batons and slipped them back in his pant sheathes.

"That guy is a one-man mosh pit," Ella remarked.

Darius raised his nightstick again. "Alright, vigilante, you may have saved our lives, but that changes nothing. What you do is just as bad as what that gang does, and I'm going to take you in."

"Is he always this stubborn?" Moonstalker asked Ella. "He's starting to remind me of myself."

"He may be stubborn, but he believes in the law," Ella replied. "Which is why I believe in him."

Suddenly, another group of gangbangers emerged from a corridor to their left, while several more emerged from the right. The three found themselves surrounded again.

"Don't you think you should hold off on arresting me just for a minute longer, McCain?" the vigilante said.

"He's right, Darius," Ella said quietly.

"For now," the irate young officer agreed. He raised his nightstick and pointed it at the twin groups of gang members. "All right, what are you waiting for, assholes? Bring it!"

As the larger group from the left began charging forward, Moonstalker hurled a nitro-pellet in their direction while they were still far enough away for him to risk it. It exploded upon hitting the floor a foot in front of them, and the blast wave shredded both clothing and flesh as it knocked every single one of them off their feet while simultaneously popping their eardrums.

"Jesus, this guy is using explosives now?" Darius said rhetorically.

Moonstalker then hurled shurikens at two opponents charging from the right, striking each in the face and sending them to the ground. The urban crusader wasted not a fraction of a second on dealing with the remainder of the smaller second group as he turned around and side-kicked a particularly heavy gangbanger into two others running directly behind him, a move which sent all three of them to the floor. That made them easy pickings for a follow-up attack by Darius and Ella, whose nightsticks quickly delivered several skull-smashing blows.

Just as the remainder of the group from the right was almost upon them, a window was smashed open on the ground floor. Emerging through the makeshift entrance was the quartet of Breaker, Fist of God, Princess Pummel, and Street Hawk.

"I hope y'all didn't think we were gonna stay on them sidelines and let you hog all the fun," Breaker said with a grin.

"Yea!" Princess concurred. "There's enough hurt to go around here, so you gotta share!"

"Sorry, Boss," Street Hawk said while pounding his fist into an open palm to signal his readiness to fight. "But they talked me into this. And I admit it didn't take much."

Before the vigilante, his erstwhile law enforcing allies, and the assemblage of gang members could get over their initial surprise, the building shook a bit as a loud explosion from what must have been several blocks away could be heard and felt.

154

"Oh, that enormous 'boom' would be Sky High blowing up the Mulberry Street safe house that the second-in-command of the New York Boys has been using," Street Hawk explained. "We figured, why the hell not?"

Though Moonstalker was irritated at his crew for not following his orders, he was admittedly glad to see them. So, he decided to only give them a *minor* punishment after this whole fracas was over (minor by *his* standards, at any rate).

"All of you, just shut up and fight!" the vigilante ordered.

"Don't gotta be tellin' me twice!" Breaker decreed as he raised his aluminum baseball bat and followed his fellows into the battle.

"You don't give us orders, vigilante," Darius stated in regard to himself and Ella.

"That's okay, since you have no choice but to listen this time anyway," Moonstalker said.

The gray-adorned warrior then back-flipped out of his crew's way as they entered the fight with all due prejudice. Moonstalker completely looked forward to the heads that were going to roll and the blood that would be spilled; he simply needed to make sure that none of the rolling heads and spilled blood belonged to anyone on his side of the battle.

***

"I wanna cut me some gangbangers," Princess Pummel announced.

The girl with the Gem Delgado face mask made good on that decree immediately after speaking it when she shoved ten razor-sharp metallic fingernails super-glued to all the fingers of a pair of leather gloves into the lower abdomen of the closest man in adversarial colors.

"I think I gave dude here a tummy ache," she said as she pulled the synthetic metal fingernails in opposite directions to tear a nasty but non-life-threatening hole in the man's gut. His pants and shoes were stained a dark crimson just before he fell to the floor.

The Fist of God then began firing bullets into the legs of the attacking gang members, sending three of them to the floor in rapid succession.

"You see I'm only shooting to injure now, until you help me get some modified firearms," the disguised priest said to his leader.

"Watch your back, man!" Breaker shouted as he smashed a chunk of skin from the head of a gangbanger who was an inch away from shoving a knife into the Fist's back and ending his holy crusade.

"Watch yours as well, my friend," the priest retorted as he turned and fired a bullet into the shoulder of another gang member who was a second away from striking Breaker over the head with a pipe.

"Give me that gun!" Darius commanded the Fist as the incognito clergyman pistol-whipped another gangbanger in the face.

"Sorry, Officer," the holy vigilante replied. "But it's *mine*."

Moonstalker saw that his team and their two ersatz allies were still greatly outnumbered, but it now occurred to him how he might change that within the next few moments. He ran into the office and grabbed a hand-held paging horn speaker where he knew it would be stashed. The vigilante then activated the device and projected his amplified voice throughout the hallways.

"To all the students in this school who've been confined in the rooms by the gang!" he said through the voice amplifying speaker. "This is Moonstalker speaking. Me, my crew, and two police officers are fighting for your lives, and we may need some help. I'm asking all of you to overcome your fear and join the battle! Stand up to the enemy!"

Just then, he saw a door down the hall kicked open. From it emerged the bullish form of football running back Nate Green.

"All right!" the massive young athlete yelled as he conducted a full field rush into a triumvirate of the closest gang members. He bowled the threesome over with ease, thus proving himself as fearsome a force in the hallway as he was out on the playing field.

Nate then jumped into the main fray, and he stood side-by-side with Street Hawk as they each pounded several gang members into oblivion with their powerful fists. The two lacked weapons, but every time a gangbanger turned to use a knife or pipe on them, the Fist of God put a bullet through a limb, Breaker smashed another pair of kneecaps with his bat, and Princess Pummel rushed in and slashed the muscles on another guy's extremities.

As other students furtively peeked out of the rooms they were confined to upon hearing Moonstalker's amplified appeal for aid, they saw that the vigilante and his crew were indeed present, as well as fellow student Nate Green joining the motley assemblage with equal courage. This inspired them enough to heed the crime buster's call and join the battle, a move that quickly began reversing the odds.

Several girl athletes leapt onto the backs of gang members, clawing and tearing at their eyes; while several of their male counterparts – many of whom held chairs or metallic rulers as improvised weapons -- waded into the invading criminals. One girl used the cigarette lighter she thickened her eyeliner with to start the pants of a gang member on fire from behind, while another girl smashed three teeth from a different gangbanger by slamming him in the face with her pocket mirror.

Even many of the less physically gifted students joined the battle, with one of them notably distracting a few of the gang members by spewing cold foam from a fire extinguisher into their faces. One particular geek of a boy put to use a bottle of cooking oil taken from the cafeteria he had been confined to by squirting it into the eyes of two gang members, thereby blinding them.

The anger each of these students felt over their school being violated by the gang in this manner was unleashed in full, and they fought with a viciousness that almost startled the vigilantes and cops fighting alongside them. The gang members began falling in large numbers before the very unexpected mass attack of these formerly captive students. Of the almost fifty former captives, more kept continuously joining in as those who entered the battle before them provided the necessary inspiration and incentive.

Moonstalker was so confident these added numbers would help turn the tide that he decided to head back up a few floors to get Shanice out of the building. He ran up several flights of stairs faster than any track or cross-country runner could ever hope to, all the while praying to God that none of the gang members had successfully found and taken the girl he now realized meant so much to him.

***

As Moonstalker headed up towards the fourth floor, he evaded the remaining small groups of gang members who were still searching for hiding students and staff on the upper floors.

The ashen-attired vigilante quickly burst through the door that led towards the corridor where the science lab was located, and the hallway thankfully appeared vacant and silent. He allowed himself to relax a bit as he saw that he had only one more corridor to go before reaching the room where Shanice was (hopefully) still hiding.

That proved to be a costly decision as he was soon caught off-guard by an extremely fast haymaker that struck the side of his face with such force that it sent him flying into the wall, where he momentarily had the wind knocked out of him.

Moonstalker had to force himself not to black out, as he had no recollection of ever being hit so hard before, nor ever coming so close to being knocked out by a single punch. Whoever hit him was no ordinary gang member. *So, who the hell was it?* As the masked vigilante pushed himself to get back to his feet, he saw the huge, imposing figure of Assailant emerge from the doorway where he was hidden.

"So, we meet at last," the frightening gang leader said with a tenor of extreme anger.

"The leader of this silly gang, I presume?" Moonstalker replied, now having fully fought his way back to a standing position.

157

"The gang may be cast in ruin, but at least I'll get the satisfaction of crushing you before I leave to start over."

"You and what army? Oh, you mean the army that's downstairs getting their asses kicked by the same students they thought would be easy victims?"

The masked gang leader's anger was now beyond palpable. "I'll break you in two."

Assailant then charged at Moonstalker to make good on his threat. The coal-garbed crime fighter was swift to respond with a side kick to the gut, followed by a spinning kick to the jawbone, both struck with great force. The mighty gang leader astounded the vigilante by shaking off both blows and remaining on his feet. He then defiantly spit a small wad of blood on the floor.

"Is that the best you can do, *perdedor*?"

"I'm just getting started."

Moonstalker threw a fast reverse punch to the bridge of Assailant's nose, the force of which knocked his opponent back a few steps and caused two streams of blood to rush from his nostrils. But still he remained standing, appearing none the worse for wear as he laughed condescendingly.

The vigilante had had enough of this, and he launched another spinning kick at his adversary. This time, however, the masked gang leader caught his leg in one of his enormous hands before it could connect. He then displayed his incredible strength by swinging the off-balance Moonstalker through the air and slamming him hard into a nearby wall. The coal-clad warrior found himself sufficiently stunned that he was unable to resist being swung and slammed a second time against the opposite wall. The ninja-esque crime fighter could swear he felt a shoulder get dislocated upon that second slam.

Assailant continued his pompous laugh as he pulled a six-inch combat knife from his boot and raised it in anticipation of slicing off the limbs of his opponent. Moonstalker recovered just quickly enough to unsheathe one of his batons and slam his enemy in the shin with it. Assailant grumbled in pain but didn't waver. His grumble quickly became a growl of rage as he brought the blade down, thrusting it clear through Moonstalker's right hand and pinning it to the floor. That time the vigilante failed to stifle a scream of agony.

However, the urban defender refused to give up despite his obviously facing the toughest opponent of his life. He extended the curved blade of his baton with a flick of his free wrist and swung the kama so it perforated the muscle on Assailant's right leg directly behind the knee. This attack caused the much larger man to lose his footing and fall to one knee.

Moonstalker then used his free hand to swing the kama at his opponent's face, slicing through the top of his mask and the flesh above his left eye. This proven tactic caused blood to pour down into the sensitive organ and initiate that all too-familiar stinging pain and occlusion of vision.

As Assailant was distracted by the blood in his eye, Moonstalker reached over with his good hand and pulled the combat knife out of the other, thereby freeing his limb from where it was trapped. Before he could use it against its owner, however, the gang leader had already recovered, and he kicked the vigilante in the face, sending him sliding over a yard across the floor.

Moonstalker again found himself struggling to resist losing consciousness, a battle he quickly lost this time due to the combined injuries of a gaping hole in his palm, a wrenched shoulder, and a cracked jawbone.

Assailant used his own exceedingly strong will to force himself to locate and retrieve his dropped combat knife. He then began moving towards the limp form of his vigilante adversary.

"I'm going to open your guts and strangle you with your own intestines," the gang leader promised.

Moonstalker's reaction was no reaction at all as his opponent approached him with the business end of the gleaming blade just inches away from its ghastly goal of disembowelment.

Chapter 18: School is a Battlefield

As Assailant struggled to eviscerate Moonstalker, he realized his blade's cutting power was obstructed by a type of protective mesh in the suit. The powerful gang leader therefore redoubled his efforts, and the blade began making progress, finally reaching and penetrating the flesh of the vigilante's lower abdomen. Blood began to flow freely, with vulnerable organs mere inches from the tip of the razor-sharp blade.

***

Shanice Morris began growing stir crazy as she remained under the science lab table in accordance with Alan's insistence that she not move until he came for her. Other than the occasional sound of footsteps running through the outside corridor with voices accompanying them -- all too muffled by the closed door to possibly identify them -- things remained silent.

The young woman nevertheless found her situation petrifying, and she remained concerned that her incessant shaking would cause her to spill the corrosive acid contained within the flask she held on the skin of her hand. To prevent this, she set the container down on the floor next to her, being careful not to accidentally knock it over and spill its contents. Even though she prayed there would be no need to use it, she still didn't want to take the chance of being without it.

Geez, I should have asked Alan what to do if I had to use the bathroom. I really need to go, and I can't hold it any longer. What should I do? He told me not to get out from under this table for any reason. But it's totally quiet out there and has been for like almost a half hour straight now. What the hell is going on out there? Is it all over? Why hasn't Alan come back? Damn it, I can't hold it any longer, and I hope he doesn't expect me to just go in my pants. I'm not gonna do that even under these circumstances!

Since there was no access to a rest room in the lab, the young woman realized she had to opt for another solution, as much as she hated to resort to it. *C'mon, girl, it's not like anyone will see you, and I would hear it if someone tried to pound open the door.* Shanice quickly crawled out from under the table and climbed atop the basin of the lab sink, which was part of the room's front desk. She dropped her pants, squatted over the basin, and relieved herself. After pulling her pants back up she turned on the water and washed all traces of the urine down the drain.

Unfortunately, she picked the wrong time to do that. Seconds after she closed the faucet the young woman's ears picked up a gruff, unfamiliar male voice outside the door.

"Yo, man, I just heard the water turned on in that room," it said.

Shanice was mortified. *Shit! Oh no...*

"You're hearing things, dude," another voice responded. "Come on, let's go."
Yes!

"No, I swear I heard the faucet being turned on. I'm tellin' you, someone's in there."

No...

"Maybe we should check it out, Finney," came a third voice. "Len has no rep for hearing things."

Shanice heard a distinct pushing on the door.

"It's still locked!" noted the third voice.

"Then Len couldn't have really heard anything in there, right?" a fourth voice opined.

My god, how many of them are out there? Oh god...

"We need to be sure, Derrick," replied the third voice. "Saul, you help me push this door open."

"I got you," said Saul.

Shanice crawled back under the table as quietly as she could, and she grasped the flask full of acid as if it was the most precious thing she had ever held. She tried forcing herself not to shake so much that she spilled the corrosive fluid on herself, which would cause her to scream in pain. Her stomach began cramping, and she did her best to ignore the growing aches and swirling sensation of hyperactive gastric acid.

The endangered young woman couldn't help crying as all four gangbangers started smashing their shoulders against the door. The slamming reverberations seemed to coincide with the equally loud beats of the girl's heart as her central circulatory muscle felt as if it would burst through her rib cage. She continually wiped the tears from her eyes to prevent them from obscuring her vision while trying to carefully hold the flask with her other hand.

Her gastric acid seemed on the verge of burning a hole through her stomach lining as she noticed the lock on the door beginning to give way under the relentless efforts of the thuggish quartet.

***

On the first floor, another quartet – these on the opposite camp to the New York Boys – continued to stand beside the nightstick-wielding police officers Darius McCain and Ella Farrell against a large number of attacking gang members. Both groups likely wouldn't have lasted this long if not for Moonstalker having rallied the formerly captive student body into joining the fight.

Street Hawk sent one of the gangbangers sailing into a drinking fountain with a single well-placed haymaker to the jaw. "Keep on fighting, don't give ground!" he shouted.

Breaker ignored his split lip and a bruised rib as he cold-cocked another opponent across the side of the face with his aluminum bat. "Problem is they ain't about to give no ground either!"

Darius and Ella continued smacking aside one gang member after another with their nightsticks. The former sent two incisors flying from the mouth of one of his attackers with a single blow; the latter again took advantage of her impressive size by smashing her baton directly atop the skull of another, a blow that fractured the bone along the young criminal's crown in a neat zig-zag pattern between the skin.

"It would be nice if the SWAT team would get here!" she opined aloud.

"It would be nice if we got a raise sometime soon too," Darius spat in reply as he continued striking and parrying with his weapon. "But that isn't gonna happen either. So, we have to make do."

Darius suddenly felt his airway painfully cut off when a gangbanger came up behind him and wrapped a metal chain around his throat. As the lawman struggled to break free, Ella noticed his plight and began moving to assist him. That plan was thwarted, however, when two gang members rushed and grabbed her in tandem. She struck at both furiously but realized she wouldn't get free in time to prevent her fellow officer from having his windpipe broken.

Darius suddenly felt the choking grip grow lax due to his attacker being smashed on the head by Breaker's bat. The law enforcer threw the chain to the ground and coughed several times to clear his throat, thankful his windpipe and larynx were both still intact.

"Gotta look out for each other," Breaker said to the officer as he turned and continued warding off another gang member with several swings of his bat.

Darius retrieved his nightstick and prepared to assist Ella, only to see her body slam one of the gang members who jumped her onto the hard floor. The other who attacked her was already laying on the ground unconscious with blood pouring from his mouth and nostrils.

"Are you okay, McCain?" she asked him.

"My throat is sore, but otherwise, yeah," he replied. "That... vigilante with the bat bailed me out."

"It looks like we can return the favor now," Ella noted while she turned and ran several feet to her left.

It seemed Princess Pummel was gradually being overwhelmed by five gang members who surrounded her, all punching and kicking at her mercilessly. One of them suddenly shouted and grabbed his stomach, and blood began streaming through his closed fingers in what looked like gallons. He had clearly run afoul of the girl's metal fingernails. The other four continued their onslaught, however, and she was only able to inflict superficial cuts on them due to the unremitting nature of their attack.

Ella pulled one of them off the vigilante girl, lifted him off his feet, and slammed his skull against a locker door. The metal indented in the shape of the criminal's head along being smeared with a large splotch of his blood as he fell to the floor with a severe cranial wound.

Darius took a cue from his previous attacker by grasping another by the throat from behind with his nightstick and dragging him off Princess Pummel. He squeezed as hard as he could, cutting off the young man's airway. The gangbanger coughed and choked with his tongue protruding from his mouth before passing out several seconds later.

This left one gang member who continued his attack on Princess. That assault also ended, however, as Street Hawk entered the fray and landed a bash to the side of the criminal's face that dislocated his jaw. A follow-up punch to the thug's diaphragm took him out of the fight completely.

The young crime fighter helped the bruised but still active young woman to her feet.

"Whoa, thanks, Hawker," she said through a smashed lip and cracked face mask.

"Thank them also," he said, pointing to Darius and Ella. "We owe you two, and it's appreciated."

"Let's just finish this clean-up so you can thank us on the way 'downtown'," Darius remarked curtly.

"Wow, that's cold," Princess said as she adjusted her broken Gem Delgado mask.

"No, it's just *true*," Darius corrected. "Now back to business!"

(Due to the intensity of the situation, no one seemed to notice that the Fist of God had vanished from the melee.)

***

Images of Shanice's pretty visage, the faces of his concerned parents, and Master Kai delivering important lessons about staying strong during the most trying of circumstances flashed through Moonstalker's psyche alongside a stinging sensation on his lower abdomen.

"Maintain your ground no matter the opposition, no matter the temptation to concede defeat," a floating image of the Master's weathered but authoritative face expounded, just as he did so often in the dojo through the years.

"Alan, please get up..." the teary-eyed apparition of Shanice's countenance pleaded.

"Remember who you are, and all that you stand for," Master Kai instructed. "Never give up! Always strike back!"

"Alan Garret Perez, don't you dare leave us!" Lenore Perez's image admonished her son. "Your father and I need you."

"Alan! Please..." the impassioned projection of Shanice continued.

"Do you hear me, young man?" Master Kai interjected as his image replaced that of Shanice's. "You are above defeat! We may go down from time to time, but defeat is only permanent if we refuse to get up again! Never allow that to occur!"

The coal-attired avenger's eyes flickered underneath his full-head ninja-like hood.

More of his abdominal flesh was torn as the Assailant continued to force his combat blade through the uniform's mesh. Though his adversary was gradually succeeding in the evisceration attempt, it was going too slow for one of his limited patience. Almost a minute had passed, and though he observed a good amount of blood, he still saw no hint of the bowel's distinct pinkish hue. So, he decided to change execution methods.

"As much as I wish I could expose your intestines to the air," the brutal gang leader said, "it seems it'll be much quicker to slit your throat instead."

With this alteration of plans, Assailant moved the blade to his unconscious enemy's neck. He touched the razor point of the knife to his trachea and prepared to slice the flesh open with one quick horizontal slash of the blade.

"Never accept defeat!" Master Kai's voice again echoed through the vigilante's mindscape as if through a psychic bullhorn.

In a sudden flash of movement Moonstalker slammed his gloved knuckles into Assailant's eyes. The mighty gang leader howled in shock and agony as he dropped his blade and recoiled from his enemy's body. The salty lachrymose that seeped out of his tear ducts stung the sensitive organs as if they were wind-blown sand particles.

Moonstalker then sprung up in a sitting position fully awake. *Thank you, Master Kai, for being with me even when you're not with me.*

The crime smasher ignored the biting pain emanating from the open wound on his stomach, his injured shoulder, and his aching jawbone as he sprung back to his feet into a prepared fighting stance. He quickly meditated on the symbol of the lotus flower, which represented strength of will and greatly aided in his ability to nullify sensitivity to pain.

"You were going to gut me!" Moonstalker said angrily.

"Like a goddamned fish," Assailant confirmed as his eyes finally cleared.

The vigilante focused his rage into action, beginning with a reverse punch to the bridge of his adversary's nose. That was the initial blow was immediately followed by a palm heel strike to the side of his jaw and culminated with a spinning kick to his lower neck. The finishing move of that combo sent the formidable gang leader back against a row of lockers.

Assailant gasped as some of the wind was knocked out of him, but quickly shook off the multi-move attack as if he were none the worse for wear. Only his still deeply reddened eyes and bleeding mouth displayed any sign of his being in a fight.

"Pathetic," he said just before spitting out a wad of blood.

Moonstalker responded to that jeer by attempting a roundhouse kick to the face, his strongest move. However, Assailant managed to block it with a quick motion of his arm. The vigilante quickly rebounded with a turning kick in the opposite direction that hit the gang leader in his plexus, forcing most of the remaining air out of his lungs. Taken by surprise, the big man keeled forward a bit, after which Moonstalker delivered an equally powerful sidekick to the right side of his jaw. That move sent the king of the streets off his feet and onto the hard floor.

A startled look was evident on Assailant's face even through his Luchadorian mask; this wasn't surprising, as he hadn't been knocked down in a fight since before he was twelve years of age. And that was by his father, not any fellow street tough.

Moonstalker sought to exploit his advantage by launching another side kick when Assailant was down, but the much larger man managed to trap the leg with both arms. The coal-clad vigilante made a swift mental note to never underestimate his opponent's reflexes again.

This vow may have come too late, however, since Assailant lifted his smaller adversary in the air by his grasped limb and bashed him against the same lockers the gang master was himself slammed up against a minute earlier.

The King of the Streets put an arm up against the vigilante's throat and attempted to break his windpipe with a few seconds of intense pressure, something he had done to others on several previous occasions.

While Moonstalker was unable to outmuscle his opponent, he nevertheless slapped Assailant's ears as hard as he could with each palm, sending waves of air into the canals and all but popping one of the delicate ear drums. The gang leader released his grtip and flew back against the wall on the opposite side of the corridor, bellowing in agony. Now it was his turn to make a mental note to never again underestimate the speed and resourceful skill of his enemy.

Moonstalker was determined to press his advantage while his opponent was reeling, and he could still block out most of the pain from his own injuries. To that end, he unleashed a lightning-fast combo of blows, striking him on each side of the jaw several times, followed by a thrusting side kick just below the left knee that resulted in a small fracture.

The coal-garbed vigilante then pooled every iota of energy he had left into a spinning roundhouse that impacted the side of Assailant's face and sent him flying back towards one of the windows lining the side of the corridor. His head and right arm went smashing through the glass, embedding several small shards in his face mask and bicep. The brutal master of the streets turned and coughed up a glob of bloody phlegm as he struggled to stay on his feet.

That's game! Moonstalker rushed towards his foe to deliver the finishing blow when Assailant dealt him a nasty surprise by quickly slashing at him with his blade, which he somehow managed to recover upon going down. The business end of the knife tore through the rip already made in the vigilante's uniform around the lower abdominal area, and greatly increased the size of the wound. The twilight-themed warrior backed up against the lockers while watching blood pour out of the huge gash.

Please please *let my intestines stay where they belong.*

The Assailant pushed himself back to his feet, ignoring the pain from the hairline fracture in his right leg. He forced himself past his dazed state to admire the handiwork he had just wrought against his foe, and he smiled yet again he saw his enemy's blood dripping from the tip of his blade.

"Time to finish what I started earlier, *gilipollas*," he said with a rancorous sneer.

Chapter 19: Casualties of War

Shanice managed to force herself not to have an anxiety attack as the lock on the lab door was finally smashed open by the four gangbangers who forcefully sought ingress.

"Yoo hoo?" Finney called out sarcastically.

"Chill, man," Saul said. "There's no one in here."

"I *know* I heard that faucet," Len insisted. "And look, it's dripping. Someone was just getting a drink or somethin'."

"It looks like this is the science lab," Derrick observed. "We need to check every inch of this place. Start looking."

Shanice began shaking so hard that she was seriously worried the corrosive would spill all over her hands. She was unable to help herself as the terror and anxiety mounted. *Please, oh please let them overlook this table. Please help me, God. Alan, where are you? You always know what to do.*

No sooner did those thoughts pass through her mind than Saul's pock-marked face was looking under the table and directly into her face.

"Hey!" He shouted. "There's a bitch under this ta…"

Saul never finished the words before the young woman splashed more than half the corrosive in the flask over his eyes and nose. Saul bellowed in unimaginable agony as the powerful acid rapidly ate off his eyelids, blinded him, and dissolved the skin around his nasal area. He was writhing about the floor screaming when his three comrades-in-crime ran to his side.

In the meantime, Shanice quickly scampered out of her hiding place, still holding the flask with a quarter of its fluid contents left under one arm.

"Jesus!" Derrick exclaimed upon running to his still-screaming comrade's side. "That bitch threw some shit on Saul and it's eating his face off!"

"There she goes! I got her!" Len hollered as he clutched the young woman's free arm in a very strong grip.

Shanice went into a form of mental remote control as panic took over her mental functions. She smashed the flask over Len's face just after he grabbed her. His right cheek and temple was severely burned by the remainder of the corrosive, and the broken decanter sent small shards of glass into one of his eyes. He fell to the ground to join Saul in uttering agonized wails.

The now unarmed girl ran towards the exit, but the highly athletic Derrick outpaced her and grasped her in a steely grip from behind. She struggled as hard as she could, but to no avail; the small young woman was no match for the tall, well-built gang member.

"I got her! I got her!" he called out.

Finney stepped over his blaring and quivering cohorts to brandish a switchblade. "Look what she did to Len and Saul! She threw some kinda acid or something on them! I'm gonna carve that bitch up!"

"Aw, c'mon, Finn," Derrick griped. "Do you gotta mess up such a nice piece of ass? Let's at least enjoy the spoils of war first."

"Don't worry, man," Finney assured his ally. "I'll make sure I don't cut up any of the important parts. At least not till after we're finished with them."

"You filthy pig!" Shanice shrieked while instinctively slamming her foot down on Derrick's right foot, a stomp that effectively fractured his big toe.

The much bigger gang member howled in pain and released his grip on her. The young woman then elbowed her captor in the diaphragm, causing him to fall back against the chalk board.

"You're dead meat, whore!" Finney yelled as he chased her around the front desk.

Shanice realized she wasn't likely to outrun this pursuer either, so she leapt for a Bunsen burner she saw sitting in the middle of the table. As always, the flame-producing device was conveniently plugged into the rubber tube leading to the gas nozzle designed to send a stream of flammable methane through it.

She managed to turn its needle valve sufficiently to manifest a roaring blue flame just as Finney slashed her right arm, tearing through her sweater sleeve and ripping into her skin. The girl yelped in pain, but she was determined not to let that override the adrenaline surging through her system.

Shanice ignored the agony searing across her arm to grab the now flaring Bunsen burner by the sides of its small heatproof coaster and thrust the blue flame into Finney's face. The intense heat instantly caused his entire nasal area to blister into a discolored patch of third degree burns. He joined his two mates on the floor as a writhing and wailing mass of pain.

Derrick, the final gang member in the lab, had by now recovered and charged at Shanice. The girl initially held him at bay by waving the flaming Bunsen burner around at him. The sporty young gangbanger managed to kick the device out of her hand, however. He then grabbed her by the hair, pulled her head down, and punched her in the back of the neck. Shanice fell directly to the tiled floor, and Derrick quickly stomped on her back as hard as he could, taking much of the fight out of her.

"I'm gonna burn all your hair off!" he exclaimed as he kneeled down and recovered the still flaming Bunsen burner by its attached heat proof coaster.

As Derrick began moving the flaming nozzle towards her ebony locks to make good on his ghastly threat, Shanice noticed Finney's switchblade on the floor a few inches from her. The girl's actions were again governed by a state of panic as she grabbed the blade and stabbed her attacker in the area right underneath his groin. The sudden terrible wound sent him sprawling and screaming to the floor alongside his three friends. None of them would be continuing their malign pursuit of Shanice.

The battered and panic-stricken girl then fled from the laboratory with the bloody switchblade still in hand. She turned to the left of the corridor only to find herself confronted by two other gang members.

"Well, what have we here?" one of them said with a smirk of delight.

"Stay away from me or I'll kill you!" she screeched at the top of her lungs while swiping the blade in their direction to show she meant business.

"You ain't the only one with a blade, bitch," the second gang member said as both of them produced knives of their own, making it clear she was "outgunned."

Shanice turned to run down the opposite corridor, where she found herself face-to-face with a third gangbanger. He held a lead pipe in his hand, which he repeatedly slapped against his hand in a show of impending force.

"Looks like it's the end of the line, girl," the burly young man said.

"I believe that situation is reserved for *you*, vile sinner," a fourth voice decreed from behind the two gang members to the left.

That admonition was followed by the sound of two gun shots. A bloody hole appeared in the lower leg of one of the pair, and another such artificial cavity was blasted into the buttocks of the other. After they fell to the floor, Shanice saw the form of the trench-coat-wearing Fist of God holding his still smoking .22 behind them.

"My compadres seem to have things well in hand on the first floor, what with the rest of the captives joining the battle," he said. "Hence, I felt free to see if anyone up here was in need. It would appear God guided me to your side, young lady."

Shanice ran to into the comforting arms of the strange man with the long gray coat and old-fashioned hat pulled low over his eyes. The final gang member stood still, obviously intimidated by the new arrival's firearm.

"I give, man!" he said. "You got no need to shoot me."

"Shoot him!" Shanice shrieked. "Do you know what his friends were gonna do to me? Shoot him!"

The girl's very uncharacteristic behavior presented a clear sign she was in the midst of a breakdown. This was not only the result of what was done to her, but also the acts she was forced to commit in self-defense. The incognito priest could see this, and he did his best to calm her down.

"Everything is all right, young lady," the Fist told her in his reassuring voice. "God is with you now." He then returned his full attention to the last gang member standing several feet down the hallway in front of him. "As for you, sinner…"

The Fist pointed the gun at the young man's left leg and pulled the trigger. Unfortunately, the gun proved out of ammo, and it would take him at least twenty seconds to grab a spare magazine out of his inner coat pocket to reload.

"Ha! Looks like God wasn't on your side today after all, old man," the gangbanger said as he ran towards the now unarmed vigilante of the cloth.

"No!" Shanice yelled as she ran towards the stout young criminal.

The young girl slashed the knife at her attacker like a madwoman, screeching in fury the entire time. He likewise swung his bludgeon at her, but she managed to keep out of its striking range. A few seconds later, however, one of her erratic slashes sliced through his left shoulder. He squealed in pain and lashed out with his free hand, striking her small form in the face and sending her sprawling to the floor.

The young felon then lifted his lead truncheon with the intention of bringing it down on her skull when he was suddenly shot through the shoulder. A spurt of his blood sprayed all over Shanice as the bullet tore through the flesh and collarbone of her opponent. His face seemed to take on an expression of extreme horror for a split second before his large form came crashing to the floor a half inch from his intended victim.

Shanice lifted her bruised, blood-spattered, but still lovely face to see that the shot came from exactly the source she expected.

"Thank you for giving me time to reload," the Fist said. "That was quite proactive of you, young lady."

The girl dropped the blade and ran crying into the arms of the priest. "Oh God! Oh God!"

He patted her on the back of her head, trying to comfort the young woman as best he could. "It's all right, it's all right. You went through a harrowing experience, but God got you through it. It's okay, let it out, let it all out."

***

The horde of gang members still fighting on the first floor had been reduced to just a dozen in the twenty minutes since their former captives had entered the fight. Severe injuries were had on both sides, but there were soon more students standing than gangbangers, as the former's numerical advantage was augmented by the somewhat involuntary partnering of vigilantes and police officers.

One of the final standing gang members was pounded into oblivion courtesy of a skillful combo of punches from Street Hawk. Officer Darius McCain took out another with a swing of his baton to the criminal's ribs, cracking three in a single blow with his hardwood baton. Princess Pummel was on the back of yet another, and she ripped her metal nails across his forehead, sending trickles of blood into his eyes that blinded him.

"Here's one for you, tall cop lady!" she hollered in Ella's direction.

The Amazonian lawwoman ran towards the bleeding young gang member and decked him with a right hook. He landed on the floor with a broken jaw and smashed lower lip to add to the multiple bloody scratches on his face. Princess rolled out from under where he had fallen on her.

"Just my luck dude had to be a heavy one," she grumbled.

Breaker ran to her side. "Are you okay, um, Princess?"

"Oh, I'm good," she assured him as he offered his hand to help the young woman back to her feet.

Street Hawk had just finished off the last fighting gang member with a well-placed low blow when he turned to acknowledge the team's success. "That guy on the ground there holding his balls and crying seems to be the last one. To all the students who helped us: you did well! You took the school back!"

The students left standing didn't waste a moment cheering or hi-fiving each other. Instead, they immediately went to give aid to their compatriots who had fallen.

Darius then addressed the student body with a set of firm commands. "All of you, head to the cafeteria. I want two of you who are un-injured to head to the nurse's office and get some first aid kits; bring one of them here, and the rest back to the cafeteria. Then, everyone who is still able-bodied needs to tend to those who are wounded until we can get ambulances to the school. A few of you also need to stand guard in case there are any gang members left. Officer Farrell and I will keep an eye out for any stragglers in the hallways."

The student body quickly did as the authoritative police officer said. Within several minutes, most of them were safely ensconced in the spacious cafeteria, with a few more headed to the nurse's office to retrieve first aid paraphernalia. Within moments, one student dropped off such a kit to the officers and then hurried to join the others in the school commissary.

"We'll head to the cafeteria and help stand guard," Street Hawk said.

"No, you three will *not* be helping," Darius rejoined before either could answer. "You three are criminals like all of these gang members, and we're taking you in along with them. You'll stay here on the floor in cuffs until the SWAT team finally arrives."

"Seriously, man?" Princess said. "We just helped your ass!"

"Princess, ya'll need to calm down," Breaker warned.

"Yes, *seriously!*" Darius responded. "I'm not going to make exceptions for you! If I do, every vigilante out there will expect the same treatment. This would send the message that at least sometimes, we approve of what you people do. We don't! Helping the police, even saving our lives, doesn't justify what you do, or merit special treatment!"

"Wow," Princess said. "Inflexible much?"

"Young lady, please don't make this any worse for yourself," Ella advised.

Darius extended his index finger to the sassy young masked woman. "Shut up and get up against the wall! All three of you! Then we'll find that one with the gun, if he's still in the school. And then we're taking in Moonstalker too, because I know he's still somewhere in this building."

"Listen, Officer," Street Hawk said calmly, approaching the lawman with his hands held up in a conciliatory gesture. "What you're talking about is treating the law like it's absolute. Princess did have a point about inflexibility. I know we broke the law, but we as citizens can't rely on the police to protect us 24/7…"

"Taking the law into your own hands is not acceptable under any circumstances, no matter the rationalization!" Darius shouted. "The police, and police procedure, exist for a good reason. We can't have a free-for-all with private justice. Now get up against the wall, all of you!"

"You really suck, copper," Princess remarked with an extended tongue.

"Shut up!" Darius retorted, pointing his baton at her.

"Officer, let's all try to calm down here," Street Hawk said while putting a hand on his shoulder.

"Don't you *ever* touch me!" Darius exclaimed as he punched the young vigilante in the face.

"Hey!" Princess Pummel shouted.

Street Hawk looked up at Darius and wiped blood from his mouth. "Don't do that again, Officer."

"Watch me!" the lawman decreed and took a second swing at the young masked man.

This time, however, Street Hawk displayed impressive speed and reflexes by blocking the blow and returning one in kind, snapping the officer's head back and sending a trail of blood flying from his mouth. Darius almost went down, but the policeman proved more robust than that.

The officer attacked next with his nightstick, a swing which Street Hawk quickly ducked. He then grabbed the cop's baton-wielding wrist, twisted it hard, and delivered a blow to his sternum, causing him to drop his weapon. The young vigilante had clearly been taking to Moonstalker's recent training quite well, already proving to be adept at disarming a well-trained law enforcement officer.

Darius McCain wasn't just any police officer, however. He was as tough as they come as far as cops go, and he again resisted going down from Street Hawk's combo. His free hand delivered a punch to his adversary's stomach; this caused the masked youth to keel over a bit, but he remained standing.

Darius swung two more times, but both intended blows were blocked. Street Hawk then retaliated with a bash to the lawman's face, stunning him. He followed that up with a second punch to the officer's jaw, which finally sent Darius flying to the floor.

"Woohoo!" Princess cheered, jumping up and down. "You got him good, Hawkie!"

"Shut up, girl!" an angered Ella yelled just before delivering a haymaker to the young woman that knocked her down. The blow also sent the girl's broken mask flying clear off her face.

Street Hawk then turned to the statuesque policewoman. "I didn't want to do that, Officer," he said, "but your partner didn't leave me any choice. Can we please talk this out?"

"No!" Ella exclaimed as she helped a dazed but still conscious Darius McCain to his feet. "I'm taking you down now!"

Before she could make another move, though, the female officer fell to the floor right after a gunshot was heard. She put her hand to her numbed right leg to find it spattered with blood. A bullet had torn through her calf. The culprit stood several feet away, glaring at her from under his fedora.

"Miss me?" the Fist of God queried sardonically.

"Oh mannn..." Breaker bemoaned.

"Fist, don't you think that was going too far?" Street Hawk lamented.

"Of course, it wasn't," the holy crusader opined.

"What do you mean, 'of course it wasn't?'" Street Hawk snapped. "You just shot a cop!"

"They assaulted you when you were doing the work of God," the priest said. "You were serving a much higher set of laws than any written by man."

"Not again," Breaker whined.

Just then, the Fist was struck in the chest by a nightstick that was hurled through the air by Darius. The unexpected blow caused the holy man to fall to the ground and drop his firearm, just as the lawman intended. Darius then rolled across the floor and picked up the fallen gun, which he quickly pointed at Street Hawk.

"Easy, Officer McCain," the young man behind the mask said.

"You're in big trouble!" Darius avowed angrily.

The officer's left eye was nearly swollen shut from the last punch he took, so he was unable to focus clearly. As a result, when Street Hawk again put his hands up in a conciliatory gesture, the policeman mistook it for a hostile attempt to disarm him.

Darius thus reacted to that sudden movement as such. "Stay back!"

The lawman pulled the trigger, sending a bullet straight into the masked man's stomach.

"Oh my god! Hawks!" Princess screamed.

Before she could run to his side, however, Street Hawk grasped his bleeding belly, and appeared to make several futile attempts at gasping for air. A moment later he fell to the floor in a manner which, to Princess Pummel's horrified perception, appeared be in slow motion.

"Dear Lord…" the Fist said as he recovered his wits.

"No!" Breaker shouted as he ran to his friend.

"I had no choice!" Darius bellowed. "He was moving towards me!"

The three extra-legal crime fighters tried tending to Street Hawk, who was now lying in the center of an increasingly expanding pool of his own blood.

Chapter 20: Down and Out at Riverfield High

A quick check with his hand revealed to Moonstalker that his viscera were still where they belonged. The last remaining vestiges of his synthetic chainmail outfit prevented Assailant's blade from carving directly into his gut and exposing the organs he often referred to as his "gastro-intestinals." Nevertheless, he wouldn't be so lucky if he was cut in that area again; or at a place where his uniform mesh was less effective.

"So, that's how you want to play it?" the coal-clad vigilante said to his knife-wielding opponent. "I never leave home without my weapons either."

Moonstalker likewise dispensed with a strictly hand-to-hand battle by unsheathing each of his batons from the pockets in his pant legs. He then displayed another feature he recently added to them during his convalescent hiatus: he could connect the two of them to form a bo staff. He began whirling this combined staff about him with a speed that made it resemble a helicopter's propeller.

"You think that stick will be enough to take me out?" Assailant asked derisively.

"I don't think that," Moonstalker replied while still whirling his weapon about. "I *know* it."

The King of the Streets howled in fury as he charged his ninja-like foe like a rabid dog out of the depths of Hell. Moonstalker parried his opponent's first attempted knife thrust with a move from his staff, but the gang leader skillfully followed that up by taking a swing with his free fist. The crime fighter quickly ducked the blow, which displayed its fearsome might by leaving a severe indentation in the locker it struck in his stead.

Moonstalker followed up himself with a staff strike to the left side of Assailant's jaw, and then spun with the grace of a ballet performer to deliver a direct blow to the gang leader's sternum with one of its blunt edges.

Assailant was knocked backwards, and he calmly tilted his head and spit out a bloody tooth. He turned back to his adversary and smiled, displaying how his ejected bicuspid was no big deal to him. Moonstalker stood his ground with his staff in a prepared stance, incredulous over his foe's resilience.

What will it take to put this guy down once and for all? He's not a metahuman, but he seems like the next best thing. I need to prove myself by putting an end to this!

To that end, Moonstalker decided to unexpectedly take the offensive. He swung his staff at Assailant's right cheekbone, striking it with a loud cracking sound that sent the gang leader reeling. However, the street master ducked the follow-up swing, and managed to rush in and deliver a haymaker directly to the vigilante's face. The impact sent the modern ninja flying off his feet, and he landed hard on the floor. A quick movement of his tongue detected two loose teeth in his mouth, and his swollen jaw was obviously suffering from a light fracture.

I'm need to re-apply for Medicaid, since it seems I'm going to need the services of the dentist on a regular basis. I'll have to tell him this happens due to training mishaps in the dojo.

Assailant then made the error of attempting to rush in and stab his opponent in the belly. Moonstalker countered with a sudden front kick to the gang leader's groin, painfully knocking the big man back a few feet.

The vigilante fought both the pain he suffered and the temptation to just let himself black out by reaching to his side and recovering his bo staff. He disconnected it into its two distinct batons and ejected the sickle-shaped ceramic blades in each, transforming them into kama mode.

The urban avenger's enemy had already recovered by then and was running towards him with his knife upraised. Moonstalker swung one of his kamas in front of him, cutting a deep horizontal gash in Assailant's stomach. For the first time, his enemy truly bellowed in pain and was given serious pause.

As the King of the Queen City Streets bent over, his hand covering his profusely bleeding belly, Moonstalker saw this as his opportunity to end the brutal donnybrook. Hence, the vigilante leapt forward and swung his kama at the side of his adversary's face.

Unfortunately, despite his injury, Assailant's reflexes and disciplined street-fighting acumen were to prove far greater than anything Moonstalker had ever seen before in a gang member. The brawny man caught the bludgeon in his other hand before its curved blade could connect with his cheekbone.

The leader of the New York Boys then struck Moonstalker beneath the chin with his forearm, stunning him and causing him to drop both his batons. The vigilante fought off the growing daze by retaliating with a forehead slam to the bridge of the gang master's nose, smashing his septum across the center.

Assailant still all but ignored the fountains of crimson spurting from his nostrils and grabbed Moonstalker by the throat with both hands. He lifted his gray-clad enemy off the ground as if he weighed a mere twenty pounds and slammed him hard against the wall. The gang master then pressed his sausage-thick thumbs into the coal avenger's trachea and pushed inwards with incredible force.

"I'm gonna crush your throat!" Assailant decreed. "I'm gonna make you puke blood!"

The degree of pain Moonstalker felt made it quite clear that the declarations from his foe were no idle boasts. He had but a few seconds before his trachea was pushed inwards like a clump of tinfoil and he choked to death on his own blood. Reacting with pure adrenalin and desperation, Moonstalker raised his legs and kicked them both into the still bleeding gash on Assailant's abdomen.

The sheer force of the double kick combined with the pain of ripping an already serious wound even further open to force Assailant into both releasing his grip and being thrust several feet backwards. The gang master again yelled in agony as he instinctively covered the gaping wound with both of his hands.

Moonstalker slid down to the floor and began coughing profusely, trying urgently to recover his ability to breathe and rise back to his feet. He also struggled to regain the full measure of his vision, as multi-colored splotches kept appearing before his eyes.

Unfortunately, pulling off his mask to help catch his breath was most certainly not an option at that moment. He hoped and prayed to the great spirit of Buddha that the loss of blood from Assailant's gaping stomach wound would cause his opponent to pass out.

As Moontalker finally regained his visual acuity and cleared his airways, however, he could see that the big man was still on his feet despite trembling from the pain and blood loss. *Exactly how much more can this guy take? Maybe more importantly, how much more can I take?*

"I'm gonna kill you, kill you!" Assailant shouted as he pulled a .44 Magnum from a pocket inside his open leather jacket and pointed it at the crime fighter.

Oh shit! Moonstalker reacted faster than he ever had before when he undertook a daring move which took all his will and physical acumen to perform, especially considering the degree of his injuries and his dazed state: He performed a front flip to evade the oncoming bullet and managed to avoid a direct hit. Nevertheless, the deadly projectile still grazed his right calf, cutting through the mesh of his pant leg and slicing his skin open.

The smoke-garbed avenger forced himself not to shout in pain upon landing on his wounded leg. He quickly retaliated by hurling a shuriken from one of his hidden pockets at his foe. Assailant managed to aim his piece again, but the ceramic sickle embedded directly into his wrist and spoiled the shot. The wayward bullet instead blasted clear through one of the corridor windows, sending hundreds of shards of glass to the street below.

Moonstalker still couldn't relax for even a split second, however. He ran towards Assailant and again steeled himself against the severe agony emanating from his injured leg by using it to propel him through the air to deliver a flying kick to his opponent's chin. The impact caused the formidable gang leader to drop his firearm and go flying back against the lockers.

The vigilante then pooled together all the willpower he could muster as he ran towards his much larger adversary and bombarded him with a repeating combo of reverse punches to each side of his jaw.

"You... will... go... down!" he exclaimed while releasing the volley of crippling blows.

But Assailant withstood the fierce assault, notwithstanding the blood that spattered from every facial orifice with each hit. He then raised both of his massive arms – despite one wrist still having a shuriken embedded in it – and he simultaneously brought them down on his smaller opponent.

"I... will... *crush*... you!"

Moonstalker's reflexes remained quick enough that he was able to block with both his forearms in crisscross fashion. But the double impact of Assailant's fists nevertheless sent the modern ninja to his knees. He felt his wrenched shoulder sting as if it were on fire.

The urban avenger took full advantage of being knocked down to his knees by delivering a spear hand thrust directly into Assailant's cavernous stomach wound. He penetrated his fingers as far into the bloody opening as it would go, and cruelly rotated his hand inside the torn muscles. The bellow of pain released by his enemy was like that of a man thrown into a meat grinding machine while still fully conscious.

Both of the gang leader's hands grasped the sliced open flesh as soon as his opponent withdrew his sturdy fingers.

Moonstalker then pushed himself to his feet and put every last erg of energy he had into leaping in the air and delivering a powerful roundhouse kick to Assailant's jaw. *This has to do it!*

The big man's screams gave way to a gurgling sound as another trickle of blood flowed out of his mouth to match the ones already streaming out his nostrils; not to mention the thick droplets pouring out of his abdominal tear. The gang master fought desperately to remain on his feet and began stumbling about.

"Go *down*!" Moonstalker roared at the highest volume his larynx could muster as he ran up to his wobbling foe and side-kicked him directly in the chin.

Finally, the leader of the New York Boys was pushed beyond the limits of even his incredible endurance, and his body fell to the floor with a resounding thud.

Finally…

Moonstalker took a few moments to lean up against the wall near the shattered windows, lift up his mask, and take a series of deep breaths. He lamented lacking the energy to release the resounding victory cry he felt was now his due. *Man, I thought he would never go down…*

***

"My God, Breaker, he's gonna die!" Princess Pummel shouted as she used both her hands to exert as much pressure as she could on Street Hawk's bloody bullet wound.

"Just keep up that pressure, we don't want him bleeding out on us," the older man stated.

"I'll… call an ambulance for him when the SWAT team gets here," Darius McCain said in a gentler than usual tone. "But you're all still going to jail."

"You will go to Hell for this, you foolish young man," the Fist pontificated. "You shot a hero acting on God's will."

"Oh, shut up, you deluded holy-rolling dick!" Darius spat as he continued to hold the vigilante priest and his friends at bay with the purloined gun.

"He saved your life!" the man of the cloth exclaimed.

"That didn't and couldn't matter!" Darius rejoined. "He was still a dangerous criminal who resisted arrest!"

"He wasn't givin' no resistance!" Breaker insisted.

"Could have fooled me," Darius insisted.

A second later, the firearm was knocked out of the lawman's hand by a blow from behind. Before the officer could fully turn around, he received a strong kick to the face which knocked him to the floor right beside the now barely conscious Officer Ella Farrell.

Darius covered his bleeding nose and looked up to see a very beaten and worn-looking Moonstalker standing above him. The gray-garbed crime fighter was bleeding from several different injuries, and he moved with a noticeable limp.

"You're an asshole, McCain," was all the vigilante said before he turned to see to the condition of Street Hawk.

The Fist of God recovered his weapon and pointed it at the two downed police officers. "I would stay on the floor and relax if I were either of you."

"It's bad, Boss-man," Breaker said to his leader as he put a consoling hand on the shoulder of Princess Pummel. "He's barely breathin', and I don't like where that bullet went at all. If we don't get him to a hospital with the quickness…"

"We will," Moonstalker assured his ally. "I contacted Sky High, so all we need to do is get him to the back entrance. But we have to do it before the reinforcements for the police get here."

"You shore you can make it, Boss?" Breaker queried. "You look like hell paved over."

"I'll… make it," Moonstalker replied. "But first I have to see to…"

"The girl you're thinking of is okay," the Fist interjected quietly, just out of earshot of the two officers, neither of whom were in any shape to listen very closely anyway. "I saved her from some ruffians, and I sent her to the cafeteria where the other students are. She is… very shaken up, but she accorded herself like a warrior born."

"She'll have to keep for now," Moonstalker said. "Let's lift Hawk up carefully and get him to the back entrance."

It was a thankfully short journey there as Moonstalker, Breaker, and Princess Pummel each ignored their various injuries to carry the terribly wounded young man. The Fist of God kept close watch behind them to make sure Officers Darius and/or Ella didn't unexpectedly recover and attempt to bushwhack them from the opposite direction.

"I'm… gonna get those bastards yet," Darius said as he wrapped a sterile cloth from the first aid kit around the bleeding hole in his partner's leg. "They can't just violate the law like that!"

Ella sighed weakly. "McCain, can you give it a rest just long enough to properly tie that damn rag around my wound?"

***

As the vigilante crew carried their seriously injured comrade to the back entrance of the school, they saw that only two armed gangbangers were left to guard it. The remaining police from the unit they had the shoot-out with had evidently retreated to wait for reinforcements.

"Damn, we still gotta get by that pair," Breaker bemoaned.

"Just wait for it," Moonstalker said.

Within a few seconds, a large black SUV came crashing clear through the fence surrounding the schoolyard. The two gang members were taken by surprise and were quickly struck by the vehicle just hard enough to send their bodies flying through the air. They were unconscious with several broken bones by the time gravity had yanked them back to the concrete.

"Whoa!" Princess Pummel uttered.

The vehicle pulled up to the side of the door where Moonstalker's team waited. They could see the disguised face of Sky High at the wheel.

"Did someone here order an escape vehicle?" he quipped.

***

Moonstalker tore off Street Hawk's mask and distinguishing jacket, leaving no trace of his vigilante identity, and took over the application of pressure on his wound. The van traveled several blocks just before stopping on the corner of Carlton Street.

"You three, get out of the van and head for the dojo!" he yelled to the trio of allies who were still standing. "Don't let anyone see you enter and stay there until I contact you again. Call Sensei Dell and Janice from the dojo phone after arriving; they'll see to your injuries!"

Breaker looked at his leader incredulously. "But, Boss…"

"Just do it, goddamn it!" Moonstalker yelled.

Without further question, the Fist of God, Breaker, and Princess Pummel left the SUV and stealthily headed for Master Kai's Dojo. The van then took off again.

"We need to get him to the hospital ASAP!" Moonstalker told his driver as he endured excessive pain from his injuries to remove his own uniform and stash it in a hidden compartment recently added to the back of Eli Matthews's vehicle.

"Buffalo General Hospital is just five minutes away," Sky High said. "Just keep that pressure on his wound and hang in there! And let me remind you that you need hospital treatment too."

"No, you bring me to *your* place! Right now, just concentrate on getting Reggie to the hospital! No arguing!"

"Understood. At least this time you have a good reason to explain the shape you're in to your parents. Just make sure to call them as soon as I'm done patching you up. The situation at the school must have gotten on the news by now, and your folks have to be terrified for you."

"Just worry about getting Reggie to the hospital."

"Will do, kid."

Alan Perez was thankful it was now finally over, but he was overcome with sorrow that it may end up costing a brave young ally like Reggie Diaz everything. *Dammit, if only they stayed at the goddamned dojo like I told them to! They weren't ready for something like this yet…*

Epilogue: Open Wounds...

Officer Darius McClain sat up in his uncomfortable E.R. bed at Kenmore Miracle Hospital. His nose was bandaged up, and the sight of it pissed him off every time he had cause to look in a mirror.

It's just my luck so many of those injured students went to Buffalo General that the place is strapped for beds, leaving me stuck here in the emergency room. But yeah, I understand the kids have to come first. Still sucks, though.

A moment later Officer Ted Claymore walked in. Darius was expecting this visit, and he became quite animated once his fellow lawman entered the room.

"Ted!" Darius whooped. "Did you get me that info?"

"Yeah, I did," Ted replied. "But can't you worry about it after you're done recuperating? You're up for a promotion when you get out of here, so you'll have plenty of means at your hands to…"

"Let *me* worry about my recuperation, dammit! I'm still a cop, even when I'm indisposed like this, and I still have a job to do. That's doubly the case if the promotion comes to pass! I need to know if anyone with injuries fitting the guy I shot, or those I saw on Moonstalker, were admitted to any local hospital, especially Buffalo General."

"Well, I dunno about that Moonstalker guy, since from what you and Farrell said, his injuries could match up with those of any of the dozens of kids admitted to the hospital after the gang siege. Yesterday there were three patients admitted to Buffalo General who were being treated for gunshot wounds, though. Two were due to bullet wounds to the lower abdomen, like the vigilante you shot. Their names are Calvin Cruz and Reginald Diaz."

"Find out more info on both of them."

"I will. Just be glad the investigation into your gun usage is tied up with Internal Affairs thanks to the unit getting involved in that shoot-out with the gang. So many shots were fired it's gonna take months for the big wigs in I.A. to sort through it all. And besides, you know they usually weigh in favor of their own anyway."

"Yeah, no doubt. But just get me the full skinny on both of those guys you mentioned. I'm certain one of them is that Street Hawk, and when I find out who he really is, it's only a matter of time 'till I discover who his 'boss' really is too. I'll have his ass, and the asses of his merry little band, in jail if it's the last thing I do in my career. And my career has just taken off!"

**

Alan Perez sat up on Eli Matthews's new couch bed (an item of furniture he correctly surmised he would have need of) with all his recent injuries patched up. Eli personally sewed up the severe cut Assailant made to Alan's stomach, which luckily didn't touch any of his internals, or he would have had no choice but to have the young man hospitalized. The vigilante's wrenched shoulder was nicely back in place, and his terribly bruised face and jaw were well bandaged.

"You look as close to presentable as one could expect for when your parents get here," Eli told him. "I just hope they don't get too pissed at me for bringing you here instead of the hospital, like all of your fellow students who got caught in the siege. You know how they got last time I did that."

"Yeah, about that," Alan said. "We need to set up a way for the Moon Crew to receive serious medical aid outside of a regular hospital when things get a little rough. We'll have to put our heads together and find a place and team we can trust, and a way for you to use your position at the hospital trauma center to get the necessary equipment."

"I see I have a lot to look forward to during your latest recuperation period." The older gentleman sighed. "But seriously, the 'Moon Crew?'"

"Well, Dee Dee came up with it, and I can't say it doesn't fit."

"I suppose so."

Eli then heard his doorbell ring, and knowing who it was, he answered with much trepidation. The visitors ran past him and right up to his recurring house guest.

"I can't believe you came here instead of the hospital again, Alan Garrett!" Lenore Perez complained to her son.

"Mom, I didn't want us to have to pay for a hospital when Eli was fully capable of patching me up himself," Alan replied. "We aren't insured right now, and…"

"Money isn't important, boy!" Bradford Perez sniped at his son.

"You know that isn't really true, Dad," Alan said solemnly.

"Yes, it is true!" Bradford insisted.

"Your health is the most important thing to your father and I!" Lenore added firmly. "And it should be to you too!"

183

"Mom, my injuries weren't so bad that Eli couldn't handle them," Alan said. "He doesn't mind doing it in exchange for a few free martial arts lessons down at the dojo."

"Which you won't be able to give him for a while yet!" Lenore pointed out.

"Oh, that's okay, Lenore," Eli insisted politely. "I'll get him back on his feet in no time at all, and I can wait a few months before getting those lessons. He's welcome to stay here for the duration. After all, his school is going to be closed down for a few weeks after what went down there earlier."

"The city needs to pay for better security at that school!" Bradford exclaimed. "I can't believe this happened!"

"Your father is right, Alan," Lenore agreed as she hugged her son tightly.

"Ouch!" Alan moaned uncomfortably. "Um, Mom, I appreciate the love, but you're going to end up pulling my shoulder out again."

"Oh, I'm sorry," she said, crying. "I'm just so glad you're okay. After what happened to you and the other kids, you can bet we're going to get together with the other parents and sue the hell out of the school!"

"The school probably has less money than we do, Mom," Alan pointed out.

"Then we'll sue the goddamned city!" she cried.

"Have fun with that, Mom," Alan said, trying to sound as cheery as possible. "We all need to have a hobby. And it could have been worse. Think about what happened to Buffalo Historical a few months ago, when those metahumans blasted the front of it to bits and tore up its whole schoolyard."

"That's exactly what we're so concerned about, son," Bradford said. "What happened at your school *could* have been much worse. But what did happen was still *more* than bad enough."

"Are you sure we can't pay you anything for taking care of Alan for a few days, Eli?" Lenore asked their new family friend.

"If you can make enough of those incredible meals of yours for two when you bring dinner over here for your son, that would more than suffice," Eli said.

"It's a deal," Lenore replied with a smile.

"Are you sure you don't need us here longer, son?" Bradford queried with concern. "You've just been through one hell of an experience."

"Dad, you know I got worse in the schoolyards when I was a kid," Alan responded. "My years of training at the dojo got me through it. It was dope as hell how all the students stood up to the gang after they invaded the school. I'll be fine. You and Mom can go home and relax. I'll see you both around dinner time."

"I also heard that scary vigilante Moonstalker was at the school too," Lenore mentioned with concern. "Is that true?"

"Possibly, but who could notice with all the ruckus going on there?" Alan replied. "All I saw were gang members coming at me left and right. And a few police officers here and there."

After his parents departed, Alan made a point to call Shanice on her cell. He was surprised when her mother answered.

"Shanice was treated at Buffalo General for her injuries, and she's home now. But she isn't well enough to talk."

"Oh, so she is home," Alan said with a dejected tone. *And she didn't call me first? That's totally not like her.* "How bad were here injuries, Mrs. Morris?"

"It's not all physical, Alan," Shanice's mom replied. "What she ended up having to do in self-defense, well… she doesn't want to talk about it right now. Not with anyone; and neither do I."

"Can you let her know I called?"

"I will. Bye."

Before Alan could say another word, Mrs. Morris had ended the connection. He scowled.

"Is Shanice okay?" Eli inquired.

"No, she isn't," Alan said. "It's not like her to miss calling me herself. Even if her mom did confiscate her cell, she would have used a friend's phone to call. She's avoiding me."

"She just needs time to process all of this. You heard Father Merle tell you exactly what she had to do in order to get out of that situation."

"Yes! And I want to tell her how proud I am of her. The way she used that corrosive I gave her, and that switchblade… I honestly never thought she had it in her. But she did."

"Maybe that's not what she needs to hear right now, Alan."

"Huh?"

"I think maybe she doesn't feel proud of what she had to do. Have you considered that she isn't the same kind of person that you are?"

Before Alan could say another word, the special encrypted cell he acquired from the dojo jingled with the beat of the vintage rap hit "Follow the Leader" from Eric B. & Rakim. This indicated Fred Gifford was calling him. Or, more specifically, calling Moonstalker.

Alan made sure to respond in a rough tone to disguise his true voice. "Yes?"

"Boss, me an' the other two are at Buffalo General," Fred informed him. "I done told the desk I'm Reggie's uncle, and Dee Dee is his cousin. Father Merle said he was his pastor an' was let into the room to bless him. It's… it's not good."

"What do you mean?"

"I mean… he's…"

185

Dee Dee began crying profusely, and she ran into Fred's arms. He held her tightly with the arm which wasn't holding the phone. He soon stopped talking and held her with both arms and put his face down on her head, not wanting anyone to see his own tears.

It was then that Father Merle Harris arrived in the waiting room, took the cell from Fred's hand, and replaced him on the call.

"I just returned from giving the boy my blessings," Merle said. "He lost so much blood he's in a deep coma. His spine was hit by the bullet, and even if he regains consciousness, I'm afraid he'll never walk again. I will say a prayer for all of us to receive peace of mind. He was a good champion on behalf of God during the brief time he took up the cause."

At that point, Alan dropped the phone to the floor and covered his eyes. "No…"

Eli knew exactly what the news must have been, and he put a consoling hand on Alan's good shoulder. "I'm sorry."

"That cop shot him!"

"Alan, it was a bad situation…"

"I will have *words* with him! Law or not, he won't away with this."

***

In the infirmary of the Buffalo Holding Center, Paco Esteban Juarez lay confined to a bed. He was better known by his street name of Assailant, a handle that had symbolic meaning on many levels. His smashed nose was bandaged up, and his stomach had several layers of gauze wrapped around it to cover the stiches of his terrible abdominal wound. His left leg was held up a cast.

Most uncomfortably, however, he was tied to the bed with several strong leather straps, including one around his neck to prevent him from reaching up and biting. His heavily muscled form was so tightly restricted that he could scarcely move a muscle; he had to use a catheter to urinate and a bed pan secured under him to eliminate.

A doctor was just finishing up with giving him his diagnosis.

"In addition to those injuries," the physician said, "you're also suffering from multiple lacerations and contusions, Mr. Juarez. I'm afraid it will be some time before you will be mobile enough to go to trial. Do you have any questions?"

The heavily bandaged young man was now bereft of his mask, exposing both his fearsome visage – which included a deep scar near his right eye – and his shaved head. Needless to say, he greatly disliked being seen without his Luchador-like mask. His mouth, which was wired due to a jaw injury, obscured a series of words he attempted to say.

The doctor courteously ceased talking so he could hear the dangerous felon more clearly.

"Can you please repeat that, Mr. Juarez? I didn't quite catch it."

This time Paco's words were clear despite being muffled by the jaw wiring: "I will *kill* him… and everyone he holds dear."

The doctor shuddered at the intensity of those words and the sheer conviction behind them, even though they weren't directed at him. He felt extreme sympathy for the unfortunate soul they were intended for and prayed that the man called Assailant would never escape from the state prison he was soon headed for.

However, such prayers have often proved futile in the past.

END

Moonstalker will return in *MOONSTALKER: THE CITY IS MINE,* so watch for it! And coming soon after that to an online store near you: *MOONSTALKER VS. CENTURION.*

For those who enjoyed Moonstalker's debut exploit, please do consider leaving a review on Amazon, BookBub, your own blog, the works! Reviews really do help and will enable me to continue bringing more of Moonstalker and many other heroes from the Warp Event Universe to you on a regular basis! For those readers who may not have considered this initial outing up to par, my apologies; but rest assured I will strive to make each subsequent adventure of Moonstalker an improvement over the last! Your purchase and reading of this book was much appreciated, as I would be nowhere without all of you!

Bonus Short Story: In case anyone was wondering exactly what the mysterious Master Kai was like, and under what circumstances he first met and recruited Alan Perez – well, just continue reading for a major blast (read: several punches and kicks) from Moonstalker's past.

MASTER KAI'S GREATEST RECRUIT

Christofer Nigro

The year, to those who place importance on recording such details, was 2005. The place, which most chroniclers will agree to be important, was Buffalo, New York; specifically, on the Queen City's Lower East Side, in the schoolyard of a decrepit urban middle school called School No. 46. Of supreme relevance, however, is the main participant of the scene in question: 12-year-old Alan Garrett Perez, who happened to be engaged in one of his usual altercations with the newest would-be bully to transfer to his school after being expelled from several others.

Alan was relatively thin and a mere '5'5", but despite a swollen left eye and a trickle of blood flowing from his left nostril, he remained standing against the much larger and heavier bully -- a veteran scrapper named Dan Decker -- following a few minutes of furiously exchanged blows. Dan's features were equally marred and bloody, and he was clearly surprised at the level of natural fighting acumen, unexpected strength, and levels of aggression that his smaller opponent brought to bear against him. The two were facing off with upraised fists and stances of preparedness as a crowd of fellow students gathered around for both the dark entertainment value provided by the schoolyard donnybrook, and to cheer on (though "egg on" may be more accurate) their combatant of choice.

Alan had the majority of supporters, as he was more established at this school, and hence already enjoyed a proven rep. Dan was eager to earn his own by undermining the "respect points" that Alan possessed, and he had a few supporters of his own (mostly those he had made a preemptive "deal" with to take effect after his promised demolishing of Alan).

"You wanna make something of it, bitch?" Dan queried rhetorically through his bleeding mouth. "Huh? Still wanna get your ass kicked?"

"You haven't kicked it yet!" Alan rejoined.

"Just get 'im, Dan!" came the cry of one of the new bully's supporters in the crowd, a tall boy named Kenny Brooks who had previously run afoul of Alan's fists.

Dan complied with the taunting request and launched a right hook at Alan. The smaller, lanky boy managed to barely block it with his left arm and returned fire with a right of his own. It hit his bigger adversary directly in the nose, and this caused Dan to pause for a second as a sting of pain wracked his face. A second later, a stream of blood began seeping out of each nostril like spilled crimson paint.

Dan screamed an "f-bomb" at Alan as he struck back, hitting his opponent in the side of the jaw. Alan was knocked back several steps by the powerful clout, which allowed Dan to rush in and attempt to tackle his stunned challenger to the ground. He figured his greater weight and size would give him the advantage there, a point he had learned from years of bullying and fighting. Alan winced as the nearly 200-pound, '5'11" tall boy smashed into him with the force of a thrown 50-pound sandbag.

This brought the adolescent Alan straight down to the concrete, just as his opponent had planned. Dan then began pounding on the sides of the thinner boy's ribs.

"That's it!" Kenny cried out. "Alan is gonna need a *body bag!* Hah!"

"Get up, Alan!" yelled Tyrone "Ty" Reynolds, the long time-time friend of Alan, as he stepped forward to provide possible assistance if the situation became particularly bad. "Don't let that dude wail on you!"

Kenny grabbed Ty in his two large flabby arms, holding him tight. "Don't interfere, man! Alan is a big boy; he's gotta do this himself, right?"

As Ty found himself unable to break from Kenny's grip despite his best efforts, Alan's BFF realized he had no choice but to comply.

He quickly realized he had little reason to worry, however. Alan managed to pull his arms from under Dan's bulk while the much larger boy was busy pummeling his sides. The thin scrapper used his now freed limbs to slam his cupped hands against each of his corpulent aggressor's ears. Dan jumped up and screamed as a torrent of air rushed into both auditory canals and nearly punctured his tympanic membranes. Alan followed that cruel and eminently effective move by jumping up and striking his fist against Dan's nose again, this time completely breaking the cartilage.

The larger boy's light blue shirt was stained with blood spurting from his septum as Alan grabbed his foe's throat and pushed Dan's large frame off him completely. He then leapt on top of the pain-wracked bully and began savagely pounding Dan until his entire face was a swollen and bloody mess.

"Don't you ever start shit with me or Ty again!" Alan shouted as carried out the merciless thrashing.

"Whoa!" Kenny exclaimed as he released Ty and backed away.

"Alan is killin' 'im!" one of his own supporters yelled as he jumped up and down excitedly.

The newly freed Ty approached the melee and tapped Alan on his shoulder from the side, careful to make it clear that he wasn't one of Dan's small group of (now former) supporters jumping in.

"Alan, that's enough, man!" Ty hollered. "You beat him!"

"I'm not finished beating him!" Alan replied as his enraged visage turned towards his friend.

"I meant, he's down!" Ty clarified. "It's over. If Principal Barnes even bothers to call you in, you know everyone will admit that Dan started it. Maybe he'll finally get shipped off to Queen City Alternative now."

Alan took several deep breathes to forcibly calm himself as he allowed Ty to gently pull him off of Dan. A few male members of the crowd approached Alan and offered him hi-fives, while a few of the girls gave him quick hugs. The rest of the crowd remained gathered around the fallen Dan Decker, who continued to writhe and moan painfully on the cold schoolyard ground as his blood pooled up in a puddle around his head.

Ty made a point to direct Alan towards the nearby exit leading out of the school grounds and into the mean streets surrounding it.

"That's one way to get the attention of the girls, man," Ty quipped with a tinge of sorrow. "Not my preferred way, though. Me, I go with the right words and the right moves, not with kicking the shit out of other guys."

"You know that's not why I blasted him, Ty," Alan said. "He started something, so I finished it; or, more specifically, I finished *him*. But he totally deserved it, and it was fun."

"Well, okay," Ty replied. "Ya'll don't ever pick on the weaker or the innocents, and you even stand up for them sometimes, so I guess I can't complain too much. But speakin' of the girls, I got some time alone at home before Mom comes home. And, well, Cecelia wants to come over to, ya know, play some video games. So, I'll catch you later."

"Have fun, and later, man!"

Ty gave his best friend the traditional combo gesture of hi-five and handshaking shared between male friends on the American urban landscape just before departing down a side street.

Alan likewise headed for home, which was located several blocks away. Though he ordinarily took a Metro bus from school to his house, today he was filled with an adrenal "high" following his latest fight and he wanted to walk it off. He also wanted to get his bloody nose under control before arriving and having to explain to his parents that he got into yet another skirmish. The scrappy middle-schooler had no idea how he would conceal the black eye that marred his light-colored facial skin, however.

Alan's parents were often prepared for the worst when he came home, since despite their son's high level of intelligence, they knew part of that was his natural gift for fisticuffs and strategical thinking on his feet in a street-wise manner. Moreover, he was as proud of these skills as he was with his allure to the girls and recording hip hop instrumentals. He would never allow himself to be talked out of utilizing something that cemented a high degree of respect for him with his peers -- both in the 'hood and at the school he had little interest in attending save for the social factors involved.

Though Lenore and Bradford Perez often argued that his pugilistic skills weren't a nice thing to be good at, Alan would always counter that such attributes were nevertheless *necessary* to survive and to obtain respect in the world he grew up in. Thus, he placed high value on these skills and rarely hesitated to execute them on those he deemed to be "deserving of an ass whipping."

As Alan walked towards a familiar street lamp on the corner of Franklin Street, he was startled when an older man of obvious Japanese descent with a bald pate surrounded by graying hair on the sides and a short white beard stepped from nowhere he could readily discern to directly bar his path. The man was dressed in a mauve yukata garment that one may expect a man of his culture to be wearing. If he was out and about in his native land, that is.

Alan had long ago learned not to be taken unawares by thugs who made "coming out of nowhere" an art form to surprise pedestrians. Hence, he was truly taken aback by this individual accomplishing such a feat with him.

"Huh?" Alan gasped while jumping back into a defensive stance.

"My apologies for startling you," the older Oriental gentleman replied in a slow but firm tone, and with a clear accent. "But this has shown that you're not as adept at avoiding a surprise encounter as you may think."

"What? Who do you think you are? Mr. Miyagi?"

192

"I am not certain who your 'Mr. Miyagi' is, but I can assure you that I do not think I am that person. Rather, I *know* I am Master Kai, and that I have chosen you to be one of the few students I admit to the inner circle of my dojo to train free of financial obligation. Provided, that is, you are willing to dedicate yourself to mastering the priceless arts I will teach you there."

The expression on Alan's face was now one of extreme incredulity as he continued to use a school cafeteria napkin to stop the remaining trickles of blood from dribbling out of his nostrils.

"*Huh*? You're offering me free training at some dojo? How do I know you're not some type of sex fiend who pretends to be a martial arts instructor? What would you get out of training someone for free in a world that puts a price on food, shelter, and um, pretty much everything?"

"Your concern is understandable given the popular narratives and fears of your culture, young one. Please allow me to prove I am what I purport to be by having you follow me into that establishment over there."

The mysterious Master Kai pointed to a tavern on the opposite side of the street known as Chevy's Place.

Alan's youthful Hispanic features immediately took on a startled expression once more. "Seriously? That scum hole is filled with gang members, drug dealers, gun runners, and the worst of the worst on Buffalo's East Side. Not even I go near that place. And I'm too young to go in there anyways."

Master Kai smiled slightly and motioned for Alan to follow as he began crossing the street. "Just come and enter that drinking establishment with me. I will insure the attention will be directed towards myself, so you will scarcely be noticed."

The young man found himself oddly compelled to put his reluctance aside and follow this enigmatic personage into the doors of what many law-abiding citizens in his neighborhood referred to as "The Devil's Place."

As the two entered the bar, Alan could see that it truly lived up to its wretched reputation. It was filled with clouds of smoke from both cigarettes and blunts. Several unsavory figures were standing about laughing loudly, gossiping about the anatomy of every woman within their view, and striking illicit bargains away from prying eyes. But it was over at the pool table dominating the center of the dingy hostelry where the individuals representing the treasure trove sought by the interloping Master Kai were congregating.

"See those men in the repulsive-looking jackets and mismatched colors over there?" the older gent pointed out to his younger companion.

"You mean, over by the pool table?" Alan asked. "Those are members of the Savage Baboons, one of the worst street gangs around here. Don't mess with them."

"But 'messing with them' is precisely how I will prove my claims to you. And in a most satisfying manner, I must say, considering how those barbaric *fūdoramu* regularly prey upon the innocents in this section of your city."

"Foo-du-who?"

Master Kai sighed. "You Westerners are as overly reliant on the English language as my countrymen are with the Japanese tongue."

"Can I help you, man?" the swarthy looking bartender asked the out-of-place Master Kai after finally spotting him.

"No, I am quite capable of helping myself," the older man replied as he approached the four Savage Baboons gathered around the pool table.

"Hey, what are you doing in here, kid?" the bartender inquired to Alan.

"Just watching the action, I guess," was all the lad could think of to say in response. Which was, essentially, the truth of the matter.

As Master Kai approached the closest gang member, he calmly tapped the bulky young man on the shoulder to get his attention.

"Excuse me," he said.

"Yeah? What the hell do you want, old man?" the gangbanger asked over his shoulder.

"Merely to inform you that I find you and your fellow wearers of poor sartorial choice to be among the vilest of human beings I have ever encountered in this world. And I have encountered much in my many years."

"Oh, man," Alan whispered to himself while partially covering his bruised face in his hands.

"What?" the gangbanger interrogated loudly as he turned to fully face the smaller, thinner, and older man standing before him.

"And also," Master Kai continued, "that I have little doubt your mothers made very poor sexual choices in their misbegotten pasts. You each represent the genetic end result of such ill-advised selections in men."

"Ooohh man!" Alan exclaimed as he once again covered his face. *If those guys understood what he said, he's going to be* dead meat *in less than a second!*

"Oh, shit," the bartender said as he turned towards one of his two huge bouncers. "Eddie, I think you and Devlin better get over here now. That weird old guy seems to have come in here to commit suicide, or somethin'."

Just as the closest gang member demonstrated that he did indeed understand the insults by raising his fist to strike the older man, Master Kai slammed the muscular hood under his nose with an extremely fast and powerful palm heel strike. The master of the martial arts clearly channeled a large portion of his chi into the blow, and it was delivered so fast it appeared as a mere blur of motion to the average human eye. The gangbanger's septum was split in two, and the impact of the strike sent the big man flying onto the fuzzy green surface of the pool table. His head twitched a few times as blood sprayed out of his nostrils, after which he fell totally silent.

"Holy shit, man!" one of his three fellow Savage Baboons hollered. "Get that Chinese bastard!"

The gangbanger swung his cue stick at Master Kai, who caught it between his palms. The formidable older man followed up with a punishing front kick to his younger foe's groin, pulled the stick out of his grip, and then bashed him on the bridge of the nose with its blunted end. The loud crunching sound and spray of blood that accompanied the blow accounted for the third set of adenoidal cartilage which Alan saw crushed that day – and all in the span of about thirty seconds.

"I am Japanese, *not* Chinese," Master Kai said as the hapless thug fell to the ground in front of him. "Learn the difference before entering the world of dreams." He then struck the man on the crown of his head with the cue stick, rendering him unconscious and adding a concussion to his collection of injuries.

The master of the martial arts next grasped the cue stick in each of his hands, twirling it around at incredible speed while preparing to use it as an improvised bo staff. Another gang member charged with the ferocity of an enraged rhino and swung his stick at the older man, only to have him easily block it with his own makeshift staff.

In what amounted to another blur of motion and impressive display of prowess, Master Kai pivoted around and thrust the bottom end of the cue stick at his attacker to strike him directly in the solar plexus. The man immediately fell to his knees and vomited on the floor, only to be swiftly knocked out by a blow to the back of his neck with a single rapid motion of the aged warrior's ersatz weapon.

"You're dead!" the final gang member yelled as he pulled a handgun from his jacket pocket.

But Master Kai countered before the gangbanger could fully draw his firearm by – in another blur of motion – snatching a cue ball from the table and hurling the small but solid spherical object at his adversary's face. It struck the man between the eyes before he could fire the gun, causing him to drop the weapon and fall backwards against one of the tables.

Then, in a final haze of movement, Master Kai dropped the cue stick, ran several steps towards his stunned opponent, and leapt through the air to deliver a powerful flying kick to his face. The young criminal was knocked clear off his feet and over the table to crash down on the floor several feet behind it. He didn't rise again as bloody foam bubbled from his mouth and flowed over his chin like whiteish lava erupting from a volcano.

Every person in the bar, including the bouncers Eddie and Devlin, silently paused where they stood or sat when Master Kai snatched up the displaced firearm. Instead of turning it on anyone, however, he simply slipped the magazine out of the chamber, clicked the release to cause all six bullets to fall to the floor, and then kicked the projectiles to scatter them in all directions. He then tossed the gun over the serving counter where it could not be easily retrieved for a quick re-loading.

"These clumsy and overly loud weapons are a disgrace to the martial world," he said. "Why you Westerners ever invented them has always puzzled me."

"Guys, toss him outta here!" the bartender screeched.

Eddie and Devlin ran towards the lithe older man, only to receive a spear hand thrust to their respective trachea by each of Master Kai's hands. The enormous bouncers grasped their throat gasping and choking for a moment until the old warrior bent on his knees and struck both of them directly behind the bend of their right legs. That particular move caused them to lose their footing and fall to the floor, where they continued to gasp and hack as they rubbed their bruised Adam's apples.

Master Kai then turned towards the bartender, who backed against the liquor shelf behind him and nearly collapsed in terror as he accidently sent several bottles crashing to the floor. Every other patron in the bar remained exactly where they were, barely even speaking among themselves.

"Aw, man, please don't..." the bartender stammered as he struggled to remain on his feet. "I didn't do anything to you! I had to tell my men to throw you out 'cause you were assaulting my customers! Ya'll shouldn't take it personally..."

"Begging is pathetic even for one as unseemly as yourself," Master Kai said as he headed for the door and motioned for Alan to follow him. "Shame on you for the company you keep and serve in this den of iniquity."

The two of them then departed Chevy's Place and crossed the street, putting some distance between themselves and the notorious tavern. When Master Kai turned and faced the boy again, Alan noticed that he was a mere two inches shorter than this strange man who suddenly entered his life and wasted little time in earning his respect.

"I trust that answered your first question, young one," the older man said, almost grimacing.

"Um, yeah, I suppose it does," Alan replied. "I can't believe what you..."

"And I believe you Westerners have a saying for the veracity of events you personally witnessed: 'Seeing is believing,' *hai*?

"Now, as to your second question. How I would personally gain from training you and a select number for free? Simply in this manner: I have dedicated my life to training a small number of others to master the Teng-ryu art of my own devising. It is a series of techniques which combine the best of many Japanese, Chinese, and Korean disciplines into a unified system. Few have the attributes necessary to learn the art to its full capacity and become a true master. Fewer still can learn them quickly; that is, in a short number of years rather than over the course of many decades.

"I have a natural intuition for identifying such individuals. And since I was forced to travel to this part of the world, I had no choice but to recruit Westerners to train from that point onwards."

"Why did you get kicked out of Japan? Did you beat up a cop or something?"

"Ha! If only it were that simple! But that is a tale for another day. What is important now is what I have done since I've been here for the past six months. And that was to have a few of my finest students from Europe travel here to help me set up a dojo in this area. It is financed by the regular students I train during the daylight hours, who are fully unaware of my inner circle of the Chosen Few. That, and the pottery shop I established next door to it. Both ventures have been surprisingly profitable, I must say.

"Once we fully established the dojo as a viable business I began surreptitiously wandering about this city, hoping to find any possible recruits for my circle of the Chosen Few. To my astonishment, I have indeed found a few with, as you Americans might say, 'the right stuff.' You are the third such individual I have found in this city. Your natural aptitude for martial technique and overall intelligence give you the potential to be my greatest recruit."

"Seriously, dude?"

"*Hai.* Now for my question. Will you take up this offer of mine? Or would you prefer to allow your aptitude to remain forever undeveloped, and thus spend the remainder of your life being far less than you could have been?"

"Let me think about it." Alan put his right index finger to his mouth and looked up pensively, as if pondering a major decision… but only for a split second before responding. "Hell yeah! Just point the way to the dojo, my new sensei."

"You may call me Master Kai."

"Whatever works for you, um… *Master Kai.*"

With this decision made, the road to Moonstalker began for the boy who would turn out to be Master Kai's greatest recruit.

END

About the Author

Christofer Nigro is a writer, freelance editor, and publisher who makes his home in the United States. He is a lifelong fan of the comic book medium in general and the super-hero genre in particular. His short stories have been published by Black Coat Press, Sirens Call Publications, Pro Se Press, Grinning Skull Press, Horrified Press, and Local Hero Press. He has previously had novels published by Severed Press. Wild Hunt Press is his first foray into publishing on his own.

www.ingramcontent.com/pod-product-compliance
Lightning Source LLC
Chambersburg PA
CBHW050936120626
46552CB00001B/231